# The Haunted
# and the Haunters

Kathleen Lines, editor

The House of the Nightmare and Other Eerie Tales

The Haunted and the Haunters
*Tales of Ghosts and Other Apparitions*

# The Haunted and the Haunters

## TALES OF GHOSTS AND OTHER APPARITIONS

CHOSEN BY
### Kathleen Lines

FARRAR / STRAUS / GIROUX
NEW YORK

Library of Congress Cataloging in Publication Data

Main entry under title:
The Haunted and the haunters.
CONTENTS: Bulwer Lytton. The haunted and the
haunters.—The bloody hand.—James, M. R. Rats.—
Breinburg, P. It was Rose Hall. [etc.]
1. Ghost stories. [1. Ghost stories. 2. Short
stories] I. Lines, Kathleen.
PZ5.H3        [Fic]        75–20361
ISBN 0–374–32900–1

## Acknowledgments

Every effort has been made to trace the ownership of the copyright material in this book. It is believed that the necessary permissions from publishers, authors, and authorised agents have been obtained, but in the event of any question arising as to the right material: Edward Arnold (Publishers), Ltd., London, for any error inadvertently made, will be pleased to make the necessary correction in future editions of the book.

Thanks are due to the following for permission to reprint copyright material: Edward Arnold (Publishers) Ltd., London, for "Rats" from *Collected Ghost Stories of M. R. James;* the author for "It Was Rose Hall" © 1975 by Petronella Breinburg; the Public Trustee and Hamlyn Publishing Group, Ltd., London, for "Running Wolf," "Entrance and Exit," and "Violence" from *Tales of the Uncanny and Supernatural* by Algernon Blackwood; the Estate of Lord Tweedsmuir and Houghton Mifflin Co. for "The Wind in the Portico" from *The Rundgates Club* by John Buchan; Viking Press, for "A Little Companion" from *Such Darling Dodos* by Angus Wilson; the author and Cassell and Company, Ltd., for "The Cat 'I Am'" and "Vindicae Flammae" from *The Great Fog and Other Weird Tales* by Gerald Heard; the author and Victor Gollancz, Ltd., London, for "Gay as Cheese" from *The Windscreen Weepers* by Joan Aiken; the Estate of Cyril Hare and Collins-Knowlton-Wing, Inc., New York, for "The Mark-

*v*

hampton Miracle" from *The Best Detective Stories of Cyril Hare;* the author and Viking Press for "The Second Death" from *Collected Stories* by Graham Greene; the author for "Many-Coloured Glass" © 1970 by Lucy M. Boston; the Literary Trustees of Walter de la Mare and The Society of Authors, London, as their representative, for "The Riddle" by Walter de la Mare published by Faber and Faber, Ltd., London; Collins-Knowlton-Wing, Inc., New York, for "Balaam" by Anthony Boucher published in *Nine Tales of Space and Time* by Henry Holt and Company; Miss B. K. Barnardiston for "The Legend of Clare Friary" from *Clare Priory: Seven Centuries of a Suffolk House* published by Heffer and Sons, Ltd., Cambridge.

# Contents

# Foreword

When my previous anthology, *The House of the Nightmare and Other Eerie Stories*, was published in 1967, it was welcomed for the quality of the stories included in it. Today, eight years later, it is not distinguishable from the many other anthologies now in print. Working on a second selection, I soon discovered that I had no enthusiasm for making another book just like the first. So *The Haunted and the Haunters*, while it has in it stories by writers of high standing, has also some bits and pieces chosen for specific reasons.

There is more to be had from reading tales of the supernatural than the sensation of a chill down the spine! It is an interest that can last for years (sometimes leading to investigation and research) and one shared by many notable men and women.

As storytellers Conan Doyle, H. G. Wells, and Algernon Blackwood are well known and well remembered. H. H. Munro ("Saki") and Walter de la Mare wrote out of their own particular interests and convictions, and Lord Halifax summed up part of his life-long investigations into spell-binding, hauntings, and other manifestations of the spirit world in his *Ghost Book*. Perhaps not many people remember that during the rush-hours to and from the city, Richard Church "walked" quickly *several inches above the pavements;* or that a curiously assorted group of writers—amongst them Tennyson, Browning, Rider Haggard, Dickens, and Captain Marryat—dreamed prophetically, saw spirits, or had some other psychic experience.

Almost thirty years ago Robert Lynd in *Things One Hears* (Dent, 1945) wrote entertainingly, though seriously, about "Doubting Thomases":

*ix*

"There are still, for example, an extraordinary number of people who doubt the existence of ghosts. I have never seen a ghost . . . but people I know and whose word I trust . . . have seen them . . . and I see no more reason to doubt the truth of what they tell me than if they had told me they had seen a golden oriole. If an unsuperstitious woman . . . a female edition of George Washington . . . tells me that she has seen a ghost I must believe her . . . On the whole I cannot doubt the existence of ghosts . . . Not many things are too strange to be true."

I am very grateful to the authors (or their publishers and agents) who have given me permission to include their work; and in addition I should like to thank those who have permitted me to shorten or slightly edit the stories "Running Wolf," "Entrance and Exit," and "The Wind in the Portico." The title story by Bulwer-Lytton has also been slightly cut and edited.

*Kathleen Lines*
*Winchester, 1975*

# Ghosts and Other Mysteries

The Haunted and the Haunters
BULWER-LYTTON

The Bloody Hand
ANONYMOUS

Rats
M. R. JAMES

It Was Rose Hall
PETRONELLA BREINBURG

Running Wolf
ALGERNON BLACKWOOD

# The Haunted
# and the Haunters

## OR THE HOUSE AND THE BRAIN

A friend of mine, who is a man of letters and a philosopher, said to me one day, as if between jest and earnest: "Fancy! since we last met, I have discovered a haunted house in the midst of London."

"Really haunted?—and by what?—ghosts?"

"Well, I can't answer that question; all I know is this: six weeks ago my wife and I were in search of a furnished apartment. Passing a quiet street, we saw on the window of one of the houses a sign, 'Apartments, Furnished.' The situation suited us: we entered the house—liked the rooms—engaged them by the week—and left them the third day. No power on earth could have reconciled my wife to stay longer; and I don't wonder at it."

"What did you see?"

"Forgive me—I have no desire to be ridiculed as a superstitious dreamer—nor, on the other hand, could I ask you to accept on my affirmation what you would hold to be incredible without the evidence of your own senses. Let me say only this, it was not so much what we saw or heard (in which you might fairly suppose that we were the dupes of our own excited fancy, or the victims of imposture in others) that drove us away, as it was an undefinable terror which seized both of us whenever we passed by the door of a certain unfurnished room, in which we neither saw nor heard anything. And the strangest marvel of all was that for once in my life I agreed with my wife, silly woman though she be—and allowed, after the third night, that it was impossible to stay a fourth in that house. Accordingly, on the fourth morning I summoned the woman who kept the house and attended on us, and I told her that the rooms did not quite suit us, and we would not stay out our week. She said dryly: 'I know why; you have stayed longer than any other lodger. Few ever stayed a second night; none before you a third. But I take it they have been very kind to you.'

" 'They—who?' I asked, affecting to smile.

" 'Why, they who haunt the house, whoever they are. I don't mind them; I remember them many years ago, when I lived in this house, not as a servant; but I know they will be the death of me some day. I don't care—I'm old, and must die soon anyhow; and then I shall be with them, and in this house still.' The woman spoke with so dreamy a calmness that really it was a sort of awe that prevented my conversing with her further. I paid for my week, and too happy were my wife and I to get off so cheaply."

"You excite my curiosity," said I; "there is nothing I should like better than to a sleep in a haunted house. Pray give me the address of the one which you left so ignominiously."

My friend gave me the address; and when we parted, I walked straight towards the house thus indicated.

It is situated on the north side of Oxford Street, in a dull but respectable thoroughfare. I found the house shut up—no bill at the window, and no response to my knock. As I was turning away, a beer-boy, collecting pewter pots at the neighbouring areas, said to me: "Do you want anyone at that house, sir?"

"Yes, I heard it was to be let."

"Let! Why, the woman who kept it is dead—has been dead these three weeks, and no one can be found to stay there, though Mr J—— offered ever so much. He offered mother, who chars for him, a pound a week just to open and shut the windows, and she would not."

"Would not!—and why?"

"The house is haunted; and the old woman who kept it was found dead in her bed, with her eyes wide open. They say the devil strangled her."

"Pooh!—you speak of Mr J ——. Is he the owner of the house?"

"Yes."

"Where does he live?"

"In G—— Street, number —."

"What is he?—in any business?"

"No, sir—nothing particular; a single gentleman."

I gave the pot-boy the gratuity earned by his liberal information, and proceeded to Mr J——, in G—— Street, which was close by the street that boasted the haunted house. I was lucky enough to find Mr J—— at home—an elderly man, with intelligent countenance and prepossessing manners.

I communicated my name and my business frankly. I said I heard the house was considered to be haunted—that I had a strong desire to examine the house with so equivocal a reputation—that I should be greatly obliged if he would allow me to hire it, though only for a night. I was willing to pay for that privilege whatever he might be inclined to ask. "Sir," said Mr J——, with great courtesy, "the house is at your service, for as short or as long a time as you please. Rent is out of the question—the obligation will be on my side should you be able to discover the cause of the strange phenomena which at present deprive it of all value. I cannot let it, for I cannot even get a servant to keep it in order or answer the door. Unluckily the house is haunted, if I may use that expression, not only by night, but by day; though at night the disturbances are of a more unpleasant and some-times of a more alarming character. The poor old woman who died in it three weeks ago was a pauper whom I took out of the workhouse, for in her childhood she had been known to some of my family, and had once been in such good circumstances that she had rented that house of my uncle. She was a woman of superior education and strong mind, and was the only person I could ever induce to remain in the house. Indeed, since her death, which was sudden, and the coroner's inquest, which gave it a notoriety in the neighbourhood, I have so despaired of finding any person to take charge of the house, much more a tenant, that I would willingly let it rent free for a year to anyone who would pay its rates and taxes."

"How long is it since the house acquired this sinister character?"

"That I can scarcely tell you, but very many years since. The old woman I spoke of said it was haunted when she rented it between thirty and forty years ago. The fact is that my life has been spent in the East Indies, and in the civil service of the Company. I returned to England last year, on inheriting the fortune of an uncle, among whose possessions was the house in question. I found it shut up and uninhabited. I was told that it was haunted, that no one would inhabit it. I smiled at what seemed to me so idle a story. I spent some money in repairing it—added to its old-fashioned furniture a few modern articles—advertised it, and obtained a lodger for a year. He was a colonel on half-pay. He came in with his family, a son and a daughter, and four or five servants: they all left the house the next day; and, although each of them declared that he had seen something different from that which had scared the others, a something still was equally terrible to all. I really could not in conscience sue, nor even blame, the colonel for breach of agreement. Then I put in the old woman I have spoken of, and she was empowered to let the house in apartments. I never had one lodger who stayed more than three days. I do not tell you their stories—to no two lodgers have there been exactly the same phenomena repeated. It is better that you should judge for yourself than enter the house with an imagination influenced by previous narratives; only be prepared to see and to hear something or other, and take whatever precautions you yourself please."

"Have you never had a curiosity yourself to pass a night in that house?"

"Yes, I passed not a night, but three hours in broad daylight in that house. My curiosity is not satisfied, but is quenched. I have no desire to renew the experiment. You cannot complain, you see, sir, that I am not sufficiently candid; and unless your interest be exceedingly eager and your nerves unusually strong, I honestly add, that I advise you not to pass a night in that house."

"My interest is exceedingly keen," said I, "and though only

a coward will boast of his nerves in situations wholly unfamiliar to him, yet my nerves have been seasoned in such
variety of danger that I have the right to rely on them—even
in a haunted house."

Mr J—— said very little more; he took the keys of the
house out of his bureau, gave them to me—and, thanking
him cordially for his frankness, and his urbane concession to
my wish, I carried off my prize.

Impatient for the experiment, as soon as I reached home, I
summoned my confidential servant—a young man of gay
spirits, fearless temper, and as free from superstitious prejudice as anyone I could think of.

"F——," said I, "you remember in Germany how disappointed we were at not finding a ghost in that old castle,
which was said to be haunted by a headless apparition?
Well, I have heard of a house in London which, I have
reason to hope, is decidedly haunted. I mean to sleep there
tonight. From what I hear, there is no doubt that something
will allow itself to be seen or to be heard—something, perhaps, excessively horrible. Do you think, if I take you with
me, I may rely on your presence of mind, whatever may
happen?"

"Oh, sir! pray trust me," answered F——, grinning with
delight.

"Very well; then here are the keys of the house—this is
the address. Go now—select for me any bedroom you please;
and since the house has not been inhabited for weeks, make
up a good fire—air the bed well—see, of course, that there
are candles as well as fuel. Take with you my revolver and
my dagger—so much for my weapons—arm yourself equally
well; and if we are not a match for a dozen ghosts, we shall
be but a sorry couple of Englishmen."

I was engaged for the rest of the day on business so urgent that I had no leisure to think much on the nocturnal adventure to which I had plighted my honour. I dined alone, and very late, and while dining, read, as is my habit. I selected one of the volumes of Macaulay's essays. I thought to myself that I would take the book with me; there was so much of healthfulness in the style and practical life in the subjects that it would serve as an antidote against the influences of superstitious fancy.

Accordingly, about half-past nine, I put the book into my pocket, and strolled leisurely towards the haunted house. I took with me a favourite dog—an exceedingly sharp, bold, and vigilant bull-terrier—a dog fond of prowling about strange ghostly corners and passages at night in search of rats—a dog of dogs for a ghost.

It was a summer night, but chilly, the sky somewhat gloomy and overcast. Still there was a moon—faint and sickly, but still a moon—and if the clouds permitted, after midnight it would be brighter.

I reached the house, knocked, and my servant opened with a cheerful smile.

"All right, sir, and very comfortable."

"Oh!" said I, rather disappointed; "have you not seen or heard anything remarkable?"

"Well, sir, I must own I have heard something queer."

"What?—what?"

"The sound of feet pattering behind me; and once or twice small noises like whispers close at my ear—nothing more."

"You are not at all frightened?"

"I! Not a bit of it, sir," and the man's bold look reassured me on one point—*viz*, that happen what might, he would not desert me.

We were in the hall, the street-door closed, and my attention was now drawn to my dog. He had at first run in eagerly
enough, but had sneaked back to the door, and was scratching and whining to get out. After patting him on the head,
and encouraging him gently, the dog seemed to reconcile
himself to the situation, and followed me and F—— through
the house, but keeping close at my heels instead of hurrying
inquisitively in advance, which was his usual and normal
habit in all strange places. We first visited the subterranean
apartments, the kitchen and other offices, and especially the
cellars, in which last there were two or three bottles of wine
still left in the bin, covered with cobwebs, and evidently, by
their appearance, undisturbed for many years. It was clear
that the ghosts were not wine-bibbers. For the rest we discovered nothing of interest. There was a gloomy little backyard, with very high walls. The stones of this yard were very
damp; and what with the damp, and what with the dust and
smoke-grime on the pavement, our feet left a slight impression where we passed. And now appeared the first strange
phenomenon witnessed by myself in this strange abode. I
saw, just before me, the print of a foot suddenly form itself,
as it were. I stopped, caught hold of my servant, and pointed
to it. In advance of that footprint as suddenly dropped another. We both saw it. I advanced quickly to the place; the
footprints kept advancing before me, a small footprint—the
foot of a child: the impression was too faint thoroughly to
distinguish the shape, but it seemed to us both that it was
the print of a naked foot. This phenomenon ceased when we
arrived at the opposite wall, nor did it repeat itself on returning. We remounted the stairs, and entered the rooms on
the ground floor, a dining parlour, a small back parlour, and

a still smaller third room that had been probably appropri-ated to a footman—all still as death. We then visited the drawing-rooms, which seemed fresh and new. In the front room I seated myself in an arm-chair. F—— placed on the table the candlestick with which he had lighted us. I told him to shut the door. As he turned to do so, a chair opposite to me moved from the wall quickly and noiselessly, and dropped itself about a yard from my own chair, immediately fronting it.

"Why, this is better than the turning-tables," said I, with a half-laugh; and as I laughed, my dog put back his head and howled.

F——, coming back, had not observed the movement of the chair. He employed himself now in stilling the dog. I continued to gaze on the chair, and fancied I saw on it a pale blue misty outline of a human figure, but an outline so indistinct that I could only distrust my own vision. The dog was now quiet.

"Put back that chair opposite to me," said I to F——; "put it back to the wall."

F—— obeyed. "Was that you, sir?" said he, turning abruptly.

"I!—what?"

"Why, something struck me. I felt it sharply on the shoul-der—just here."

"No," said I. "But we have jugglers present, and though we may not discover their tricks, we shall catch them before they frighten us."

We did not stay long in the drawing-rooms—in fact, they felt so damp and so chilly that I was glad to get to the fire upstairs. We locked the doors of the drawing-rooms—a pre-

caution which, I should observe, we had taken with all the
rooms we had searched below. The bedroom my servant had
selected for me was the best on the floor—a large one, with
two windows fronting the street. The four-posted bed, which
took up no inconsiderable space, was opposite to the fire,
which burnt clear and bright; a door in the wall to the left,
between the bed and the window, communicated with the
room which my servant appropriated to himself. This last
was a small room with a sofa-bed, and had no communication with the landing-place—no other door but that which
conducted to the bedroom I was to occupy. On either side of
my fireplace was a cupboard, without locks, flush with the
wall, and covered with the same dull-brown paper. We examined these cupboards—only hooks to suspend female
dresses—nothing else; we sounded the walls—evidently
solid—the outer walls of the building. Having finished the
survey of these apartments, warmed myself a few moments,
and lighted my cigar, I then, still accompanied by F——,
went forth to complete my reconnoitre. In the landing-place
there was another door; it was closed firmly. "Sir," said my
servant, in surprise, "I unlocked this door with all the others
when I first came; it cannot have got locked from the inside,
for——"

Before he had finished his sentence, the door, which
neither of us then was touching, opened quietly of itself. We
looked at each other a single instant. The same thought
seized both—some human agency might be detected here. I
rushed in first, my servant followed. A small, blank, dreary
room without furniture—a few empty boxes and hampers in
a corner—a small window—the shutters closed—not even a
fireplace—no other door but that by which we had entered

—no carpet on the floor, and the floor seemed very old, uneven, worm-eaten, mended here and there, as was shown by the whiter patches on the woods; but no living being, and no visible place in which a living being could have hidden. As we stood gazing round, the door by which we had entered closed as quietly as it had before opened: we were imprisoned.

For the first time I felt a creep of indefinable horror. Not so my servant. "Why, they don't think to trap us, sir; I could break that trumpery door with a kick of my foot."

"Try first if it will open to your hand," said I, shaking off the vague apprehension that had seized me, "while I unclose the shutters and see what is without."

I unbarred the shutters—the window looked on the little backyard I have before described; there was no ledge without—nothing to break the sheer descent of the wall. No man getting out of that window would have found any footing till he had fallen on the stones below.

F——, meanwhile, was vainly attempting to open the door. He now turned round to me and asked my permission to use force. And I should here state, in justice to the servant, that, far from evincing any superstitious terrors, his nerve, composure, and even gaiety amidst circumstances so extraordinary, compelled my admiration, and made me congratulate myself on having secured a companion in every way fitted to the occasion. I willingly gave him the permission he required. But though he was a remarkably strong man, his force was as idle as his milder efforts; the door did not even shake to his stoutest kick. Breathless and panting, he desisted. I then tried the door myself, equally in vain. As I ceased from the effort, again that creep of horror came over me; but this time it was more cold and stubborn. I felt as if some strange and ghastly exhalation were rising up from the chinks of that rugged floor, and filling the atmosphere with a venomous influence hostile to human life. The door now very slowly and quietly opened as of its own accord. We precipitated ourselves into the landing-place. We both saw a large pale light—as large as the human figure, but shapeless and unsubstantial—move before us, and ascend the stairs that led from the landing into the attics. I followed the light, and my servant followed me. It entered to the right of the landing a small garret, of which the door stood open. I entered in the same instant. The light then collapsed into a small globule, exceedingly brilliant and vivid: rested a moment on a bed in the corner, quivered, and vanished. We approached the bed and examined it—a half-tester, such as is commonly found in attics devoted to servants. On the drawers that stood near it we perceived an old faded silk kerchief, with the needle still left in a rent half repaired. The kerchief was covered with dust; probably it had belonged to the old woman who had last died in that house, and this might have been her sleeping-room. I had sufficient curiosity to open the drawers: there were a few odds and ends of female dress, and two letters tied round with a narrow ribbon of faded yellow. I took the liberty to possess myself of the letters. We found nothing else in the room worth noticing—nor did the light reappear; but we distinctly heard, as we turned to go, a pattering footfall on the floor—just before us. We went through the other attics (in all four), the footfall still preceding us. Nothing to be seen—nothing but the footfall heard. I had the letters in my hand: just as I was descending the stairs I distinctly felt my wrist seized, and a faint soft effort made to draw the letters from my clasp. I only held them the more tightly, and the effort ceased.

We regained the bed-chamber appropriated to myself, and I then remarked that my dog had not followed us when we had left it. He was thrusting himself close to the fire, and trembling. I was impatient to examine the letters; and while I read them, my servant opened a little box in which he had deposited the weapons I had ordered him to bring, took them out, and placed them on a table close at my bed-head, and then occupied himself in soothing the dog, who, however, seemed to heed him very little.

The letters were short—they were dated; the dates exactly thirty-five years ago. They were evidently from a lover to his mistress, or a husband to some young wife. Not only the terms of expression, but a distinct reference to a former voyage, indicated the writer to have been a seafarer. The spelling and hand writing were those of a man imperfectly educated, but still the language itself was forcible. In the expressions of endearment there was a kind of rough, wild love; but here and there were dark, unintelligible hints at some secret not of love—some secret that seemed of crime. "We ought to love each other," was one of the sentences I remember, "for how everyone else would execrate us if all was known." Again: "Don't let anyone be in the same room with you at night—you talk in your sleep." And again "What's done can't be undone; and I tell you there's nothing against us unless the dead could come to life." Here there was underlined in a better handwriting (a female's), "They do!" At the end of the letter latest in date the same female hand had written these words: "Lost at sea the 4th of June, the same day as——."

I put down the letters, and began to muse over their

contents. Fearing, however, that the train of thought into which I fell might unsteady my nerves, I fully determined to keep my mind in a fit state to cope with whatever of the Marvellous the advancing night might bring forth. I roused myself—laid the letters on the table—stirred up the fire, which was still bright and cheering, and opened my volume of Macaulay. I read quietly enough till about half-past eleven. I then threw myself dressed upon the bed, and told my servant he might retire to his own room, but must keep himself awake. I bade him leave open the door between the two rooms. Thus alone, I kept two candles burning on the table by my bed-head. I placed my watch beside my weapons, and calmly resumed my Macaulay. Opposite to me the fire burned clear; and on the hearth-rug, seemingly asleep, lay the dog. In about twenty minutes I felt an exceedingly cold air pass my cheek, like a sudden draught. I fancied the door to my right, communicating with the landing-place, must have got open; but no—it was closed. I then turned my glance to my left, and saw the flame of the candles violently swayed as by a wind. At the same moment the watch beside the revolver softly slid from the table—softly, softly—no visible hand—it was gone. I sprang up, seizing the revolver with one hand, the dagger with the other; I was not willing that my weapons should share the fate of the watch. Thus armed, I looked round the floor—no sign of the watch. Three slow, loud, distinct knocks were now heard at the bed-head; my servant called out, "Is that you, sir?"

"No; be on your guard."

The dog now roused himself and sat on his haunches, his ears moving quickly backwards and forwards. He kept his eyes fixed on me with a look so strange that he concentrated all my attention on himself. Slowly, he rose up, all his hair bristling, and stood perfectly rigid, and with the same wild stare. I had no more time, however, to examine the dog, for my servant emerged from his room; and if ever I saw horror in the human face, it was then.

I should not have recognized him had we met in the street, so altered was every lineament. He passed by me quickly, saying in a whisper that seemed scarcely to come from his lips, "Run—run! it is after me!" He gained the door to the landing, pulled it open, and rushed forth. I followed him into the landing involuntarily, calling him to stop; but without heeding me, he bounded down the stairs, clinging to the balusters, and taking several steps at a time. I heard, where I stood, the street-door open—heard it again clap to. I was left alone in the haunted house.

It was but for a moment that I remained undecided whether or not to follow my servant; pride and curiosity alike forbade so dastardly a flight. I re-entered my room, closing the door after me, and proceeded cautiously into the interior chamber. I encountered nothing to justify my servant's terror. I again carefully examined the walls, to see if there was any concealed door. I could find no trace of one—not even a seam in the dull-brown paper with which the room was hung. How, then, had the Thing, whatever it was, which had so scared him, obtained ingress except through my own chamber? I returned to my room, shut and locked the door that opened upon the interior one, and stood on the hearth, expectant and prepared. I now perceived that the dog had slunk into an angle of the wall, and was pressing himself close against it, as if literally striving to force his way into it. I approached the animal and spoke to it; the poor brute was evidently beside itself with terror. It showed all its teeth, the slaver dropped from its jaws, and would certainly have bitten me if I had touched it. It did not seem to recognise me. Whoever has seen at the Zoological Gardens a rabbit, fascinated by a serpent, cowering in a corner, may form some idea of the anguish which the dog exhibited. Finding all efforts to soothe the animal in vain, and fearing that his bite might be as venomous in that state as in the madness of hydrophobia, I left him alone, placed my weapons on the table beside the fire, seated myself, and recommenced my Macaulay.

Perhaps, in order not to appear seeking credit for a courage or rather a coolness which the reader may conceive I exaggerate, I may be pardoned if I pause to indulge in one or two egotistical remarks.

As I hold presence of mind, or what is called courage, to be precisely proportioned to familiarity with the circumstances that lead to it, so I should say that I had been long sufficiently familiar with all experiments that appertain to the Marvellous. I had witnessed many very extraordinary phenomena in various parts of the world—phenomena that would be either totally disbelieved if I stated them, or ascribed to supernatural agencies. Now, my theory is that the Supernatural is the Impossible, and that what is called supernatural is only a something in the laws of nature of which we have been hitherto ignorant. Therefore, if a ghost rises before me, I have not the right to say, "So, then, the supernatural is possible," but rather, "So, then, the apparition of a ghost is contrary to received opinion, within the laws of nature—i.e., not supernatural."

Now, in all that I had hitherto witnessed, and indeed in all the wonders which the amateurs of mystery in our age record as facts, a material living agency is always required. Hence all that I had experienced up till now, or expected to see, in this strange house, I believed to be occasioned through some agency or medium as mortal as myself; and this idea necessarily prevented the awe with which those who regard as supernatural things that are not within the ordinary operations of nature, might have been impressed by the adventures of that memorable night.

As, then, it was my conjecture that all that was presented, or would be presented to my senses, must originate in some human being gifted by constitution with the power so to present them, and having some motive so to do. I felt an interest in my theory which, in its way, was rather philosophical than superstitious. And I can sincerely say that I was in as tranquil a temper for observation as any practical experimentalist could be in awaiting the effects of some rare, though perhaps perilous, chemical combination. Of course, the more I kept my mind detached from fancy, the more the temper fitted for observation would be obtained; and I therefore riveted my eye and thought on the strong daylight sense in the page of my Macaulay.

I now became aware that something interposed between the page and the light—the page was overshadowed: I looked up, and I saw what I shall find it very difficult, perhaps impossible, to describe.

It was Darkness shaping itself forth from the air in very undefined outline. I cannot say it was of a human form, and yet it had more resemblance to a human form, or rather shadow, than to anything else. As it stood, wholly apart and distinct from the air and the light around it, its dimensions seemed gigantic, the summit nearly touching the ceiling. While I gazed, a feeling of intense cold seized me. An iceberg before me could not have chilled me more; nor could the cold of an iceberg have been more purely physical. I feel convinced that it was not the cold caused by fear. As I continued to gaze, I thought—but this I cannot say with precision—that I distinguished two eyes looking down on me from the height. One moment I fancied that I distinguished them clearly, the next they seemed gone; but still two rays of a pale-blue light frequently shot through the darkness, as from the height on which I half believed, half doubted, that I had encountered the eyes.

I strove to speak, "Is this fear? It is not fear!" I strove to rise—in vain; I felt as if weighed down by an irresistible force. Indeed, my impression was that of an immense and overwhelming Power opposed to my volition; that sense of utter inadequacy to cope with a force beyond men's, which one may feel physically in a storm at sea, in a conflagration, or when confronting some terrible wild beast, or rather, perhaps, the shark of the ocean, I felt morally. Opposed to my will was another will, as far superior to its strength as storm, fire, and shark are superior in material force to the force of man.

And now, as this impression grew on me—now came, at last, horror—horror to a degree that no words can convey. Still I retained pride, if not courage; and in my own mind I said: "This is horror, but it is not fear; unless I fear I cannot be harmed; my reason rejects this thing; it is an illusion—I do not fear." With a violent effort I succeeded at last in stretching out my hand towards the weapon on the table: as

I did so, on the arm and shoulder I received a strange shock, and my arm fell to my side powerless. And now, to add to my horror, the light began slowly to wane from the candles —they were not, as it were, extinguished, but their flame seemed very gradually withdrawn: it was the same with the fire—the light extracted from the fuel; in a few minutes the room was in utter darkness. The dread that came over me, to be thus in the dark with that dark Thing, whose power was so intensely felt, brought a reaction of nerve. In fact, terror had reached that climax, that either my senses must have deserted me, or I must have burst through the spell. I did burst through it. I found voice, though the voice was a shriek. I remember that I broke forth with words like these: "I do not fear, my soul does not fear"; and at the same time I found strength to rise. Still in that profound gloom I rushed to one of the windows—tore aside the curtain—flung open the shutters; my first thought was—Light. And when I saw the moon high, clear, and calm, I felt a joy that almost compensated for the previous terror. There was the moon, there was also the light from the gas-lamps in the deserted slumberous street. I turned to look back into the room; the moon penetrated its shadow very palely and partially—but still there was light. The dark Thing, whatever it might be, was gone—except that I could yet see a dim shadow, which seemed the shadow of that shade, against the opposite wall.

My eye now rested on the table, and from under the table (which was without cloth or cover—an old mahogany round table) there rose a Hand, visible as far as the wrist. It was a hand, seemingly, as much of flesh and blood as my own, but the hand of an aged person—lean, wrinkled, small too—a woman's hand. That hand very softly closed on the

two letters that lay on the table: hand and letters both
vanished. There then came the same three loud measured
knocks I had heard at the bed-head before this extraordinary
drama had commenced.

As those sounds slowly ceased, I felt the whole room
vibrate sensibly; and at the far end there rose, as from the
floor, sparks or globules like bubbles of light, many-coloured
—green, yellow, fire-red, azure. Up and down, to and fro,
hither, thither, as tiny will-o'-the-wisps, the sparks moved,
slow or swift, each at its own caprice. A chair (as in the
drawing-room below) was now advanced from the wall
without apparent agency, and placed at the opposite side of
the table. Suddenly, as forth from the chair, there grew a
shape—a woman's shape. It was distinct as a shape of life—
ghastly as a shape of death. The face was that of youth, with
a strange mournful beauty; the throat and shoulders were
bare, the rest of the form in a loose robe of cloudy white. It
began sleeking its long yellow hair, which fell over its shoulders; its eyes were not turned towards me but to the door; it
seemed listening, watching, waiting. The shadow of the
shade in the background grew darker; and again I thought I
beheld the eyes gleaming out from the summit of the
shadow—eyes fixed upon that shape.

As if from the door, though it did not open, there grew out
another shape, equally distinct, equally ghastly—a man's
shape—a young man's. It was in the dress of the last century, or rather in a likeness of such dress (for both the male
shape and the female, though defined, were evidently unsubstantial, impalpable—simulacra—phantasms); and there
was something incongruous, grotesque, yet fearful, in the
contrast between the elaborate finery, the courtly precision
of that old-fashioned garb, with its ruffles and lace and

buckles, and the corpse-like aspect and ghost-like stillness of the flitting wearer. Just as the male shape approached the female, the dark Shadow started from the wall, all three for a moment were wrapped in darkness. When the pale light returned, the two phantoms were as if in the grasp of the Shadow that towered between them; and there was a blood-stain on the breast of the female; and the phantom male was leaning on its phantom sword, and blood seemed trickling fast from the ruffles, from the lace; and the darkness of the intermediate Shadow swallowed them up—they were gone. And again the bubbles of light shot, and sailed, and undulated, growing thicker and thicker and more wildly confused in their movements.

The closet door to the right of the fireplace now opened, and from the aperture there came the form of an aged woman. In her hand she held letters—the very letters over which I had seen the Hand close; and behind her I heard a footstep. She turned round as if to listen, and then she opened the letters and seemed to read; and over her shoulder I saw a livid face, the face as of a man long drowned—bloated, bleached—seaweed tangled in its dripping hair; and at her feet lay a form as of a corpse, and beside the corpse there cowered a child, a miserable squalid child, with famine in its cheeks and fear in its eyes. And as I looked in the old woman's face, the wrinkles and lines vanished, and it became a face of youth—hard-eyed, stony, but still youth; and the Shadow darted forth, and darkened over those phantoms as it had darkened over the last.

Nothing now was left but the Shadow, and on that my eyes were intently fixed, till again eyes grew out of the Shadow—malignant, serpent eyes. And the bubbles of light again rose and fell, and in their disordered, irregular, turbu-

lent maze, mingled with the wan moonlight. And now from
these globules themselves, as from the shell of an egg, mon-
strous things burst out; the air filled with them, larvae so
bloodless and so hideous that I can in no way describe them
except to remind the reader of the swarming life which a
solar microscope brings before his eyes in a drop of water—
things transparent, supple, agile, chasing each other, devour-
ing each other—forms like nought ever beheld by the naked
eye. As the shapes were without symmetry, so their movements were without order. In the very vagrancies there was
no sport; they came round me and round, thicker and faster
and swifter, swarming over my head, crawling over my right
arm, which was outstretched in involuntary command
against all evil beings. Sometimes I felt myself touched, but
not by them; invisible hands touched me. Once I felt the
clutch as of cold, soft fingers at my throat. I was still equally
conscious that if I gave way to fear I should be in bodily
peril; and I concentrated all my faculties in the single focus
of resisting, stubborn will. And I turned my sight from the
Shadow—above all, from those strange serpent eyes—eyes
that had now become distinctly visible. For there, though in
nought else around me, I was aware that there was a Will,
and a will of intense, creative, working evil, which might
crush down my own.

The pale atmosphere in the room began now to redden as
if in the air of some near conflagration. The larvae grew
lurid as things that live in fire. Again the room vibrated;
again were heard the three measured knocks; and again all
things were swallowed up in the darkness of the dark
Shadow, as if out of that darkness all had come, into that
darkness all returned.

As the gloom receded, the Shadow was wholly gone. Slowly, as it had been withdrawn, the flame grew again into the candles on the table, again into the fuel in the grate. The whole room came once more calmly, healthfully into sight.

The two doors were still closed, the door communicating with the servant's room still locked. In the corner of the wall, into which he had so convulsively niched himself, lay the dog. I called to him—no movement; I approached—the animal was dead; his eyes protruded; his tongue out of his mouth; the froth gathered round his jaws. I took him in my arms; I brought him to the fire; I felt acute grief for the loss of my poor favourite—acute self-reproach; I accused myself of his death; I imagined he had died of fright. But what was my surprise on finding that his neck was actually broken. Had this been done in the dark?—must it not have been by a hand human as mine?—must there not have been a human agency all the while in that room? Good cause to suspect it. I cannot tell. I cannot do more than state the fact fairly; the reader may draw his own inference.

Another surprising circumstance—my watch was restored to the table from which it had been so mysteriously withdrawn; but it had stopped at the very moment it was so withdrawn; nor, despite all the skill of the watchmaker, has it ever gone since—that is, it will go in a strange erratic way for a few hours, and then come to a dead stop—it is worthless.

Nothing more chanced for the rest of the night. Nor, indeed, had I long to wait before the dawn broke. Nor till it was broad daylight did I quit the haunted house. Before I did so, I revisited the little blind room in which my servant and myself had been for a time imprisoned. I had a strong

impression—for which I could not account—that from that
room had originated the mechanism of the phenomena—if I
may use the term—which had been experienced in my
chamber. And though I entered it now in the clear day, with
the sun peering through the filmy window, I still felt, as I
stood on its floors, the creep of the horror which I had first
there experienced the night before, and which had been so
aggravated by what had passed in my own chamber. I could
not, indeed, bear to stay more than half a minute within
those walls. I descended the stairs, and again I heard the
footfall before me; and when I opened the street door, I
thought I could distinguish a very low laugh. I gained my
own home, expecting to find my runaway servant there. But
he had not presented himself, nor did I hear more of him for
three days, when I received a letter from him, dated from
Liverpool, to this effect:

Honoured Sir:
    I humbly entreat your pardon, though I can scarcely hope
that you will think that I deserve it, unless—which Heaven
forbid!—you saw what I did. I feel that it will be years before
I can recover myself; and as to being fit for service, it is out
of the question. I am therefore going to my brother-in-law at
Melbourne. The ship sails tomorrow. Perhaps the long voyage may set me up. I do nothing now but start and tremble,
and fancy IT is behind me. I humbly beg you, honoured
sir, to order my clothes, and whatever wages are due to me,
to be sent to my mother's at Walworth—John knows her
address.

The letter ended with additional apologies, somewhat
incoherent, and explanatory details as to effect that had been
under the writer's charge.

This flight may perhaps warrant a suspicion that the man wished to go to Australia, and had been somehow or other fraudulently mixed up with the events of the night. I say nothing in refutation of that conjecture; rather, I suggest it as one that would seem to many persons the most probable solution of improbable occurrences. My belief in my own theory remained unshaken. I returned in the evening to the house, to bring away in a hack cab the things I had left there, together with my poor dog's body. In this task I was not disturbed, nor did any incident worth note befall me, except that still, on ascending and descending the stairs, I heard the same footfall in advance. On leaving the house, I went to Mr J——'s. He was at home. I returned him the keys, told him that my curiosity was sufficiently gratified, and was about to relate quickly what had passed, when he stopped me, and said, though with much politeness, that he had no longer any interest in a mystery which none had ever solved.

I determined at least to tell him of the two letters I had read, as well as of the extraordinary manner in which they had disappeared, and I then inquired if he thought they had been addressed to the woman who had died in the house, and if there was anything in her early history which could possibly confirm the dark suspicions to which the letters gave rise. Mr J—— seemed startled, and, after musing a few moments, answered: "I am but little acquainted with the woman's earlier history, except, as I before told you, that her family were known to mine. But you revive some vague reminiscences to her prejudice. I will make inquiries, and inform you of their result. Still, even if we could admit the popular superstition that a person who had been either the perpetrator or the victim of dark crimes in life could revisit, as a restless spirit, the scene in which those crimes had been committed, I should observe that the house was infested by strange sights and sounds before the old woman died—you smile—what would you say?"

"I would say this, that I am convinced, if we could get to the bottom of these mysteries, we should find a living human agency."

"What! You believe it is all an imposture? For what object?"

"Not an imposture in the ordinary sense of the word. If suddenly I were to sink into a deep sleep, from which you could not awake me, but in that sleep could answer questions with an accuracy which I could not pretend to when awake—tell you what money you had in your pocket—nay, describe your very thoughts—it is not necessarily an imposture, any more than it is necessarily supernatural. I should be, unconsciously to myself, under a mesmeric influence, conveyed to me from a distance by a human being who had acquired power over me by previous rapport."

"But if a mesmeriser could so affect another living being, can you suppose that a mesmeriser could also affect inanimate objects: move chairs—open and shut doors?"

"Or impress our senses with the belief in such effects—we never having been en rapport with the person acting on us? No. What is commonly called mesmerism could not do this; but there may be a power akin to mesmerism and superior to it—the power that in the old days was called Magic. That such a power may extend to all inanimate objects of matter, I do not say; but if so, it would not be against nature—it would only be a rare power in nature which might be given

to a constitution with certain peculiarities, and cultivated b,
practice to an extraordinary degree. That such a power
might extend over the dead—that is, over certain thoughts
and memories that the dead may still retain—and compel,
not that which ought properly to be called the Soul, and
which is far beyond human reach, but rather a phantom of
what has been most earth-stained on earth to make itself
apparent to our senses—is a very ancient though obsolete
theory, upon which I will hazard no opinion. But I do not
conceive the power would be supernatural. Such an apparition comes for little or no object—seldom speaking: if it does
speak it conveys no ideas above those of ordinary people on
earth. American spiritualists have published volumes of
communications, in prose and verse, which they assert to be
given in the names of the most illustrious dead—Shakespeare, Bacon—Heaven knows whom. Those communications, taking the best, are certainly not a whit of higher
order than would be communications from living persons of
fair talent and education; they are wondrously inferior to
what Bacon, Shakespeare, and Plato said and wrote when on
earth. Nor, what is more noticeable, do they ever contain an
idea that was not on earth before. Wonderful, therefore, as
such phenomena may be ( granting them to be truthful), I
see much that philosophy may question, nothing that it is
incumbent on philosophy to deny—*viz*, nothing supernatural. They are but ideas conveyed somehow or other (we
have not yet discovered the means) from one mortal brain to
another. Whether, in so doing, tables walk of their own
accord, or fiend-like shapes appear in a magic circle, or
bodyless hands rise and remove material objects, or a Thing
of Darkness, such as presented itself to me, freeze our blood

—still am I persuaded that these are but agencies conveyed, as by electric wires, to my own brain from the brain of another. In some constitutions there is a natural chemistry, and those constitutions may produce chemic wonders—in others a natural fluid, call it electricity, and these may produce electric wonders. But the wonders differ from Normal Science in this—they are alike objectless, purposeless, puerile, frivolous. They lead on to no grand results: and therefore the world does not heed, and true sages have not cultivated them. But sure I am, that of all I saw or heard, a man, human as myself, was the remote originator; and I believe unconsciously to himself as to the exact effects produced, for this reason: no two persons, you say, have ever told you that they experienced exactly the same thing. Well, observe, no two persons ever experienced the same dream. If this were an ordinary imposture, the machinery would be arranged for results that would but little vary; if it were a supernatural agency permitted by the Almighty, it would surely be for some definite end. These phenomena belong to neither class; my persuasion is that they originate in some brain now far distant; that that brain had no distinct volition in anything that occurred; that what does occur reflects but its devious, motley, ever-shifting, half-formed thoughts; in short, that it has been but the dreams of such a brain put into action and invested with a semi-substance. That this brain is of immense power, that it can set matter into movement, that it is malignant and destructive, I believe; some material force must have killed my dog; the same force might, for aught I know, have sufficed to kill myself, had I been as subjugated by terror as the dog—had my intellect or my spirit given me no countervailing resistance in my will."

"It killed your dog! That is fearful! Indeed it is stra
that no animal can be induced to stay in that house; not even
a cat. Rats and mice are never found in it."

"The instincts of the brute creation detect influences
deadly to their existence. Man's reason has a sense less
subtle, because it has a resisting power more supreme. But
enough; do you comprehend my theory?"

"Yes, though imperfectly—and I accept any crotchet
(pardon the word), however odd, rather than embrace at
once the notion of ghosts and hobgoblins we imbibed in our
nurseries. Still, to my unfortunate house the evil is the same.
What on earth can I do with the house?"

"I will tell you what I would do. I am convinced from my
own internal feelings that the small unfurnished room at
right angles to the door of the bedroom which I occupied
forms a starting-point or receptacle for the influences which
haunt the house; and I strongly advise you to have the walls
opened, the floor removed—nay, the whole room pulled
down. I observe that it is detached from the body of the
house, built over the small backyard, and could be removed
without injury to the rest of the building."

"And you think, if I did that—"

"You would cut off the telegraph wires. Try it. I am so
persuaded that I am right, that I will pay half the expense if
you will allow me to direct the operations."

"Nay, I am well able to afford the cost; for the rest, allow
me to write to you."

About ten days later, I received a letter from Mr J——
telling me that he had visited the house since I had seen
him; that he had found the two letters I had described,
replaced in the drawer from which I had taken them; that he

had read them with misgivings like my own; that he had instituted a cautious inquiry about the woman to whom I rigidly conjectured they had been written. It seemed that thirty-six years ago (a year before the date of the letters) she had married, against the wish of her relations, an American of very suspicious character; in fact, he was generally believed to have been a pirate. She herself was the daughter of very respectable tradespeople, and had served in the capacity of a nursery governess before her marriage. She had a brother, a widower, who was considered wealthy, and who had one child of about six years. A month after the marriage, the body of this brother was found in the Thames, near London Bridge; there seemed some marks of violence about his throat, but they were not deemed sufficient to warrant the inquest in any other verdict than that of "found drowned."

The American and his wife took charge of the little boy, the deceased brother having by his will left his sister the guardian of his only child—and in the event of the child's death, the sister inherited. The child died about six months afterwards—it was supposed to have been neglected and ill-treated. The neighbours deposed to have heard it shriek at night. The surgeon who had examined it after death said that it was emaciated as if from want of nourishment, and the body was covered with livid bruises. It seemed that one winter night the child had sought to escape—crept out into the backyard—tried to scale the wall—fallen back exhausted, and been found at morning on the stones in a dying state. But though there was some evidence of cruelty, there was none of murder; and the aunt and her husband had sought to palliate cruelty by alleging the exceeding stubbornness and perversity of the child, who was declared to be half-witted. Be that as it may, at the orphan's death the aunt inherited her brother's fortune. Before the first wedded year was out, the American quitted England abruptly, and never returned to it. He obtained a cruising vessel, which was lost in the Atlantic two years afterwards. The widow was left in affluence: but reverses of various kinds had befallen her: a bank broke—an investment failed—she went into a small business and became insolvent—then she entered into service, sinking lower and lower, from housekeeper down to maid-of-all-work—never long retaining a place, though nothing decided against her character was ever alleged. She was considered sober, honest, and peculiarly quiet in her ways; still, nothing prospered with her. And so she had dropped into the workhouse, from which Mr J—— had taken her, to be placed in charge of the very house which she had rented as mistress in the first year of her wedded life.

Mr J—— added that he had passed an hour alone in the unfurnished room which I had urged him to destroy, and that his impressions of dread while there were so great, though he had neither heard nor seen anything, that he was eager to have the walls bared and the floors removed as I had suggested. He had engaged persons for the work, and would commence any day I would name.

The day was accordingly fixed. I repaired to the haunted house—we went into the blind, dreary room, took up the skirting, and then the floors. Under the rafters, covered with rubbish, was found a trap-door, quite large enough to admit a man. It was closely nailed down, with clamps and rivets of iron. On removing these we descended into a room below,

the existence of which had never been suspected. In this
room there had been a window and a flue, but they had been
bricked over, evidently for many years. By the help of
candles we examined this place; it still retained some moul-
dering furniture—three chairs, an oak settle, a table—all of
the fashion of about eighty years ago. There was a chest of
drawers against the wall, in which we found, half-rotted
away, old-fashioned articles of a man's dress, such as might
have been worn eighty or a hundred years ago by a gentleman of some rank—costly steel buckles and buttons, like
those yet worn in court dresses, a handsome court sword. In
a waistcoat which had once been rich with gold lace, but
which was now blackened and foul with damp, we found
five guineas, a few silver coins, and an ivory ticket, probably
for some place of entertainment long since passed away. But
our main discovery was in a kind of iron safe fixed to the
wall, the lock of which it cost us much trouble to get picked.

In this safe were three shelves, and two small drawers.
Ranged on the shelves were several small bottles of crystal,
hermetically stopped. They contained colourless volatile
essences, of the nature of which I shall only say that they
were not poisons—phosphor and ammonia entered into some
of them. There were also some very curious glass tubes, and
a small pointed rod of iron, with a large lump of rock-crystal,
and another of amber—also a lodestone of great power.

In one of the drawers we found a miniature portrait set in
gold, and retaining the freshness of its colours most remarkably, considering the length of time it had probably been
there. The portrait was that of a man who might be somewhat advanced in middle life, perhaps forty-seven or forty-
eight.

It was a remarkable face—a most impressive face. If you could fancy some mighty serpent transformed into man, pre-serving in the human lineaments the old serpent type, you would have a better idea of that countenance than long descriptions can convey: the width and flatness of frontal— the tapering elegance of contour disguising the strength of the deadly jaw—the long, large, terrible eye, glittering and green as the emerald—and withal a certain ruthless calm, as if from the consciousness of an immense power.

Mechanically I turned round the miniature to examine the back of it, and on the back was engraved a pentacle; in the middle of the pentacle a ladder, and the third step of the ladder was formed by the date 1765. Examining still more minutely, I detected a spring; this, on being pressed, opened the back of the miniature as a lid. Withinside the lid was engraved, "Marianna to thee— Be faithful in life and in death to ——." Here follows a name that I will not mention, but it was not unfamiliar to me. I had heard it spoken of by old men in my childhood as the name borne by a dazzling charlatan who had made a great sensation in London for a year or so, and had fled the country on the charge of a double murder within his own house—that of his mistress and his rival. I said nothing of this to Mr J——, to whom reluctantly I resigned the miniature.

We had found no difficulty in opening the first drawer within the iron safe; we found great difficulty in opening the second: it was not locked, but it resisted all efforts, till we inserted in the chinks the edge of a chisel. When we had thus drawn it forth, we found a very singular apparatus in the nicest order. Upon a small thin book, or rather tablet, was placed a saucer of crystal; this saucer was filled with a clear liquid—on that liquid floated a kind of compass, with a needle shifting rapidly round; but instead of the usual points of a compass were seven strange characters, not very unlike those used by astrologers to denote the planets. A peculiar, but not strong nor displeasing odour, came from this drawer, which was lined with a wood that we afterwards discovered to be hazel. Whatever the cause of this odour, it produced a material effect on the nerves. We all felt it, even the two workmen who were in the room—a creeping tingling sensation from the tips of the fingers to the roots of the hair. Impatient to examine the tablet, I removed the saucer. As I did so the needle of the compass went round and round with exceeding swiftness, and I felt a shock that ran through my whole frame, so that I dropped the saucer on the floor. The liquid was spilt—the saucer was broken—the compass rolled to the end of the room—and at that instant the walls shook to and fro, as if a giant had swayed and rocked them.

The two workmen were so frightened that they ran up the ladder by which we had descended from the trap-door; but seeing that nothing more happened, they were easily induced to return.

Meanwhile I had opened the tablet: it was bound in plain red leather, with a silver clasp; it contained but one sheet of thick vellum, and on that sheet were inscribed, within a double pentacle, words in old monkish Latin, which are literally to be translated thus: "On all that it can reach within these walls—sentient or inanimate, living or dead—as moves the needle, so work my will! Accursed be the house, and restless be the dwellers therein."

We found no more. Mr J—— burnt the tablet and its anathema. He razed to the foundations the part of the building containing the secret room with the chamber over it. He had then the courage to inhabit the house himself for a month, and a quieter, better-conditioned house could not be found in all London. Subsequently he let it to advantage, and his tenant has made no complaints.

ANONYMOUS

# The Bloody Hand

In a certain village on the South Coast, a widow and her two daughters were living in a house standing rather apart from its neighbours on either side. It was situated on a wooded cliff, and about a quarter of a mile from the garden was a waterfall of some height. The two daughters were much attached to each other. One of them, Mary, was very good-looking and attractive. Among her admirers there were two men especially distinguished for their devotion of her, and one of them, John Bodneys, seemed on the point of realising the ambition of his life, when a new competitor of a very different disposition appeared and completely conquered Mary's heart.

The day was fixed for the marriage, but though Mary wrote to the Bodneyses to announce her engagement and to ask John to be present at her wedding, no reply was received from him. On the evening before the day, Ellen, the other sister, was gathering ferns in the wood when she heard a faint rustling behind her and, turning quickly round, thought she had a momentary glimpse of the figure of John Bodneys; but whoever it was vanished swiftly in the twilight. On her return to the house, she told her sister what she thought she had seen, but neither of them thought much of it.

The marriage took place next day. Just before the bride was due to leave with her husband, she took her sister to the room they had shared, the window of which opened onto a balcony from which a flight of steps led down to an enclosed garden. After a few words, Mary said to her sister, "I would like to be alone for a few minutes. I will join you again presently."

Ellen left her and went downstairs, where she waited with the others. When half an hour had passed and Mary had not appeared, her sister went up to see if anything had happened to her. The bedroom door was locked. Ellen called, but had no answer. She called again more loudly; there was still no answer. Becoming alarmed, she ran downstairs and told her mother. At last the door was forced open, but there was no trace of Mary in the room. They went into the garden, but except for a white rose lying on the path, nothing was to be seen. For the rest of that day and on the following days, they hunted high and low. The police were called in, the whole countryside was roused, but all to no purpose. Mary had utterly disappeared.

The years passed by. The mother and Mary's husband were dead, and of the wedding party only Ellen and an old servant were left. One winter's night the wind rose to a furious gale and did a great deal of damage to the trees near the waterfall. When the workmen came in the morning to clear away the fallen timber and fragments of rock, they came upon a skeleton hand, on the third finger of which was a wedding ring, guarded by another ring with a red stone in it. On searching further, they found a complete skeleton, round whose dried-up bones some rags of clothes still adhered. The ring with the red stone in it was identified by Ellen as one which her sister was wearing on her wedding

day. The skeleton was buried in the churchyard, but the
shock of the discovery was so great that a few weeks later
Ellen herself was on her deathbed. On the occasion of
Mary's burial, she had insisted on keeping the skeleton hand
with the rings, putting it in a glass box to secure it from
accident; and now, when she lay dying, she left the relic to
the care of her old servant.

Shortly afterwards the servant set up a public house,
where, as may be imagined, the skeleton hand and its story
were a common topic of conversation among those who
frequented the bar. One night a stranger, muffled up in a
cloak and with his cap pulled over his face, made his way
into the inn and asked for something to drink.

"It was a night like this when the great oak was blown
down," the publican observed to one of his customers.

"Yes," the other replied. "And it must have made the
skeleton seem doubly ghastly, discovering it, as it were, in
the midst of ruins."

"What skeleton?" asked the stranger, turning suddenly
from the corner in which he had been standing.

"Oh, it's a long story," answered the publican. "You can
see the hand in that glass case, and if you like, I will tell you
how it came there."

He waited for an answer, but none came. The stranger
was leaning against the wall in a state of collapse. He was
staring at the hand, repeating again and again, "Blood,
blood," and, sure enough, blood was slowly dripping from
his finger tips. A few minutes later, he had recovered sufficiently to admit that he was John Bodneys and to ask that he
might be taken to the magistrates. To them he confessed
that, in a frenzy of jealousy, he had made his way into the

private garden on Mary's wedding day. Seeing her alone in her room, he had entered and seized her, muffling her cries, and had taken her as far as the waterfall. There she had struggled so violently to escape from him that, unintentionally, he had pushed her off the rocks and she had fallen into a cleft where she was almost completely hidden. Afraid of being discovered, he had not even waited to find out whether she were dead or alive. He had fled and had lived abroad ever since, until an overpowering longing led him to revisit the scene of his crime.

After making his confession, Bodneys was committed to the county gaol, where shortly afterwards he died, before any trial could take place.

# Rats

"And if you was to walk through the bedrooms now, you'd see the ragged, mouldy bedclothes a-heaving and a-heaving like seas." "And a-heaving and a-heaving with what?" he says. "Why, with the rats under 'em."

But was it with the rats? I ask, because in another case it was not. I cannot put a date to the story, but I was young when I heard it, and the teller was old. It is an ill-proportioned tale, but that is my fault, not his.

It happened in Suffolk, near the coast. In a place where the road makes a sudden dip and then a sudden rise; as you go northward, at the top of that rise, stands a house on the left of the road. It is a tall red-brick house, narrow for its height; perhaps it was built about 1770. The top of the front has a low triangular pediment with a round window in the centre. Behind it are stables and offices, and such garden as it has is behind them. Scraggy Scotch firs are near it: an expanse of gorse-covered land stretches away from it. It commands a view of the distant sea from the upper windows of the front. A sign on a post stands before the door; or did so stand, for though it was an inn of repute once, I believe it is so no longer.

To this inn came my acquaintance, Mr Thomson, when he was a young man, on a fine spring day, coming from the University of Cambridge, and desirous of solitude in tolerable quarters and time for reading. These he found, for the landlord and his wife had been in service and could make a visitor comfortable, and there was no one else staying in the inn. He had a large room on the first floor commanding the road and the view, and if it faced east, why, that could not be helped; the house was well built and warm.

He spent very tranquil and uneventful days: work all the morning, an afternoon perambulation of the country round, a little conversation with country company or the people of the inn in the evening over the then fashionable drink of brandy and water, a little more reading and writing, and bed; and he would have been content that this should continue for the full month he had at disposal, so well was his work progressing, and so fine was the April of that year— which I have reason to believe was that which Orlando Whistlecraft chronicles in his weather record as the "Charming Year."

One of his walks took him along the northern road, which stands high and traverses a wide common, called a heath. On the bright afternoon when he first chose this direction his eye caught a white object some hundreds of yards to the left of the road, and he felt it necessary to make sure what this might be. It was not long before he was standing by it, and found himself looking at a square block of white stone fashioned somewhat like the base of a pillar, with a square hole in the upper surface. Just such another you may see at this day on Thetford Heath. After taking stock of it he contemplated for a few minutes the view, which offered a church tower, or two, some red roofs of cottages and windows winking in the sun, and the expanse of sea—also with an occasional wink and gleam upon it—and so pursued his way.

In the desultory evening talk in the bar, he asked why the white stone was there on the common.

"A old-fashioned thing, that is," said the landlord (Mr Betts), "we was none of us alive when that was put there." "That's right," said another. "It stands pretty high," said Mr Thomson, "I dare say a sea-mark was on it some time back." "Ah! yes," Mr Betts agreed, "I 'ave 'eard they could see it from the boats; but whatever there was, it's fell to bits this long time." "Good job too," said a third, " 'twarn't a lucky mark, by which the old men used to say; not lucky for the fishin', I mean to say." "Why ever not?" said Thomson. "Well, I never see it myself," was the answer, "but they 'ad some funny ideas, what I mean, peculiar, them old chaps, and I shouldn't wonder but what they made away with it theirselves."

It was impossible to get anything clearer than this: the company, never very voluble, fell silent, and when next someone spoke it was of village affairs and crops. Mr Betts was the speaker.

Not every day did Thomson consult his health by taking a country walk. One very fine afternoon found him busily writing at three o'clock. Then he stretched himself and rose, and walked out of his room into the passage. Facing him was another room, then the stair-head, then two more rooms, one looking out to the back, the other to the south. At the south end of the passage was a window, to which he went, considering with himself that it was rather a shame to waste such a fine afternoon. However, work was paramount just at

the moment; he thought he would just take five minutes off
and go back to it; and those five minutes he would employ—
the Bettses could not possibly object—to looking at the
other rooms in the passage, which he had never seen. Nobody at all, it seemed, was indoors; probably, as it was
market day, they were all gone to the town, except perhaps a
maid in the bar. Very still the house was, and the sun shone
really hot; early flies buzzed in the window-panes. So he
explored. The room facing his own was undistinguished except for an old print of Bury St Edmunds; the two next him
on his side of the passage were gay and clean, with one
window apiece, whereas his had two. Remained the south-
west room, opposite to the last which he had entered. This
was locked; but Thomson was in a mood of quite indefen-
sible curiosity, and feeling confident that there could be no
damaging secrets in a place so easily got at, he proceeded to
fetch the key to his own room, and when that did not answer, to collect the keys of the other three. One of them
fitted, and he opened the door. The room had two windows
looking south and west, so it was as bright and the sun as hot
upon it as could be. Here there was no carpet, but bare
boards; no pictures, no washing-stand, only a bed, in the
farther corner: an iron bed, with mattress and bolster,
covered with a bluish check counterpane. As featureless a
room as you can well imagine, and yet there was something
that made Thomson close the door very quickly and yet
quietly behind him and lean against the window-sill in the
passage, actually quivering all over. It was this, that under
the counterpane someone lay, and not only lay, but stirred.
That it was some *one* and not some *thing* was certain, because the shape of a head was unmistakable on the bolster;

and yet it was all covered, and no one lies with covered head but a dead person; and this was not dead, not truly dead, for it heaved and shivered. If he had seen these things in dusk or by the light of a flickering candle, Thomson could have comforted himself and talked of fancy. On this bright day that was impossible. What was to be done? First, lock the door at all costs. Very gingerly he approached it and bending down listened, holding his breath; perhaps there might be a sound of heavy breathing, and a prosaic explanation. There was absolute silence. But as, with a rather tremulous hand, he put the key into its hole and turned it, it rattled, and on the instant a stumbling padding tread was heard coming towards the door. Thomson fled like a rabbit to his room and locked himself in: futile enough, he knew it was; would doors and locks be any obstacle to what he suspected? But it was all he could think of at the moment, and in fact nothing happened; only there was a time of acute suspense—followed by a misery of doubt as to what to do. The impulse, of course, was to slip away as soon as possible from a house which contained such an inmate. But only the day before he had said he should be staying for at least a week more, and how if he changed plans could he avoid the suspicion of having pried into places where he certainly had no business? Moreover, either the Bettses knew all about the inmate, and yet did not leave the house, or knew nothing, which equally meant that there was nothing to be afraid of, or knew just enough to make them shut up the room, but not enough to weigh on their spirits: in any of these cases it seemed that not much was to be feared, and certainly so far he had had no sort of ugly experience. On the whole the line of least resistance was to stay.

Well, he stayed out his week. Nothing took him past that door, and often as he would pause in a quiet hour of day or night in the passage and listen, and listen, no sound whatever issued from that direction. You might have thought that Thomson would have made some attempt at ferreting out stories connected with the inn—hardly perhaps from Betts, but from the parson of the parish, or old people in the village; but no, the reticence which commonly falls on people who have had strange experiences, and believe in them, was upon him. Nevertheless, as the end of his stay drew near, his yearning after some kind of explanation grew more and more acute. On his solitary walks he persisted in planning out some way, the least obtrusive, of getting another daylight glimpse into that room, and eventually arrived at this scheme. He would leave by an afternoon train—about four o'clock. When his fly was waiting, and his luggage on it, he would make one last expedition upstairs to look round his own room and see if anything was left unpacked, and then, with that key, which he had contrived to oil (as if that made any difference!), the door should once more be opened, for a moment, and shut.

So it worked out. The bill was paid, the consequent small talk gone through while the fly was loaded; "pleasant part of the country—been very comfortable, thanks to you and Mrs Betts—hope to come back some time," on one side: on the other, "very glad you've found satisfaction, sir, done our best—always glad to 'ave your good word—very much favoured we've been with the weather to be sure." Then, "I'll just take a look upstairs in case I've left a book or something out—no, don't trouble, I'll be back in a minute." And as noiselessly as possible he stole to the door and opened it.

The shattering of the illusion! He almost laughed aloud. Propped, or you might say sitting, on the edge of the bed was—nothing in the round world but a scarecrow! A scarecrow out of the garden, of course, dumped into the deserted room . . . Yes; but here amusement ceased. Have scarecrows bare bony feet? Do their heads loll onto their shoulders? Have they iron collars and links of chain about their necks? Can they get up and move, if never so stiffly, across a floor, with wagging head and arms close at their sides? and shiver?

The slam of the door, the dash to the stair-head, the leap downstairs, were followed by a faint. Awaking, Thomson saw Betts standing over him with the brandy bottle and a very reproachful face. "You shouldn't a done so, sir, really you shouldn't. It ain't a kind way to act by persons as done the best they could for you." Thomson heard words of this kind, but what he said in reply he did not know. Mr Betts, and perhaps even more Mrs Betts, found it hard to accept his apologies and his assurances that he would say no word that could damage the good name of the house. However, they *were* accepted. Since the train could not now be caught, it was arranged that Thomson should be driven to the town to sleep there. Before he went the Bettses told him what little they knew. "They says he was landlord 'ere a long time back, and was in with the 'ighwaymen that 'ad their beat about the 'eath. That's how he come by his end: 'ung in chains, they say, up where you see that stone what the gallus stood in. Yes, the fishermen made away with that, I believe, because they see it out at sea and it kep' the fish off, according to their idea. Yes, we 'ad the account from the people that 'ad the 'ouse before we come. 'You keep that room shut up,' they says, 'but don't move the bed out, and you'll find there won't be no trouble.' And no more there 'as been; not once he haven't come out into the 'ouse, though what he may do now there ain't no sayin'. Anyway, you're the first I know on that's seen him since we've been 'ere: I never set eyes on him myself, nor don't want. And ever since we've made the servants' rooms in the stablin', we ain't 'ad no difficulty that way. Only I do 'ope, sir, as you'll keep a close tongue, considerin' 'ow an 'ouse do get talked about": with more to this effect.

The promise of silence was kept for many years. The occasion of my hearing the story at last was this: that when Mr Thomson came to stay with my father it fell to me to show him to his room, and instead of letting me open the door for him, he stepped forward and threw it open himself, and then for some moments stood in the doorway holding up his candle and looking narrowly into the interior. Then he seemed to recollect himself and said: "I beg your pardon. Very absurd, but I can't help doing that, for a particular reason." What that reason was I heard some days afterwards, and you have heard now.

# It Was Rose Hall

The Hall was just what Nurse Minta had expected. It was a large English-looking mansion sitting on well-kept lawns, and like pictures she'd seen of the first "old country" homes in Jamaica. Its brown brick wall stared her in the face as she walked up the gravel path, passing a shrubbery and clumps of rose bushes in full flower.

When she reached the front door Nurse Minta could not resist the temptation of standing still before she knocked, and drinking in the air—air fragrant, and almost heady, with the combined scent of roses and other flowers and shrubs. Somewhere, beyond the house, a stable clock chimed the half hour. It all seemed quiet and well-ordered.

Nurse Minta lifted the bright brass knocker and let it fall—once, twice. The noise made by the knocker came back to her as from an empty house, with startling clarity and force. It was the sort of hollow sound often heard in caves or echoing in great churches. Come to think of it the lawn did look a bit like an old country churchyard. The narrow rose-bed in front of the windows might well be a grave—the grave of a long-dead owner?

Bang, bang, bang! Nurse Minta knocked again. She looked at the slip of paper in her hand: The Hall, Peak Lane, Maypen.

"I *am* at the right house," said Nurse Minta.

Then she experienced an uneasy feeling. Someone was watching her—but not from a window in the house. She turned and looked behind her. Sure as day there he was, standing by the road under a tree. That old man, waiting no doubt to hear her scream and run from the house in terror. Haunted he'd said it was when she'd asked him, a few minutes earlier, if she had reached the Hall. Haunted indeed! This well-kept, peaceful place!

Minta, occupied with her own thoughts, did not realise that the door of the Hall was opening. She gasped; the door was opening slowly, dead slow; not even a babe could have opened it as slowly as that. Now it was wide open and Minta waited for a face to appear; there was none. The door had opened seemingly on its own. A chill finger of fear crept down her spine. Beads of sweat glistened on her dark forehead.

"But, of course," and she laughed at herself. "That girl told me that the care-taker's wife was crippled—no doubt she has some gadget to control the door from her wheelchair."

So, trying to shake off any feeling of apprehension, she stepped through the doorway and into a square hall. It seemed dimly-lit and cold.

"Anyone in?" Minta called, as cheerfully as she could.

"This way, please," a pleasant voice answered.

Minta, following the sound of the voice, went down a passage, expecting to find only a pre-taped recorder that in some way was mechanically connected with the front door.

How wrong she was! She came to the entrance of a big room in which a lady sat at a small, elegant writing-table. The lady turned and said, "I am Mrs O'Harry. Do come in and sit down." No wheel-chair was in sight nor any mechanical contrivance. Minta wondered again how the front door had been opened.

Mrs O'Harry's face was one of the most lovely Minta had ever seen. And her whole appearance was that of a wealthy, beautiful and fastidious woman. Her grey hair hung in soft curls down to her shoulders; her dress, light gold in colour, was of pure silk, and her jewellery—a heavy gold chain, bracelet and several rings—was without doubt real. To Nurse Minta this beautiful woman seemed strange and at the same time familiar. She thought of fancy dress, then of "period" plays. "Oh, of course," said Minta to herself. "She is like one of those portraits we saw on 'art appreciation' visits to the picture gallery when I was at High School." Looking about her Nurse Minta thought Mrs O'Harry exactly suited the room, which she supposed must be a study or perhaps the library of the house. The walls were lined with book cases. On the writing-table two books lay open and beside them some paper on which were what looked like hand-written notes. But the paper had a yellowish tinge and the books seemed old, and almost grey—as if covered with dust.

These thoughts quickly shot through Minta's mind as she sat herself down uneasily on the edge of a chair, which had thin legs and wooden arms, and tried to think how to begin. "It is good of you . . . You are kind to see me—I got lost—that's why I'm late. That girl—she told you I'd be coming?"

"Oh yes, she did. It does not matter that you are later than she said you would be. So, come with me now and I will show you the flat."

Minta, obeying Mrs O'Harry's gesture, went first up the broad flight of stairs to the landing of the floor above. This floor had been altered and made into two flats. One was vacant and had been advertised as available for "visitors to Jamaica." Not that Minta had seen the advertisement herself. It was that girl, the friendly Jamaican girl, who had walked part of the way along Banana Grove Lane with Minta, who had told her about it.

The flat Minta could have consisted of one comfortable-looking sitting-room, a small kitchenette and a gigantic (after what she'd been used to), well-furnished bedroom.

"You are not listening, dear," Mrs O'Harry said, loudly. For Minta stood silent, looking about her, and had not heard Mrs O'Harry speak.

"Oh, I'm sorry. I was just thinking. It is all so nice, and just what I want . . . but . . . that girl, I thought she said only three shillings a week. Now I've seen it . . . I don't think I can . . . But did you say something?"

"I was saying that the kitchen is small—but that is right. Three shillings a week. You pay when you like. There are no conditions," Mrs O'Harry smiled, "and no keys either. I'll go to my room now, and leave you to have a good look round."

Minta did have a good look round. And since she was alone, she went to try the big, comfortable-looking bed. Eh—a spring mattress! She bounced up and down. Her bed in the nurses' hostel in Kingston, where she was staying, did not bounce. Then Minta lay flat on the bed, put her arms under her head and stretched out her aching legs. Eh, what comfort! It was too good to be true. "It must be only a dream," murmured Minta. "I am still in that café, trying to get up enough strength, after all my trotting round this morning, to start to climb the high hill in the hope of finding a place to stay."

At this point Nurse Minta must have dozed off, for the next thing she heard was rain drumming against the windows. Daylight was almost gone.

Oh no! She began to panic. No umbrella, no mac and trapped in a strange house during a typical Jamaican downpour! She must leave. Still dazed with sleep she scrambled up, stumbled in the half light into the passage, and, without realising it, bumped against the door of the other flat. The door opened and Minta found herself face to face with a young woman, who said, "Oh hello, you must be the new tenant." While she spoke she looked straight at Minta with her deep-set, violet-coloured eyes.

Minta, now more or less awake, looked at her with interest and answered, "Yes. Be moving in tomorrow."

"You are not going out in this rain, surely?"

"I must go. Got to go back to Kingston tonight and get my things."

"Oh, you won't need anything here. Do come in. My name is Etta."

Minta hesitated for a moment. There was something disturbing about the young woman. Something she could not put her finger on. Her hair, for example. Her hair was too golden, almost unnatural.

"But what girl has hair of natural colour today?" said Etta, answering Minta's unspoken words.

Nurse Minta felt herself blush and was acutely embarrassed because her thoughts had been read. But she allowed herself to be led into the room.

A little later, sitting in a deep armchair in the girl's pleasant room, sipping a glass of ice-cold coconut water, Minta found herself telling Etta why she was in Maypen.

"I've come from the United States to see if I can discover anything about my Jamaican ancestors," she explained.

"Oh, yes?" said Etta.

"My Dad and Mum went to Georgia and I was brought up there. I took my training in New York State, and now work in a big hospital. I'm a nurse, see? But both my grandparents were Jamaican-born, and they lived right here in Maypen. That's why I want to stay here for a bit. Even if only for two weeks, and even if I don't find out anything of the family history or discover any trace of my other ancestors, or find relations still living here."

"It's a long way to have come," said Etta.

"Well, but I had to save. Even in the States, young nurses don't get much. It took ages to raise the fare."

"I used to be a nurse. All of us here. We were all nurses during our other life."

"Your other life?"

"Yes, during my other life I was a nurse too. And Mrs O'Harry. Poor Mrs O'Harry . . ."

"What's wrong with her?"

"Nothing now. Only she was locked up here for many years. The smugglers, you see. This used to be their hideout. But you do know that, don't you? There is a secret underground passage leading right to the sandy sea-shore. Poor Mrs O'Harry was kidnapped and brought here to look after their wounded. They couldn't let her go after that, could they?"

"But that was years ago, before my granddad was born. And that was at—eh—Rose Hall. That's it. Rose Hall it was called. I was told stories about it when I was a kid."

"But this is Rose Hall," said Etta.

Minta laughed then. Etta was trying to frighten her. Rose
Hall was haunted. Nobody dared even to talk about Rose
Hall, let alone visit it. "If this was Rose Hall," said Minta
with a big laugh, "no one would be seen dead here. Not in
the evening, anyway."

"Some people do call us dead. They call me dead, call Mrs
O'Harry dead, poor Mrs O'Harry."

"But you're sitting right here. Of course you're not dead."

"I'm glad *you* think so. Most people call us dead. They
don't believe that we've just passed on to another world."

Nurse Minta began laughing, stopped short. After all,
mentally ill patients had to be sympathised with, Nurse
Minta knew that. She understood. This poor young woman
was not quite normal. She'd probably been overworking, and
was at the Hall for a rest and change. Minta got up. It was
time she left even though the storm was not quite over. Etta
stood up too. Minta stretched out her hands, meaning to put
them reassuringly upon the girl's shoulders: Nurse Minta's
arms remained extended, as though frozen in mid-air. Etta
still stood in front of her, but Minta's hands, though apparently resting upon her shoulders, had touched . . . nothing.
Minta stood, as though glued to the spot, she looked the girl
up and down.

Minta gasped—she had just noticed Etta's feet. They were
not even touching the floor. Minta cried out in real fright,
turned, ran and almost tumbled down the stairs. Mrs
O'Harry came from her room just as she reached the bottom
step.

"That lodger," gasped Minta, pointing up the stairway,
"she's . . . she's a ghost. She's a ghost," she shouted, feeling
she must make herself heard above the renewed splashing
and thudding of the rain.

Mrs O'Harry spoke gently. "Ghost? Oh dear, has Etta frightened you?"

"Yes. She's a ghost—a real ghost—a GHOST!"

"My dear, you must not upset yourself. We are not ghosts, you know, although we can't make people believe that."

Minta stepped back. "You . . . you? You said 'we'?" She looked at Mrs O'Harry and then turned quickly to look up the stairs. The girl called Etta was still standing, or rather floating, on the landing.

"Yes, dear," came Mrs O'Harry's quiet voice. "We. All of us here at Rose Hall."

This was too much. "I *am* dreaming," said Minta aloud, "I know, I went fast asleep on that comfortable bed."

"You are not asleep, dear. This *is* Rose Hall."

At these firm, though gently spoken words—Minta did indeed "wake up." "Lord save us," she muttered, "I'm in a loony bin." She felt that she must get out. "Please move away from the door," she said. And then, as Mrs O'Harry's eyes seemed to take on a steely look, she spoke more roughly, and put out a hand to shove Mrs O'Harry aside. "Out of my way—if you aren't all mad, perhaps you are a lot of crooks. I'm not staying here. Move out of my . . ." Nurse Minta stopped. Her body became stiff with fright. She thought she had pushed Mrs O'Harry. But she had not touched anything. Her hand was just out in space—in air, vacuum—nothingness.

Nurse Minta screamed. She turned to run. And there before her was another figure—appearing seemingly from nowhere. Heavens, no—it could not be the same girl. Not that girl she'd walked with in Banana Grove Lane—the girl who had given her the address of the vacant flat?

"Yes, it is." Once more Nurse Minta's thoughts were

understood, just as if she had spoken the words aloud. "And you will be my special friend," said the girl from the Grove floating towards Nurse Minta. "I saw it all. It happened on the hill just in front of the house. Yes," she repeated, almost proudly, "I saw it all. I was in the shrubbery. It was a black car, number—number—let me think—number MV 1237. Yes, it was MV 1237, sure of it."

"Dear God, let me wake up!"

"But you are not asleep," said the girl. "Don't you understand? You are coming here to live with us. You and I will be great friends. I saw it all. Yes *I* did."

The Jamaican girl stopped speaking. Nurse Minta seized her chance, dashed past her and ran out of the house. Not that she thought anyone would have prevented her escape. But she somehow knew that they *could* have stopped her if they had wanted to. They had the power.

"Mad. That's it. They are all mad," she said. Trying to reassure herself. Trying to find a rational explanation of her bewildering, terrifying experience. Then the words of the old man came back to her. "Haunted!"

She rushed from the house into the rain, tore down the path and out onto the wet road. Two headlights bore down upon her from the top of the hill. She heard the screech of brakes. The screech came too late. Much too late. Just before that sharp impact against her body, Nurse Minta saw the number of the car: it was MV 1237.

"Not my fault," cried a coarse voice. "Not my fault. She dashed out right in front of me. I tried to stop; my God, I tried to stop! She ran straight into me."

"I saw it all." Nurse Minta heard the voice of the girl from the Banana Grove.

She tried to speak: got to save that driver. "It was not his fault, was not his fault."

"No pain fortunately. Died instantly," said the ambulance people when they came.

"Not true." Again Nurse Minta tried to speak aloud. "I am still alive."

No one heeded her. The ambulance crawled away. The rain clouds had gone. All that was left on the Maypen hill was the sweet smell of flowers. Somewhere someone was playing a piano softly. Nurse Minta in spirit floated up and back along the gravel path and through the door of Rose Hall.

Inspired by a Jamaican tale,
*"The White Witch of Rosehall"*

# Running Wolf

"Go to Medicine Lake, it's fairly stiff with big fish," said Morton of the Montreal Sporting Club to his younger friend Malcolm Hyde. "Spend your holidays there—up Mattawa way, some fifteen miles west of Stony Creek. You'll have it all to yourself except for an old Indian who's got a shack there. Camp on the east side—if you'll take a tip from me." He then talked for half an hour about the wonderful sport; yet he was not otherwise very communicative, and did not suffer questions gladly, Hyde noticed. Nor had he stayed there very long himself. If it was such a paradise as Morton, its discoverer and the most experienced rod in the province, claimed, why had he himself spent only three days there?

"Ran short of grub," was the explanation offered; but to another friend he had mentioned briefly, "Flies," and to a third, so Hyde learned later, he gave the excuse that his half-breed companion "took sick," necessitating a quick return to civilisation.

Hyde, however, cared little for the explanations; his interest in these came later. "Stiff with fish" was the phrase he liked. He took the Canadian Pacific train to Mattawa, laid in his outfit at Stony Creek, and set off thence for the fifteen-mile canoe-trip without a care in the world.

Travelling light, the portages did not trouble him; the water was swift and easy, the rapids negotiable; everything came his way, as the saying is. Occasionally he saw big fish making for the deeper pools, and was sorely tempted to stop; but he resisted. He pushed on between the immense world of forests that stretched for hundreds of miles, known to deer, bear, moose, and wolf, but strange to any echo of human tread, a deserted and primeval wilderness. The autumn day was calm, the water sang and sparkled, the blue sky hung cloudless over all, ablaze with light. Towards evening he passed an old beaver-dam, rounded a little point, and had his first sight of Medicine Lake. He lifted his dripping paddle; the canoe shot with silent glide into calm water. He gave an exclamation of delight, for the loveliness took his breath away.

Though primarily a sportsman, he was not insensible to beauty. The lake formed a crescent, perhaps four miles long, its width between a mile and half a mile. The slanting gold of sunset flooded it. No wind stirred its crystal surface. Here it had lain since the redskins' god first made it; here it would lie until he dried it up again. Towering spruce and hemlock trooped to its very edge, majestic cedars leaned down as if to drink, crimson sumachs shone in fiery patches, and maples gleamed orange and red beyond belief. The air was like wine, with the silence of a dream.

It was here the red men formerly "made medicine," with all the wild ritual and tribal ceremony of an ancient day. But it was of Morton, rather than of Indians, that Hyde thought. If this lonely, hidden paradise was really stiff with big fish, he owed a lot to Morton for the information. Peace invaded him, but the excitement of the hunter lay below.

He looked about him with a quick, practised eye for a camping-place before the sun sank below the forests and the half-lights came. The Indian's shack, lying in full sunshine on the eastern shore, he found at once; but the trees lay too thick about it for comfort, nor did he wish to be so close to its inhabitant. Upon the opposite side, however, an ideal clearing offered. This lay already in shadow, the huge forest darkening it toward evening; but the open space attracted him. He paddled over quickly and examined it. The ground was hard and dry, he found, and a little brook ran tinkling down one side of it into the lake. This outfall, too, would be a good fishing spot. Also it was sheltered. A few low willows marked the mouth.

An experienced camper soon makes up his mind. It was a perfect site, and some charred logs, with traces of former fires, proved that he was not the first to think so. Hyde was delighted. Then, suddenly, disappointment came to tinge his pleasure. His kit was landed, and preparations for putting up the tent were begun, when he recalled a detail that excitement had so far kept in the background of his mind—Morton's advice. But not Morton's only, for the storekeeper at Stony Creek had reinforced it. The big fellow with straggling moustache and stooping shoulders, dressed in shirt and trousers, had handed him out a final sentence with the bacon, flour, condensed milk, and sugar. He had repeated Morton's half-forgotten words.

"Put yer tent on the east shore, I should," he had said at parting.

He remembered Morton, too, apparently. "A shortish fellow, brown as an Indian and fairly smelling of the woods. Travelling with Jake, the half-breed." That assuredly was

Morton. "Didn't stay long, now, did he?" he added to himself in a reflective tone.

"Going Windy Lake way, are yer? Or Ten Mile Water, maybe?" he had first inquired of Hyde.

"Medicine Lake."

"Is that so?" the man said, as though he doubted it for some obscure reason. He pulled at his ragged moustache a moment. "Is that so, now?" he repeated. And the final words followed him down-stream after a considerable pause—the advice about the best shore on which to put his tent.

All this now suddenly flashed back upon Hyde's mind with a tinge of disappointment and annoyance, for when two experienced men agreed, their opinion was not to be lightly disregarded. He wished he had asked the storekeeper for more details. He looked about him, he reflected, he hesitated. His ideal camping-ground lay certainly on the forbidden shore. What in the world, he wondered, could be the objection to it?

But the light was fading; he must decide quickly one way or the other. After staring at his unpackaged dunnage, and the tent, already half erected, he made up his mind with a muttered expression that consigned both Morton and the storekeeper to less pleasant places. "They must have *some* reason," he growled to himself: "fellows like that usually know what they're talking about. I guess I'd better shift over to the other side—for tonight, at any rate."

He glanced across the water before actually reloading. No smoke rose from the Indian's shack. He had seen no sign of a canoe. The man, he decided, was away. Reluctantly, then, he left the good camping-ground and paddled across the lake, and half an hour later his tent was up, firewood collected, and two small trout were already caught for supper. But the bigger fish, he knew, lay waiting for him on the other side by the little outfall, and he fell asleep at length on his bed of balsam boughs, annoyed and disappointed, yet wondering how a mere sentence could have persuaded him so easily against his own better judgment. He slept like the dead; the sun was well up before he stirred.

But his morning mood was a very different one. The brilliant light, the peace, the intoxicating air, all this was too exhilarating for the mind to harbour foolish fancies, and he marvelled that he could have been so weak the night before. No hesitation lay in him anywhere. He struck camp immediately after breakfast, paddled back across the strip of shining water, and quickly settled in upon the forbidden shore, as he now called it, with a contemptuous grin. And the more he saw of the spot, the better he liked it. There was plenty of wood, running water to drink, an open space about the tent, and there were no flies. The fishing, moreover, was magnificent. Morton's description was fully justified, and "stiff with big fish" for once was not an exaggeration.

The useless hours of the early afternoon he passed dozing in the sun, or wandering through the underbrush beyond the camp. He found no sign of anything unusual. He bathed in a cool, deep pool; he revelled in the lonely little paradise. Lonely it certainly was, but the loneliness was part of its charm; the stillness, the peace, the isolation of this beautiful backwoods lake delighted him. The silence was divine. He was entirely satisfied.

Towards evening, after a brew of tea, he strolled along the shore, looking for the first sign of a rising fish. A faint ripple on the water, with the lengthening shadows, made good conditions. *Plop* followed *plop,* as the big fellows rose, snatched at their food, and vanished into the depths. He hurried back. Ten minutes later he had taken his rods and was gliding cautiously in the canoe through the quiet water.

So good was the sport, indeed, and so quickly did the big trout pile up in the bottom of the canoe, that despite the growing lateness, he found it hard to tear himself away. "One more," he said, "and then I really will go." He landed that "one more," and was in the act of taking off the hook, when the deep silence of the evening was curiously disturbed. He became abruptly aware that someone watched him. A pair of eyes, it seemed, were fixed upon him from some point in the surrounding shadows.

Thus, at least, he interpreted the odd disturbance in his happy mood; for thus he felt it. The feeling stole over him without the slightest warning. He was not alone. The slippery big trout dropped from his fingers. He sat motionless, and stared about him.

Nothing stirred; the ripple on the lake had died away; there was no wind; the forest lay a single purple mass of shadow; the yellow sky, fast fading, threw reflections that troubled the eye and made distances uncertain. But there was no sound, no movement; he saw no figure anywhere. Yet he knew that someone watched him, and a wave of quite unreasoning terror gripped him. The nose of the canoe was against the bank. In a moment, and instinctively, he shoved it off and paddled into deeper water. The watcher, it came to him also instinctively, was quite close to him upon that bank. But where? And who? Was it the Indian?

Here, in deeper water, and some twenty yards from the shore, he paused and strained both sight and hearing to find some possible clue. He felt half ashamed, now that the first strange feeling passed a little. But the certainty remained. Absurd as it was, he felt positive that someone watched him with concentrated and intent regard. Every fibre in his being told him so; and though he could discover no figure, no new outline on the shore, he could even have sworn in which clump of willow bushes the hidden person crouched and stared. His attention seemed drawn to that particular clump.

The water dripped slowly from his paddle, now lying across the thwarts. There was no other sound. The canvas of his tent gleamed dimly. A star or two had come out. He waited. Nothing happened.

Then, as suddenly as it had come, the feeling passed, and he knew that the person who had been watching him intently had gone. It was as if a current had been turned off; the normal world flowed back; the landscape emptied as if someone had left a room. The disagreeable feeling left him at the same time, so that he instantly turned the canoe in to the shore again, landed, and paddle in hand, went over to examine the clump of willows he had singled out as the place of concealment. There was no one there, of course, nor any trace of recent human occupancy. No leaves, no branches stirred, nor was a single twig displaced; his keen and practised sight detected no sign of tracks upon the ground. Yet, for all that, he felt positive that a little time ago someone had crouched among these very leaves and watched him. He remained absolutely convinced of it. The watcher, whether Indian hunter, stray lumberman, or wandering half-breed, had now withdrawn, a search was useless, and dusk was falling. He returned to his little camp, more disturbed perhaps than he cared to acknowledge. He cooked his supper, hung up his catch on a string, so that no prowling animal could get at it during the night, and prepared to make himself comfortable until bedtime. Unconsciously, he built a bigger fire than usual, and found himself peering over his pipe into the deep shadows beyond the firelight, straining his ears to catch the slightest sound. He remained generally on the alert in a way that was new to him.

A man under such conditions and in such a place need not know discomfort until the sense of loneliness strikes him as too vivid a reality. Loneliness in a backwoods camp brings charm, pleasure, and a happy sense of calm until, and unless, it comes too near. Once it has crept within short range, however, it may easily cross the narrow line between comfort and discomfort, and darkness is an undesirable time for the transition. A curious dread may easily follow—the dread lest the loneliness suddenly be disturbed, and the solitary human feel himself open to attack.

For Hyde, now, this transition had been already accomplished; the too intimate sense of his loneliness had shifted abruptly into the worst condition of no longer being quite alone. It was an awkward moment, and he realised his position exactly. He did not like it. He sat there, with his back to the blazing logs, a very visible object in the light, while all about him the darkness of the forest lay like an impenetrable wall. He could not see a yard beyond the small circle of his camp-fire; the silence about him was like the silence of the dead. No leaf rustled, no wave lapped; he himself sat motionless as a log.

Then again he became suddenly aware that the person who watched him had returned, and the same intent and concentrated gaze as before was fixed upon him. There was no warning; he heard no stealthy tread or snapping of dry twigs, yet the owner of those steady eyes was very close to him, probably not a dozen feet away. This sense of proximity was overwhelming.

A shiver ran down his spine. This time, moreover, he felt positive that the man crouched just beyond the firelight. For some minutes he sat without stirring a single muscle, yet with each muscle ready and alert, straining his eyes in vain to pierce the darkness, but only succeeding in dazzling his sight with the reflected light. Then, as he shifted his position slowly, cautiously, to obtain another angle of vision, his heart gave two big thumps against his ribs and the hair seemed to rise on his scalp with the sense of cold that gave him goose-flesh. In the darkness facing him he saw two small and greenish circles that were certainly a pair of eyes, yet not the eyes of Indian hunter, or of any human being. It was a pair of animal eyes that stared so fixedly at him out of the night. And this certainty had an immediate and natural effect upon him.

For, at the menace of those eyes, the fears of millions of long dead hunters since the dawn of time woke in him. His hand groped for a weapon. His fingers fell on the iron head of his small camp axe, and at once he was himself again. Confidence returned; the vague, superstitious dread was gone. This was a bear or wolf that smelt his catch and came to steal it. With beings of that sort he knew instinctively how to deal, yet admitting, by this very instinct, that his original dread had been of quite another kind.

"I'll damned quick find out what it is," he exclaimed aloud, and snatching a burning brand from the fire, he hurled it with good aim straight at the eyes of the beast before him.

The bit of pitch-pine fell in a shower of sparks that lit the dry grass this side of the animal, flared up a moment, then died quickly down again. But in that instant of bright illumination he saw clearly what his unwelcome visitor was. A big timber wolf sat on its hindquarters, staring steadily at him through the firelight. He saw its legs and shoulders, he saw its hair, he saw also the big hemlock trunks lit up behind it, and the willow scrub on each side. It formed a clear-cut picture shown in vivid detail by the momentary blaze. To his amazement, however, the wolf did not turn and bolt away from the burning log, but withdrew a few yards only, and sat there again on its haunches, staring, staring as before. Heavens, how it stared! He "shoo-ed" it, but without effect; it did not budge. He did not waste another good log on it, for his fear was dissipated now; a timber wolf was a timber wolf, and it might sit there as long as it pleased, provided it did not try to steal his catch. No alarm was in him any more. He knew that wolves were harmless in the summer and autumn, and even when "packed" in the winter, they would attack a man only when suffering desperate hunger. So he sat and watched the beast, threw bits of stick in its direction, even talked to it, wondering only that it never moved. "You can stay there for ever, if you like," he remarked to it aloud, "for you cannot get my fish, and the rest of the grub I shall take into the tent with me!"

The creature blinked its bright green eyes, but made no move.

Why, then, if his fear was gone, did he think of certain things as he rolled himself in the Hudson Bay blankets before going to sleep? The immobility of the animal was strange, its refusal to turn and bolt was still stranger. Never before had he known a wild creature that was not afraid of fire. Why did it sit and watch him, as with purpose in its gleaming eyes? How had he felt its presence earlier and instantly? A timber wolf, especially a solitary wolf, was a timid thing, yet this one feared neither man nor fire. Now, as he lay there wrapped in his blankets inside the cosy tent, it sat outside beneath the stars, beside the fading embers, the chilly wind in its fur, the ground cooling beneath its planted paws, watching, steadily watching.

It was unusual, it was strange. Having neither imagination nor tradition, he called upon no store of racial visions. He lay there merely wondering and puzzled. A timber wolf was a timber wolf and nothing more. Yet this timber wolf—the idea haunted him—was different. In a word, the deeper part of his original uneasiness remained. He tossed about and shivered occasionally in his broken sleep. He woke early and unrefreshed.

Again with the sunshine and the morning wind, however, the incident of the night before was forgotten, almost unreal. His hunting zeal was uppermost. The tea and fish were delicious, his pipe had never tasted so good, the glory of this lonely lake amid primeval forests went to his head a little; he was a hunter before the Lord, and nothing else. He tried the edge of the lake, and in the excitement of playing a big fish, knew suddenly that *it*, the wolf, was there. He paused with the rod, exactly as if struck. He looked about him, he looked in a definite direction. The brilliant sunshine made every smallest detail sharp—boulders of granite, burned stems, crimson sumach, pebbles along the shore in neat, separate detail—without revealing where the watcher hid. Then, his sight wandering farther inshore among the tangled under-growth, he suddenly picked up the familiar, half-expected outline. The wolf was lying behind a granite boulder, so that only the head, the muzzle, and the eyes were visible. It merged in its background. Had he not known it was a wolf, he could never have separated it from the landscape. The eyes still shone in the sunlight.

There it lay. He looked straight at it. Their eyes, in fact, actually met full and square. "Great Scott!" he exclaimed aloud, "why, it's like looking at a human being!"

From that moment, unwittingly, he established a singular personal relation with the beast. And what followed confirmed this undesirable impression, for the animal rose instantly and came down in leisurely fashion to the shore, where it stood looking back at him. It stood and stared into his eyes like some great wild dog, so that he was aware of a new and almost incredible sensation—that it courted recognition.

"Well! well!" he exclaimed again, relieving his feelings by addressing it aloud, "if this doesn't beat everything I ever saw! What d'you want, anyway?"

He examined it now more carefully. He had never seen a wolf so big before; it was a tremendous beast, a nasty customer to tackle, he reflected, if it ever came to that. It stood there absolutely fearless, and full of confidence. In the clear sunlight he took in every detail of it—a huge, shaggy, lean-flanked timber wolf, its eyes staring straight into his own, almost with a purpose in them. He saw its great jaws, its teeth, and its tongue hanging out, dropping a little saliva.

He was amazed and puzzled beyond belief. He wished the Indian would come back. He did not understand this strange behaviour in an animal. Its eyes, the odd expression in them, gave him a queer, unusual, difficult feeling. Had his nerves failed, he wondered.

The beast stood on the shore and looked at him. He

wished for the first time that he had brought a rifle. With a resounding smack he brought his paddle down flat upon the water, using all his strength, till the echoes rang as from a pistol-shot that was audible from one end of the lake to the other. The wolf never stirred. He shouted, but the beast remained unmoved. He blinked his eyes, speaking as to a dog, a domestic animal, a creature accustomed to human ways. It blinked its eyes in return.

At length, increasing his distance from the shore, he continued his fishing, and the excitement of the marvellous sport held his attention—his outward attention, at any rate. At times he almost forgot the attendant beast; yet whenever he looked up, he saw it there. And worse; when he slowly paddled home again, he observed it trotting along the shore as though to keep him company. Crossing a little bay, he spurted, hoping to reach the other point before his undesired and undesirable attendant. Instantly the brute broke into that rapid, tireless lope that, except on ice, can beat anything on four legs in the woods. When he reached the distant point, the wolf was waiting for him. He raised his paddle from the water, pausing a moment for reflection. His camp was near; he had to land; he felt uncomfortable even in the sunshine of broad day, when, to his keen relief, about half a mile from the tent, he saw the creature suddenly stop and sit down in the open. He waited a moment, then paddled on. It did not follow. There was no attempt to move; it merely sat and watched him. After a few hundred yards he looked back. It was still sitting where he left it. And the absurd, yet significant, feeling came to him that the beast divined his thought, his anxiety, his dread, and was now showing him, as well as it could, that it entertained no hostile feeling and did not meditate attack.

He turned the canoe towards the shore; he landed; he cooked his supper in the dusk; the animal made no sign. Not far away it certainly lay and watched, but it did not advance. And to Hyde, observant now in a new way, came one sharp, vivid reminder of the strange atmosphere into which his commonplace personality had strayed: he suddenly recalled that his relations with the beast, already established, had progressed distinctly a stage further. This startled him, yet without the accompanying alarm he must certainly have felt twenty-four hours before. He had an understanding with the wolf. He was aware of friendly thoughts towards it. He even went so far as to set out a few big fish on the spot where he had first seen it sitting the previous night. "If he comes," he thought, "he is welcome to them. I've got plenty, anyway." He thought of it now as "he."

Yet the wolf made no appearance until Hyde was in the act of entering his tent. It was close on ten o'clock, whereas nine was his usual hour for turning in. He had, therefore, unconsciously been waiting for the wolf. Then, as he was closing the flap, he saw the eyes close to where he had placed the fish. He waited, hiding himself, and expecting to hear sounds of munching jaws; but all was silence. Only the eyes glowed steadily out of the background of darkness. He closed the flap. He had no slightest fear. In ten minutes he was sound asleep.

He could not have slept very long, for when he woke up he could see by the faint red light shining through the canvas that the fire had not died down completely. He rose and cautiously peeped out. The air was very cold; he saw his breath. But he also saw the wolf, for it was sitting by the dying embers, not two yards away from where he crouched behind the flap. And this time, at these very close quarters, there was something in the attitude of the big wild thing that caught his attention with a vivid thrill of startled surprise and a sudden shock of cold that held him spellbound. He stared, unable to believe his eyes; for the wolf's attitude conveyed to him something familiar that at first he was unable to explain. Its pose reached him in the terms of another thing with which he was entirely at home. What was it? Did his senses betray him? Was he still asleep and dreaming?

Then, suddenly, with a start of uncanny recognition, he thought he knew. Its attitude was that of a dog. Having found the clue, his mind then made an awful leap. For it was, after all, no dog its appearance aped, but something nearer to himself, and more familiar still. Good heavens! It sat there with the pose, the attitude, the gesture in repose of something almost human. And then, with a second shock of biting wonder, it came to him like a revelation. The wolf sat beside that camp-fire as a man might sit.

Before he could weigh his extraordinary discovery, before he could examine it in detail or with care, the animal, sitting in this fashion, seemed to feel his eyes fixed on itself. It slowly turned and looked him in the face, and for the first time Hyde felt a superstitious fear flood through his entire being. He was transfixed with that nameless terror that is said to attack human beings who suddenly face the dead, finding themselves bereft of speech and movement. This moment of paralysis certainly occurred. Its passing, however, was as singular as its advent. For almost at once he was aware of something beyond and above this mockery of human attitude and pose, something that ran along unaccustomed nerves and reached his feeling, even perhaps his

heart. He was aware of appeal, silent, half expressed, yet
vastly pathetic. He saw in the savage eyes a beseeching,
even a yearning, expression that changed his mood as by
magic from dread to natural sympathy. The great grey
brute, symbol of cruel ferocity, sat there beside his dying fire
and appealed for help.

The gulf betwixt animal and human seemed in that instant
bridged. It was, of course, incredible. Hyde, sleep still possibly clinging to his inner being with the shades and half-
shapes of dream yet about his soul, acknowledged, how he
knew not, the amazing fact. He found himself nodding to the
wolf in half-consent, and instantly, without more ado, the
lean grey shape rose like a wraith and trotted off swiftly, but
with stealthy tread, into the background of the night.

When Hyde woke in the morning his first impression was
that he must have dreamed the entire incident. His practical
nature asserted itself. There was a bite in the fresh autumn
air; the bright sun allowed no half-lights anywhere; he felt
brisk in mind and body. Reviewing what had happened, he
came to the conclusion that he was dealing with something
entirely outside his experience. His fear, however, had completely left him. The odd sense of friendliness remained. The
beast had a definite purpose, and he himself was included in
that purpose. His sympathy held good.

But with the sympathy there was also an intense curiosity.
"If it shows itself again," he told himself, "I'll go up close
and find out what it wants." The fish laid out the night
before had not been touched.

It must have been a full hour after breakfast when he next
saw the wolf; it was standing on the edge of the clearing,
looking at him in the way now become familiar. Hyde im-

mediately picked up his axe and advanced toward it boldly, keeping his eyes fixed straight upon its own. There was nervousness in him, but kept well hidden; step by step he drew nearer until some ten yards separated them. The wolf had not stirred a muscle as yet. Its jaws hung open, its eyes observed him intently; it allowed him to approach without a sign of what its mood might be. Then, with these ten yards between them, it turned abruptly and moved slowly off, looking back first over one shoulder and then over the other, exactly as a dog might do, to see if he was following.

A singular journey it was they then made together, animal and man. The trees surrounded them at once, for they left the lake behind them, entering the tangled bush beyond. The beast, Hyde noticed, obviously picked the easiest track for him to follow. Occasionally there were windfalls to be surmounted; but though the wolf bounded over these with ease, it was always waiting for the man on the other side after he had laboriously climbed over. Deeper and deeper into the heart of the lonely forest they penetrated, cutting across the arc of the lake's crescent, it seemed to Hyde; for after two miles or so, he recognised the big rocky bluff that overhung the water at its northern end. This bluff he had seen from his camp, one side of it falling sheer into the water; it was probably the spot, he imagined, where the Indians held their medicine-making ceremonies, for it stood out in isolated fashion, and its top formed a private plateau not easy of access. And it was here, close to a big spruce at the foot of the bluff upon the forest side, that the wolf stopped suddenly and for the first time since its appearance gave audible expression to its feelings. It sat down on its haunches, lifted its muzzle with open jaws, and gave vent to a subdued and long-drawn howl that was more like the wail of a dog than the fierce barking associated with a wolf.

By this time Hyde had lost not only fear, but caution too; nor, oddly enough, did this howl revive a sign of unwelcome emotion in him. In that curious sound he detected the same message that the eyes conveyed—appeal for help. He had paused, nevertheless, startled by the animal's cry, and looked about him quickly. There was young timber here; it had once been a small clearing, evidently. Axe and fire had done their work, but there was evidence to an experienced eye that it was Indians and not white men who had once been busy here. Some part of the medicine ritual, doubtless, took place in the little clearing, thought the man, as he advanced again towards his patient leader.

Hyde had not taken two steps before the animal got up and moved very slowly in the direction of some low bushes that formed a clump just beyond. It entered these, first looking back to make sure that its companion watched. The bushes hid it; a moment later it emerged again. Twice it performed this pantomime, each time, as it reappeared, standing still and staring at the man with as distinct an expression of appeal in its eyes as an animal can compass, probably. Its excitement, meanwhile, certainly increased, and this excitement was, with equal certainty, communicated to the man. Hyde made up his mind quickly. Gripping his axe tightly, and ready to use it at the first hint of malice, he moved slowly nearer to the bushes, wondering with something of a tremor what would happen.

If he expected to be surprised, his expectation was at once fulfilled; but it was the behaviour of the wolf that was startling. It positively frisked about him like a happy dog. It frisked for joy. Its excitement was intense, yet from its open mouth no sound was audible. Then, with a sudden leap, it bounded past him into the clump of bushes, against whose very edge he stood, and began scraping vigorously at the ground. Hyde stood and stared, amazement and interest now banishing all his nervousness, even when the wolf, in its violent scraping, actually touched his body with its own; for the manner of scratching at the ground seemed an impossible phenomenon. No wolf, no dog certainly, used its paws in the way those paws were working. Hyde had the odd, distressing sensation that they were hands, not paws, he watched. And yet, somehow, the natural surprise he should have felt was absent. In his heart the deep spring of sympathy and pity stirred again.

The wolf stopped in its task and looked up into his face. Hyde acted without hesitation then. Afterwards he was wholly at a loss to explain his own conduct. It seemed he knew what to do, divined what was expected of him. Between his mind and the dumb yearning of the savage animal there was intelligent and intelligible communication. He cut a stake and sharpened it, for the stones would blunt his axe-edge. He entered the clump of bushes to complete the digging his four-legged companion had begun. And while he worked, though he did not forget the proximity of the wolf, he paid no attention to it; often his back was turned as he stooped over the laborious clearing away of the hard earth; no uneasiness or sense of danger was in him any more. The wolf sat outside the clump and watched the operations. The concentrated attention, patience, intense eagerness, and the gentleness of the fierce and probably hungry animal, the obvious pleasure of having won the human to its mysterious

purpose—these were colours in the strange picture that
Hyde thought of later when dealing with the human herd
again. At the moment he was aware chiefly of pathos and
affection.

The digging continued for fully half an hour before his
labour was rewarded by the discovery of a small whitish
object. He picked it up and examined it—the finger-bone of
a man. Other discoveries then followed quickly and in quan-
tity. The *cache* was laid bare. He collected nearly the complete skeleton. The skull, however, he found last, and might
not have found at all but for the guidance of his now
strangely alert companion. As he worked the wolf lay watching intently, watching every movement, and one of its front
paws was raised a little from the ground. It made no sign of
any kind. Hyde gathered boughs enough to make a funeral
pyre, on which he laid the bones, and then carefully lit it.
He became so absorbed in feeding and tending the cere-
monial fire that he did not look once at the wolf, knowing
now with certainty that he was fulfilling its desperate, if
dumb, request. It was only when the platform of boughs
collapsed, laying their charred burden gently on the fragrant
earth among the soft wood ashes, that he turned again, as
though to show the wolf what he had done, and to find,
perhaps, some look of satisfaction in its curiously expressive
eyes. But the place where it had been was empty. The wolf
was gone.

He did not see it again; it gave no sign of its presence
anywhere; no howl was ever audible in the distant forest. He
was not watched. He fished as before, wandered through the
bush about his camp, sat smoking round his fire after dark,
and slept peacefully in his cosy little tent. He felt no eyes,

there was nothing to disturb him. The wolf that behaved like a man had gone for ever.

It was the day before he left that Hyde, noticing smoke rising from the shack across the lake, paddled over to exchange a word or two with the Indian, who had evidently now returned. The redskin came down to meet him as he landed, but it was soon plain that he spoke very little English. He emitted the familiar grunts at first; then bit by bit Hyde stirred his limited vocabulary into action. The net result, however, was slight enough, though it was certainly direct:

"You camp there?" the man asked, pointing to the other side.

"Yes."

"Wolf come?"

"Yes."

"You see wolf?"

"Yes."

The Indian stared at him fixedly, a keen, wondering look upon his coppery, creased face.

"You 'fraid wolf?" he asked after a moment's pause.

"No," replied Hyde, truthfully. He knew it was useless to ask questions of his own, though he was eager for information. The other would have told him nothing. It was sheer luck that the man had touched on the subject at all, and Hyde realised that his own best role was merely to answer but to ask no questions. Then, suddenly, the Indian became comparatively voluble. There was awe in his voice and manner.

"Him no wolf. Him big medicine wolf. Him spirit wolf."

Whereupon he drank the tea the other had brewed for him, closed his lips tightly, and said no more. His outline was discernible on the shore, rigid and motionless, an hour later, when Hyde's canoe turned the corner of the lake three miles away and landed to make the portages up the first rapid of his homeward stream.

It was Morton who, after some persuasion, supplied further details of what he called the legend. Some hundred years before, the tribe that lived in the territory beyond the lake began their annual medicine-making ceremonies on the big rocky bluff at the northern end; but no medicine could be made. The spirits, declared the chief medicine man, would not answer. They were offended. An investigation followed. It was discovered that a young brave had recently killed a wolf, a thing strictly forbidden, since the wolf was the totem animal of the tribe. To make matters worse, the name of the guilty man was Running Wolf. The offence being unpardonable, the man was cursed and driven from the tribe:

"Go out. Wander alone among the woods, and if we see you we slay you. Your bones shall be scattered in the forest, and your spirit shall not enter the Happy Hunting Grounds till one of another race shall find and bury them."

"Which meant," explained Morton laconically, his only comment on the story, "probably for ever."

# The Mind Possessed

The Wind in the Portico
JOHN BUCHAN

A Little Companion
ANGUS WILSON

The Cat "I Am"
GERALD HEARD

Violence
ALGERNON BLACKWOOD

Entrance and Exit
ALGERNON BLACKWOOD

Gay as Cheese
JOAN AIKEN

JOHN BUCHAN

# The Wind in the Portico

There is a place in Shropshire which I do not propose to visit again. It lies between Ludlow and the hills, in a shallow valley full of woods. Its name is St Sant, a village with a big house and park adjoining, on a stream called the Vaun, about five miles from the little town of Faxeter. They have queer names in those parts, and other things queerer than the names.

I was motoring from Wales to Cambridge at the close of the long vacation. All this happened before the War, when I had just got my fellowship and was settling down to academic work. It was a fine night in early October, with a full moon, and I intended to push on to Ludlow for supper and bed. The time was about half-past eight, the road was empty and good going, and I was trundling pleasantly along when something went wrong with my headlights. It was a small thing, and I stopped to remedy it beyond a village and just at the lodge-gates of a house.

On the opposite side of the road a carrier's cart had drawn up, and two men, who looked like indoor servants, were lifting some packages from it onto a big barrow. The moon was up, so I didn't need the feeble light of the carrier's lamp to see what they were doing. I suppose I wanted to stretch my legs for a moment, for when I had finished my job I strolled over to them. They did not hear me coming and the carrier on his perch seemed to be asleep.

The packages were the ordinary consignments from some big shop in town. But I noticed that the two men handled them very gingerly, and that, as each was laid in the barrow, they clipped off the shop label and affixed one of their own. The new labels were odd things, large and square, with some address written on them in very black capital letters. There was nothing in that, but the men's faces puzzled me. For they seemed to do their job in a fever, longing to get it over, and yet in a sweat lest they should make some mistake. Their commonplace task seemed to be for them a matter of tremendous importance. I moved so as to get a view of their faces, and I saw that they were white and strained. The two were of the butler or valet class, both elderly, and I could have sworn that they were labouring under something like fear.

I shuffled my feet to let them know of my presence, and remarked that it was a fine night. They started as if they had been robbing a corpse. One of them mumbled something in reply, but the other caught a package which was slipping, and in a tone of violent alarm growled to his mate to be careful. I had a notion that they were handling explosives.

I had no time to waste, so I pushed on. That night, in my room at Ludlow, I had the curiosity to look up my map and identify the place where I had seen the men. The village was St Sant, and it appeared that the gate I stopped at belonged to a considerable demesne called Vauncastle. That was my first visit.

At that time I was busy on a critical edition of Theocritus, for which I was making a new collation of the manuscripts. There was a variant of the Medicean Codex in England, which nobody had seen since Gaisford, and after a good deal of trouble I found that it was in the library of a man called Dubellay. I wrote to him at his London club, and got a reply, to my surprise, from Vauncastle Hall, Faxeter. It was an odd letter, for you could see that he longed to tell me to go to the devil, but couldn't quite reconcile it with his conscience. We exchanged several letters, and the upshot was that he gave me permission to examine his manuscript. He did not ask me to stay, but mentioned that there was a comfortable little inn in St Sant.

My second visit began on the 27th of December, after I had been at home for Christmas. We had had a week of severe frost, and then it had thawed a little; but it remained bitterly cold, with leaden skies that threatened snow. I drove from Faxeter, and as we ascended the valley I remember thinking that it was a curiously sad country. The hills were too low to be impressive, and their outlines were mostly blurred with woods; but the tops show clear, funny little knolls of grey bent that suggested a volcanic origin. It might have been one of those backgrounds you find in Italian primitives, with all the light and colour left out. When I got a glimpse of the Vaun in the bleached meadows it looked like the "wan water" of the Border ballads. The woods, too, had not the friendly bareness of English copses in winter time. They remained dark and cloudy, as if they were hiding secrets. Before I reached St Sant, I decided that the landscape was not only sad, but ominous.

I was fortunate in my inn. In the single street of one-storied cottages it rose like a lighthouse, with a cheery glow from behind the red curtains of the bar parlour. The inside proved as good as the outside. I found a bedroom with a bright fire, and I dined in a wainscoted room of preposterous old pictures of lanky hounds and hollow-backed horses. I had been rather depressed on my journey, but my spirits were raised by this comfort, and when the house produced a most respectable bottle of port I had the landlord in to drink a glass. He was an ancient man who had been a gamekeeper, with a much younger wife, who was responsible for the management. I was curious to hear something about the owner of my manuscript, but I got little from the landlord. He had been with the old squire, and had never served the present one. I heard of Dubellays in plenty—the landlord's master, who had hunted his own hounds for forty years; the Major, his brother, who had fallen at Abu Klea; Parson Jack, who had had the living till he died; and of all kinds of collaterals. The "Deblays" had been a high-spirited, open-handed stock, and much liked in the place. But of the present master of the Hall he could or would tell me nothing. The Squire was a "great scholard," but I gathered that he followed no sport and was not a convivial soul like his predecessors. He had spent a mint of money on the house, but not many people went there. He, the landlord, had never been inside the grounds in the new master's time, though in the old days there had been hunt breakfasts on the lawn for the whole countryside, and mighty tenantry dinners. I went to bed with a clear picture in my mind of the man I was to interview on the morrow. A scholarly and autocratic recluse, who collected treasures and beautified his dwelling and probably lived in his library. I rather looked forward to meeting him, for the bonhomous sporting squire was not much in my line.

After breakfast next morning I made my way to the Hall. It was the same leaden weather, and when I entered the gates the air seemed to grow bitterer and the skies darker. The place was muffled in great trees which even in their winter bareness made a pall about it. There was a long avenue of ancient sycamores, through which one caught only rare glimpses of the frozen park. I took my bearings, and realised that I was walking nearly due south, and was gradually descending. The house must be in a hollow. Presently the trees thinned, I passed through an iron gate, came out on a big untended lawn, untidily studded with laurels and rhododendrons, and there before me was the house front.

I had expected something beautiful—an old Tudor or Queen Anne façade or a dignified Georgian portico. I was disappointed, for the front was simply mean. It was low and irregular, more like the back parts of a house, and I guessed that at some time or another the building had been turned round, and the old kitchen door made the chief entrance. I was confirmed in my conclusion by observing that the roofs rose in tiers, like one of those recessed New York skyscrapers, so that the present back parts of the building were of an impressive height.

The oddity of the place interested me, and still more its dilapidation. What on earth could the owner have spent his money on? Everything—lawn, flower-beds, paths—was neglected. There was a new stone doorway, but the walls badly needed pointing, the window woodwork had not been painted for ages, and there were several broken panes. The bell did not ring, so I was reduced to hammering on the knocker, and it must have been ten minutes before the door opened. A pale butler, one of the men I had seen at the carrier's cart the October before, stood blinking in the entrance.

He led me in without question, when I gave my name, so I was evidently expected. The hall was my second surprise. What had become of my picture of the collector? The place was small and poky, and furnished as barely as the lobby of a farmhouse. The only thing I approved was its warmth. Unlike most English country houses, there seemed to be excellent heating arrangements.

I was taken into a little dark room with one window that looked out on a shrubbery, while the man went to fetch his master. My chief feeling was of gratitude that I had not been asked to stay, for the inn was paradise compared with this sepulchre. I was examining the prints on the wall, when I heard my name spoken and turned round to greet Mr Dubellay.

He was my third surprise. I had made a portrait in my mind of a fastidious old scholar, with eye-glasses on a black cord, and a finical *weltkind*-ish manner. Instead I found a man still in early middle age, a heavy fellow dressed in the roughest country tweeds. He was as untidy as his demesne, for he had not shaved that morning, his flannel collar was badly frayed, and his finger-nails would have been the better for a scrubbing brush. His face was hard to describe. It was high-coloured, but the colour was not healthy; it was friendly, but it was also wary; above all, it was *unquiet*. He gave me the impression of a man whose nerves were all wrong, and who was perpetually on his guard.

He said a few civil words, and thrust a badly tied brown paper parcel at me.

"That's your manuscript," he said jauntily.

I was staggered. I had expected to be permitted to collate the codex in his library, and in the last few minutes had realised that the prospect was distasteful. But here was this casual owner offering me the priceless thing to take away.

I stammered my thanks, and added that it was very good of him to trust a stranger with such a treasure.

"Only as far as the inn," he said. "I wouldn't like to send it by post. But there's no harm in your working at it at the inn. There should be confidence among scholars." And he gave an odd cackle of a laugh.

"I greatly prefer your plan," I said. "But I thought you would insist on my working at it here."

"No, indeed," he said earnestly. "I shouldn't think of such a thing . . . Wouldn't do at all . . . An insult to our free-masonry . . . That's how I should regard it."

We had a few minutes' further talk. I learned that he had inherited under the entail from a cousin, and had been just over ten years at Vauncastle. Before that he had been a London solicitor. He asked me a question or two about Cambridge—wished he had been at the University—much hampered in his work by a defective education. I was a Greek scholar?—Latin, too, he presumed. Wonderful people the Romans . . . He spoke quite freely, but all the time his queer restless eyes were darting about, and I had a strong impression that he would have liked to say something to me very different from these commonplaces—that he was long-ing to broach some subject but was held back by shyness or fear. He had such an odd appraising way of looking at me.

I left without having been asked to a meal, for which I was not sorry, for I did not like the atmosphere of the place. I took a short cut over the ragged lawn, and turned at the top of the slope to look back. The house was in reality a huge pile, and I saw that I had been right and that the main building was all at the back. Was it, I wondered, like the Alhambra, which behind a front like a factory concealed a treasure-house? I saw, too, that the woodland hollow was more spacious than I had fancied. The house, as at present arranged, faced due north, and behind the south front was an open space in which I guessed that a lake might lie. Far beyond I could see in the December dimness the lift of high dark hills.

That evening the snow came in earnest, and fell continuously for the better part of two days. I banked up the fire in my bedroom and spent a happy time with the codex. I had brought only my working books with me and the inn boasted no library, so when I wanted to relax I went down to the taproom, or gossiped with the landlady in the bar parlour. The yokels who congregated in the former were pleasant fellows, but, like all the folk on the Marches, they did not talk readily to a stranger, and I heard little from them of the Hall. The old squire had reared every year three thousand pheasants, but the present squire would not allow a gun to be fired on his land, and there were only a few wild birds left. For the same reason the woods were thick with vermin. This they told me when I professed an interest in shooting. But of Mr Dubellay they would not speak, declaring that they never saw him. I dare say they gossiped wildly about him, and their public reticence struck me as having in it a touch of fear.

The landlady, who came from a different part of the shire, was more communicative. She had not known the former Dubellays and so had no standard of comparison, but she was inclined to regard the present squire as not quite right in the head. "They do say," she would begin; but she, too, suffered from some inhibition, and what promised to be sensational would trail off into the commonplace. One thing apparently puzzled the neighbourhood above others, and that was his rearrangement of the house. "They do say," she said in an awed voice, "that he have built a great church." She had never visited it—no one in the parish had, for Squire Dubellay did not allow intruders—but from Lyne Hill you could see it through a gap in the woods. "He's no good Christian," she told me, "and him and Vicar has quarrelled this many a day. But they do say as he worships summat there." I learned that there were no women servants in the house, only the men he had brought from London. "Poor benighted souls, they must live in a sad hobble," and the buxom lady shrugged her shoulders and giggled.

On the last day of December I decided that I needed exercise and must go for a long stride. The snow had ceased that morning, and the dull skies had changed to a clear blue. It was still very cold, but the sun was shining, the snow was firm and crisp under foot, and I proposed to survey the country. So after luncheon I put on thick boots and gaiters, and made for Lyne Hill. This meant a considerable circuit, for the place lay south of the Vauncastle park. From it I hoped to get a view of the other side of the house.

I was not disappointed. There was a rift in the thick woodlands, and below me, two miles off, I suddenly saw a strange building, like a classical temple. Only the entablature and the tops of the pillars showed above the trees, but they stood out vivid and dark against the background of snow. The spectacle in that lonely place was so startling that for a little I could only stare. I remember that I glanced behind me to the snowy line of the Welsh mountains, and felt that I might have been looking at a winter view of the Apennines two thousand years ago.

My curiosity was now alert, and I determined to get a nearer view of this marvel. I left the track and ploughed through the snowy fields down to the skirts of the woods. After that my troubles began. I found myself in a very good imitation of a primeval forest, where the undergrowth had been unchecked and the rides uncut for years. I sank into deep pits, I was savagely torn by briars and brambles, but I struggled on, keeping a line as best I could. At last the trees stopped. Before me was a flat expanse which I knew must be a lake, and beyond rose the temple.

It ran the whole length of the house, and from where I stood it was hard to believe that there were buildings at its back where men dwelt. It was a fine piece of work—the first glance told me that—admirably proportioned, classical, yet not following exactly any of the classical models. One could imagine a great echoing interior, dim with the smoke of sacrifice, and it was only by reflecting that I realised that the peristyle could not be continued down the two sides, that there was no interior, and that what I was looking at was only a portico.

The thing was at once impressive and preposterous. What madness had been in Dubellay when he embellished his house with such a grandiose garden front? The sun was setting and the shadow of the wooded hills darkened the interior, so I could not even make out the back wall of the portico. I wanted a nearer view, so I embarked on the frozen lake.

Then I had an odd experience. I was not tired, the snow

lay level and firm, but I was conscious of extreme weariness. The biting air had become warm and oppressive. I had to drag boots that seemed to weigh tons across that lake. The place was utterly silent in the stricture of the frost, and from the pile in front no sign of life came.

I reached the other side at last and found myself in a frozen shallow of bullrushes and skeleton willow-herbs. They were taller than my head, and to see the house I had to look upward through their snowy traceries. It was perhaps eighty feet above me and a hundred yards distant, and, since I was below it, the delicate pillars seemed to spring to a great height. But it was still dusky, and the only detail I could see was on the ceiling, which seemed either to be carved or painted with deeply shaded monochrome figures.

Suddenly the dying sun came slanting through the gap in the hills, and for an instant the whole portico to its farthest recesses was washed in clear gold and scarlet. That was wonderful enough, but there was something more. The air was utterly still, with not the faintest breath of wind—so still that, when I had lit a cigarette half an hour before, the flame of the match had burned steadily upward like a candle in a room. As I stood among the sedges not a single frost crystal stirred . . . But there was a wind blowing in the portico.

I could see it lifting feathers of snow from the base of the pillars and fluffing the cornices. The floor had already been swept clean, but tiny flakes drifted onto it from the exposed edges. The interior was filled with a furious movement, though a yard from it was frozen peace. I felt nothing of the action of the wind, but I knew that it was hot, hot as the breath of a furnace.

I had only one thought, dread of being overtaken by night

near that place. I turned and ran. Ran with labouring steps across the lake, panting and stifling with a deadly hot oppression, ran blindly by a sort of instinct in the direction of the village. I did not stop till I had wrestled through the big wood and come out on some rough pasture above the highway. Then I dropped on the ground, and felt again the comforting chill of the December air.

The adventure left me in an uncomfortable mood. I was ashamed of myself for playing the fool, and at the same time hopelessly puzzled, for the oftener I went over in my mind the incidents of that afternoon the more I was at a loss for an explanation. One feeling was uppermost, that I did not like this place and wanted to be out of it. I had already broken the back of my task, and by shutting myself up for two days I completed it; that is to say, I made my collation as far as I had advanced myself in my commentary on the text. I did not want to go back to the Hall, so I wrote a civil note to Dubellay, expressing my gratitude and saying that I was sending up the manuscript by the landlord's son, as I scrupled to trouble him with another visit.

I got a reply at once, saying that Mr Dubellay would like to give himself the pleasure of dining with me at the inn before I went, and would receive the manuscript in person.

It was the last night of my stay in St Sant, so I ordered the best dinner the place could provide, and a magnum of claret, of which I discovered a bin in the cellar. Dubellay appeared promptly at eight o'clock, arriving, to my surprise, in a car. He had tidied himself up and put on a dinner jacket, and he looked exactly like the city solicitors you see dining in the Junior Carlton.

He was in excellent spirits, and his eyes had lost their air of being on guard. He seemed to have reached some conclusion about me, or decided that I was harmless. More, he seemed to be burning to talk to me. After my adventure I was prepared to find fear in him, the fear I had seen in the faces of the men-servants. But there was none; instead, there was excitement, overpowering excitement.

He neglected the courses in his verbosity. His coming to dinner had considerably startled the inn, and instead of a maid the landlady herself waited on us. She seemed to want to get the meal over, and hustled the biscuits and the port onto the table as soon as she decently could. Then Dubellay became confidential.

He was an enthusiast, it appeared, an enthusiast with a single hobby. All his life he had pottered among antiquities, and when he succeeded to Vauncastle he had the leisure and money to indulge himself. The place, it seemed, had been famous in Roman Britain—Vauni Castra—and Faxeter was a corruption of the same. "Who was Vaunus?" I asked. He grinned, and told me to wait.

There had been an old temple up in the high woods. There had always been a local legend about it, and the place was supposed to be haunted. Well, he had had the site excavated and he had found— Here he became the cautious solicitor, and explained to me the law of treasure trove. As long as the objects found were not intrinsically valuable, not gold or jewels, the finder was entitled to keep them. He had done so—had not published the results of his excavations in the proceedings of any learned society—did not want to be bothered by tourists. I was different, for I was a scholar.

What had he found? It was really rather hard to follow his babbling talk, but I gathered that he had found certain carvings and sacrificial implements. And—he sunk his voice—most important of all, an altar, an altar of Vaunus, the tutelary deity of the vale.

When he mentioned this word his face took on a new look—not of fear but of secrecy, a kind of secret excitement. I have seen the same look on the face of a street-preaching Salvationist.

Vaunus had been a British god of the hills, whom the Romans in their liberal way appear to have identified with Apollo. He gave me a long confused account of him, from which it appeared that Mr Dubellay was not an exact scholar. Some of his derivations of place-names were absurd—like St Sant from Sancta Sanctorum—and in quoting a line of Ausonius he made two false quantities. He seemed to hope that I could tell him something more about Vaunus, but I said that my subject was Greek, and that I was deeply ignorant about Roman Britain. I mentioned several books, and found that he had never heard of Haverfield.

One word he used, "hypocaust," which suddenly gave me a clue. He must have heated the temple, as he heated his house, by some very efficient system of hot air. I know little about science, but I imagined that the artificial heat of the portico, as contrasted with the cold outside, might create an air current. At any rate that explanation satisfied me, and my afternoon's adventure lost its uncanniness. The reaction made me feel friendly towards him, and I listened to his talk with sympathy, but I decided not to mention that I had visited his temple.

He told me about it himself in the most open way. "I couldn't leave the altar on the hillside," he said. "I had to make a place for it, so I turned the old front of the house into a sort of temple. I got the best advice, but architects are ignorant people, and I often wished I'd been a better scholar. Still, the place satisfies me."

"I hope it satisfies Vaunus," I said jocularly.

"I think so," he replied quite seriously, and then his thoughts seemed to go wandering, and for a minute or so he looked through me with a queer abstraction in his eyes.

"What do you do with it now you've got it?" I asked.

He didn't reply, but smiled to himself.

"I don't know if you remember a passage in Sidonius Apollinaris," I said, "a formula for consecrating pagan altars to Christian uses. You begin by sacrificing a white cock or something suitable, and tell Apollo with all friendliness that the old dedication is off for the present. Then you have a Christian invocation—"

He nearly jumped out of his chair.

"That wouldn't do—wouldn't do at all . . . Oh Lord, no! . . . Couldn't think of it for one moment!"

It was as if I had offended his ears by some horrid blasphemy, and the odd thing was that he never recovered his composure. He tried, for he had good manners, but his ease and friendliness had gone. We talked stiffly for another half-hour about trifles, and then he rose to leave. I returned him his manuscript neatly parcelled up, and expanded in thanks, but he scarcely seemed to heed me. He stuck the thing in his pocket, and departed with the same air of shocked absorption.

After he had gone I sat before the fire and reviewed the situation. I was satisfied with my hypocaust theory, and had no more perturbation in my memory about my afternoon's adventure. Yet a slight flavour of unpleasantness hung about

it, and I felt that I did not quite like Dubellay. I set him
down as a crank who had tangled himself up with a half-
witted hobby, like an old maid with her cats, and I was not
sorry to be leaving the place.

My third and last visit to St Sant was in the following June
—the midsummer of 1914. I had all but finished my Theocritus, but I needed another day or two with the Vauncastle manuscript, and, as I wanted to clear the whole thing
off before I went to Italy in July, I wrote to Dubellay and
asked if I might have another sight of it. The thing was a
bore, but it had to be faced, and I fancied that the valley
would be a pleasant place in that hot summer.

I got a reply at once, inviting, almost begging me to come,
and insisting that I should stay at the Hall. I couldn't very
well refuse, though I would have preferred the inn. He
wired about my train, and wired again saying he would meet
me. This time I seemed to be a particularly welcome guest.

I reached Faxeter in the evening, and was met by a car
from a Faxeter garage. The driver was a talkative young
man, and, as the car was a closed one, I sat beside him for
the sake of fresh air. The term had tired me, and I was glad
to get out of stuffy Cambridge, but I cannot say that I found
it much cooler as we ascended the Vaun valley. The woods
were in their summer magnificence, but a little dulled and
tarnished by the heat, the river was shrunk to a trickle, and
the curious hilltops were so scorched by the sun that they
seemed almost yellow above the green of the trees. Once
again I had the feeling of a landscape fantastically un-
English.

"Squire Dubellay's been in a great way about your coming, sir," the driver informed me. "Sent down three times to

the boss to make sure it was all right. He's got a car of his own, too, a nice little Daimler, but he don't seem to use it much. Haven't seen him about in it for a month of Sundays."

As we turned in at the Hall gates he looked curiously about him. "Never been here before, though I've been in most gentlemen's parks for fifty miles round. Rum old-fashioned spot, isn't it, sir?"

If it had seemed a shuttered sanctuary in mid-winter, in that June twilight it was more than ever a place enclosed and guarded. There was almost an autumn smell of decay, a dry decay like touchwood. We seemed to be descending through layers of ever-thickening woods. When at last we turned through the iron gate I saw that the lawns had reached a further stage of neglect, for they were as shaggy as a hayfield.

The white-faced butler let me in, and there, waiting at his back, was Dubellay. But he was not the man whom I had seen in December. He was dressed in an old baggy suit of flannels, and his unwholesome red face was painfully drawn and sunken. There were pouches under his eyes, and these eyes were no longer excited, but dull and pained. Yes, and there was more than pain in them—there was fear. I wondered if his hobby were becoming too much for him.

He greeted me like a long-lost brother. Considering that I scarcely knew him, I was a little embarrassed by his warmth. "Bless you for coming, my dear fellow," he cried. "You want a wash and then we'll have dinner. Don't bother to change, unless you want to. I never do." He led me to my bedroom, which was clean enough, but small and shabby like a servant's room. I guessed that he had gutted the house to build his absurd temple.

We dined in a fair-sized room which was a kind of library.

It was lined with old books, but they did not look as if they had been there long; rather it seemed like a lumber room in which a fine collection had been stored. Once no doubt they had lived in a dignified Georgian chamber. There was nothing else, none of the antiques which I had expected.

"You have come just in time," he told me. "I fairly jumped when I got your letter, for I had been thinking of running up to Cambridge to insist on your coming down here. I hope you're in no hurry to leave."

"As it happens," I said, "I *am* rather pressed for time, for I hope to go abroad next week. I ought to finish my work here in a couple of days. I can't tell you how much I'm in your debt for your kindness."

"Two days," he said. "That will get us over midsummer. That should be enough." I hadn't a notion what he meant.

I told him that I was looking forward to examining his collection. He opened his eyes. "Your discoveries, I mean," I said, "the altar of Vaunus . . ."

As I spoke the words his face suddenly contorted in a spasm of what looked like terror. He choked and then recovered himself. "Yes, yes," he said rapidly. "You shall see it—you shall see everything—but not now—not tonight. Tomorrow—in broad daylight—that's the time."

After that the evening became a bad dream. Small talk deserted him, and he could only reply with an effort to my commonplaces. I caught him often looking at me furtively, as if he were sizing me up and wondering how far he could go with me. The thing fairly got on my nerves, and, to crown all, it was abominably stuffy. The windows of the room gave on a little paved court with a background of laurels, and I might have been in Seven Dials for all the air there was.

When coffee was served I could stand it no longer. "What about smoking in the temple?" I said. "It should be cool there with the air from the lake."

I might have been proposing the assassination of his mother. He simply gibbered at me. "No, no," he stammered. "My God, no!" It was half an hour before he could properly collect himself. A servant lit two oil-lamps, and we sat on in the frowsty room.

"You said something when we met before," he ventured at last, after many a sidelong glance at me. "Something about a ritual for re-dedicating an altar."

I remembered my remark about Sidonius Apollinaris.

"Could you show me the passage? There is a good classical library here, collected by my great-grandfather. Unfortunately my scholarship is not equal to using it properly."

I got up and hunted along the shelves, and presently found a copy of Sidonius, the Plantin edition of 1609. I turned up the passage, and roughly translated it for him. He listened hungrily, and made me repeat it twice.

"He says a cock," he hesitated. "Is that essential?"

"I don't think so. I fancy any of the recognised ritual stuff would do."

"I am glad," he said simply. "I am afraid of blood."

"Good God, man," I cried out, "are you taking my nonsense seriously? I was only chaffing. Let old Vaunus stick to his altar!"

He looked at me like a puzzled and rather offended dog.

"Sidonius was in earnest . . ."

"Well, I'm not," I said rudely. "We're in the twentieth century and not in the third. Isn't it about time we went to bed?"

He made no objection, and found me a candle in the hall. As I undressed I wondered into what kind of lunatic asylum I had strayed. I felt the strongest distaste for the place, and longed to go straight off to the inn; only I couldn't make use of a man's manuscripts and insult his hospitality. It was fairly clear to me that Dubellay was mad. He had ridden his hobby to the death of his wits and was now in its bondage. Good Lord! He had talked of his precious Vaunus as a votary talks of a god. I believed he had come to worship some figment of his half-educated fancy.

I think I must have slept for a couple of hours. Then I woke dripping with perspiration, for the place was simply an oven. My window was as wide open as it would go, and, though it was a warm night, when I stuck my head out the air was fresh. The heat came from indoors. The room was on the first floor near the entrance and I was looking onto the overgrown lawns. The night was very dark and utterly still, but I could have sworn that I heard wind. The trees were as motionless as marble, but somewhere close at hand I heard a strong gust blowing. Also, though there was no moon, there was somewhere near me a steady glow of light; I could see the reflection of it round the end of the house. That meant that it came from the temple. What kind of saturnalia was Dubellay conducting at such an hour?

When I drew in my head I felt that if I was to get any sleep something must be done. There could be no question about it; some fool had turned on the steam heat, for the room was a furnace. My temper was rising. There was no bell to be found, so I lit my candle and set out to find a servant.

I tried a cast downstairs and discovered the room where

we had dined. Then I explored a passage at right angles, which brought me up against a great oak door. The light showed me that it was a new door, and that there was no apparent way of opening it. I guessed that it led into the temple, and, though it fitted close and there seemed to be no keyhole, I could hear through it a sound like a rushing wind . . . Next I opened a door on my right and found myself in a big store cupboard. It had a funny, exotic, spicy smell, and, arranged very neatly on the floor and shelves, was a number of small sacks and coffers. Each bore a label, a square of stout paper with very black lettering. I read "*Pro servitio Vauni.*"

I had seen them before, for my memory betrayed me if they were not the very labels that Dubellay's servants had been attaching to the packages from the carrier's cart that evening in the past autumn. The discovery made my suspicions an unpleasant certainty. Dubellay evidently meant the labels to read "For the service of Vaunus." He was no scholar, for it was an impossible use of the word "*servitium,*" but he was very patently a madman.

However, it was my immediate business to find some way to sleep, so I continued my quest for a servant. I followed another corridor, and discovered a second staircase. At the top of it I saw an open door and looked in. It must have been Dubellay's, for his flannels were tumbled untidily on a chair; but Dubellay himself was not there and the bed had not been slept in.

I suppose my irritation was greater than my alarm—though I must say I was getting a little scared—for I still pursued the evasive servant. There was another stair which apparently led to attics, and in going up it I slipped and made a great clatter. When I looked up the butler in his nightgown was staring down at me, and if ever a mortal face held fear it was his. When he saw who it was he seemed to recover a little.

"Look here," I said, "for God's sake turn off that infernal hot air. I can't get a wink of sleep. What idiot set it going?"

He looked at me owlishly, but he managed to find his tongue.

"I beg your pardon, sir," he said, "but there is no heating apparatus in this house."

There was nothing more to be said. I returned to my bedroom, and it seemed to me that it had grown cooler. As I leaned out of the window, too, the mysterious wind seemed to have died away, and the glow no longer showed from behind the corner of the house. I got into bed and slept heavily till I was roused by the appearance of my shaving water about half-past nine. There was no bathroom, so I bathed in a tin pannikin.

It was a hazy morning which promised a day of blistering heat. When I went down to breakfast I found Dubellay in the dining-room. In the daylight he looked a very sick man, but he seemed to have taken a pull on himself, for his manner was considerably less nervy than the night before. Indeed, he appeared almost normal, and I might have reconsidered my view but for the look in his eyes.

I told him that I proposed to sit tight all day over the manuscript, and get the thing finished. He nodded. "That's all right. I've a lot to do myself, and I won't disturb you."

"But first," I said, "you promised to show me your discoveries."

He looked at the window where the sun was shining on the laurels and on a segment of the paved court.

"The light is good," he said—an odd remark. "Let us go there now. There are times and seasons for the temple."

He led me down the passage I had explored the previous night. The door opened, not by a key but by some lever in the wall. I found myself looking suddenly at a bath of sunshine with the lake below as blue as a turquoise.

It is not easy to describe my impressions of that place. It was unbelievably light and airy, as brilliant as an Italian colonnade in midsummer. The proportions must have been good, for the columns soared and swam, and the roof (which looked like cedar) floated as delicately as a flower on its stalk. The stone was some local limestone, which on the floor took a polish like marble. All around was a vista of sparkling water and summer woods and far blue mountains. It should have been as wholesome as the top of a hill.

And yet I had scarcely entered before I knew that it was a prison. I am not an imaginative man, and I believe my nerves are fairly good, but I could scarcely put one foot before the other, so strong was my distaste. I felt shut off from the world, as if I were in a dungeon or on an ice-floe. And I felt, too, that though far enough from humanity, we were not alone.

On the inner wall there were three carvings. Two were imperfect friezes sculptured in low relief, dealing apparently with the same subject. It was a ritual procession, priests bearing branches, the ordinary *dendrophori* business. The faces were only half-human, and that was from no lack of skill, for the artist had been a master. The striking thing was that the branches and the hair of the hierophants were being tossed by a violent wind, and the expression of each was of a being in the last stage of endurance, shaken to the core by terror and pain.

Between the friezes was a great roundel of a Gorgon's
head. It was not a female head, such as you commonly find,
but a male head, with the viperous hair sprouting from chin
and lip. It had once been coloured, and fragments of a green
pigment remained in the locks. It was an awful thing, the
ultimate horror of fear, the last dementia of cruelty made
manifest in stone. I hurriedly averted my eyes and looked at
the altar.

That stood at the west end on a pediment with three steps.
It was a beautiful piece of work, scarcely harmed by the
centuries, with two words inscribed on its face—APOLL.
VAUN. It was made of some foreign marble, and the hollow
top was dark with ancient sacrifices. Not so ancient either,
for I could have sworn that I saw there the mark of recent
flame.

I do not suppose I was more than five minutes in the
place. I wanted to get out, and Dubellay wanted to get me
out. We did not speak a word till we were back in the
library.

"For God's sake give it up!" I said. "You're playing with
fire, Mr Dubellay. You're driving yourself into Bedlam. Send
those damned things to a museum and leave this place. Now,
now, I tell you. You have no time to lose. Come down with
me to the inn straight off and shut up this house."

He looked at me with his lip quivering like a child about
to cry.

"I will. I promise you I will . . . But not yet . . . After
tonight . . . Tomorrow I'll do whatever you tell me . . .
You won't leave me?"

"I won't leave you, but what earthly good am I to you if
you won't take my advice?"

"Sidonius . . ." he began.

"Oh, damn Sidonius! I wish I had never mentioned him. The whole thing is arrant nonsense, but it's killing you. You've got it on the brain. Don't you know you're a sick man?"

"I'm not feeling very grand. It's so warm today. I think I'll lie down."

It was no good arguing with him, for he had the appalling obstinacy of very weak things. I went off to my work in a shocking bad temper.

The day was what it had promised to be, blisteringly hot. Before midday the sun was hidden by a coppery haze, and there was not the faintest stirring of wind. Dubellay did not appear at luncheon—it was not a meal he ever ate, the butler told me. I slogged away all the afternoon, and had pretty well finished my job by six o'clock. That would enable me to leave next morning, and I hoped to be able to persuade my host to come with me.

The conclusion of my task put me into a better humour, and I went for a walk before dinner. It was a very close evening, for the heat haze had not lifted; the woods were as silent as a grave, not a bird spoke, and when I came out of the cover to the burnt pastures the sheep seemed too languid to graze. During my walk I prospected the environs of the house, and saw that it would be very hard to get access to the temple except by a long circuit. On one side was a mass of outbuildings, and then a high wall, and on the other the very closest and highest hedge I have ever seen, which ended in a wood with savage spikes on its containing wall. I returned to my room, had a cold bath in the exiguous tub, and changed.

Dubellay was not at dinner. The butler said that his master was feeling unwell and had gone to bed. The news pleased me, for bed was the best place for him. After that I settled myself down to a lonely evening in the library. I browsed among the shelves and found a number of rare editions which served to pass the time. I noticed that the copy of Sidonius was absent from its place.

I think it was about ten o'clock when I went to bed, for I was unaccountably tired. I remember wondering whether I oughtn't to go and visit Dubellay, but decided that it was better to leave him alone. I still reproach myself for that decision. I know now I ought to have taken him by force and haled him to the inn.

Suddenly I came out of heavy sleep with a start. A human cry seemed to be ringing in the corridors of my brain. I held my breath and listened. It came again, a horrid scream of panic and torture.

I was out of bed in a second, and only stopped to get my feet into slippers. The cry must have come from the temple. I tore downstairs expecting to hear the noise of an alarmed household. But there was no sound, and the awful cry was not repeated.

The door in the corridor was shut, as I expected. Behind it pandemonium seemed to be loose, for there was a howling like a tempest—and something more, a crackling like fire. I made for the front door, slipped off the chain, and found myself in the still, moonless night. Still, except for the rending gale that seemed to be raging in the house I had left.

From what I had seen on my evening's walk I knew that my one chance to get to the temple was by way of the quickset hedge. I thought I might manage to force a way between the end of it and the wall. I did it, at the cost of much of my raiment and my skin. Beyond was another rough lawn set with tangled shrubberies, and then a precipitous slope to the level of the lake. I scrambled along the sedgy margin, not daring to lift my eyes till I was on the temple steps.

The place was brighter than day with a roaring blast of fire. The very air seemed to be incandescent and to have become a flaming ether. And yet there were no flames—only a burning brightness. I could not enter, for the waft from it struck my face like a scorching hand and I felt my hair singe . . .

I am short-sighted, as you know, and I may have been mistaken, but this is what I think I saw. From the altar a great tongue of flame seemed to shoot upwards and lick the roof, and from its pediment ran flaming streams. In front of it lay a body—Dubellay's—a naked body, already charred and black. There was nothing else, except that the Gorgon's head in the wall seemed to glow like a sun in hell.

I suppose I must have tried to enter. All I know is that I found myself staggering back, rather badly burned. I covered my eyes, and as I looked through my fingers I seemed to see the flames flowing under the wall, where there may have been lockers, or possibly another entrance. Then the great oak door suddenly shrivelled like gauze, and with a roar the fiery river poured into the house.

I ducked myself in the lake to ease the pain, and then ran back as hard as I could by the way I had come. Dubellay, poor devil, was beyond my aid. After that I am not very clear what happened. I know that the house burned like a haystack. I found one of the men-servants on the lawn, and I think I helped to get the other down from his room by one of the rain-pipes. By the time the neighbours arrived the house was ashes, and I was pretty well mother-naked. They took me to the inn and put me to bed, and I remained there till after the inquest. The coroner's jury were puzzled, but they found it simply death by misadventure; a lot of country houses were burned that summer. There was nothing found of Dubellay; nothing remained of the house except a few blackened pillars; the altar and the sculptures were so cracked and scarred that no museum wanted them. The place has not been rebuilt, and for all I know they are there today. I am not going back to look for them.

ANGUS  WILSON

# A Little Companion

They say in the village that Miss Arkwright has never been
the same since the war broke out, but she knows that it all
began a long time before that—on 24th July 1936, to be
exact, the day of her forty-seventh birthday.

She was in no way a remarkable person. Her appearance
was not particularly distinguished and yet she was without
any feature that could actively displease. She had enough
personal eccentricities to fit into the pattern of English village life, but none so absurd or anti-social that they could
embarrass or even arouse gossip beyond what was pleasant
to her neighbours. She accepted her position as an old maid
with that cheerful good humour and occasional irony which
are essential to English spinsters since the deification of Jane
Austen, or more sacredly Miss Austen, by the upper middle
classes, and she attempted to counteract the inadequacy of
the unmarried state by quiet, sensible, and tolerant social
work in the local community. She was liked by nearly everyone, though she was not afraid of making enemies where she
knew that her broad but deeply felt religious principles were
being opposed. Any socially pretentious or undesirably extravagant conduct, too, was liable to call forth from her an
unexpectedly caustic and well-aimed snub. She was invited

everywhere and always accepted the invitations. You could
see her at every tea or cocktail party, occasionally drinking a
third gin, but never more. Quietly but well dressed, with one
or two very fine old pieces of jewellery that had come down
to her from her grandmother, she would pass from one
group to another, laughing or serious as the occasion demanded. She smoked continuously her own rather expensive
brand of cigarettes—"My one vice," she used to say, "the
only thing that stands between me and secret drinking." She
listened with patience, but with a slight twinkle in her eye,
to Mr Hodgson's endless stories of life in Dar es Salaam or
Myra Hope's breathless accounts of her latest system of diet.
John Hobday in his somewhat ostentatiously gentleman-
farmer attire would describe his next novel about East
Anglian life to her before even his beloved daughter had
heard of it. Richard Trelawney, just down from Oxford,
found that she had read and really knew Donne's sermons,
yet she could swop detective stories with Colonel Wright by
the hour, and was his main source for quotations when *The
Times* crossword was in question. She it was who incorpo-
rated little Mrs Grantham into village life, when that rather
underbred, suburban woman came there as Colonel Grantham's second wife, checking her vulgar remarks about "the
lower classes" with kindly humour, but defending her
against the formidable battery of Lady Vernon's antagonism.
Yet she it was also who was first at Lady Vernon's when Sir
Robert had his stroke and her unobtrusive kindliness and
real services gained her a singular position behind the grim
reserve of the Vernon family. She could always banter the
vicar away from his hobby horse of the Greek rite when at
parish meetings the agenda seemed to have been buried for

ever beneath a welter of Euchologia and Menaia. She
checked Sir Robert's anti-bolshevik phobia from victimising
the County Librarian for her Fabianism, but was fierce in
her attack on the local council when she thought that class
prejudice had prevented Commander Osborne's widow from
getting a council house. She led in fact an active and useful
existence, yet when anyone praised her she would only
laugh—"My dear," she would say, "hard work's the only
excuse old maids like me have got for existing at all, and
even then I don't know that they oughtn't to lethalise the lot
of us." As the danger of war grew nearer in the thirties her
favourite remark was "Well, if they've got any sense this
time they'll keep the young fellows at home and put us
useless old maids in the trenches," and she said it with real
conviction.

With her good carriage, ample figure, and large, deep blue
eyes, she even began to acquire a certain beauty as middle
age approached. People speculated as to why she had never
married. She had in fact refused a number of quite person-
able suitors. The truth was that from girlhood she had
always felt a certain repulsion from physical contact. Not
that she was in any way prudish, she was remarkable for a
rather eighteenth-century turn of coarse phrase, indeed
verbal freedom was the easier for her in that sexual activity
was the more remote. Nor would psychoanalysts have found
anything of particular interest in her; she had no abnormal
desires, as a child she had never felt any wish to change her
sex or observed any peculiarly violent or crude incident that
could have resulted in what is called a psychic trauma. She
just wasn't interested, and was perhaps as a result a little
over-given to talking of "all this fuss and nonsense that's

made over sex." She would however have liked to have had a
child. She recognised this as a common phenomenon among
childless women and accepted it, though she could never
bring herself to admit it openly or laugh about it in the
common-sensical way in which she treated her position as an
old maid. As the middle years approached she found a sudden interest and even sometimes a sudden jealousy over
other people's babies and children growing upon her, attack-
ing her unexpectedly and with apparent irrelevancy to time
or place. She was equally wide-awake to the dangers of the
late forties and resolutely resisted such foolish fancies,
though she became as a result a little snappish and over-
gruff with the very young. "Now, my dear," she told herself,
"you *must* deal with this nonsense or you'll start getting
odd." How very odd she could not guess.

The Granthams always gave a little party for her on her
birthdays. "Awful nonsense at my age," she had been saying
now for many years, "but I never say no to a drink." Her
forty-seventh birthday party was a particular success; Mary
Hatton was staying with the Granthams and like Miss Arkwright she was an ardent Janeite so they'd been able to talk
Mr Collins and Mrs Elton and the Elliots to their hearts'
content, then Colonel Grantham had given her some tips
about growing meconopsis, and finally Mrs Osborne had
been over to see the new rector at Longhurst, so they had a
good-natured but thoroughly enjoyable "cat" about the state
of the rectory there. She was just paying dutiful attention to
her hostess' long complaint about the grocery deliveries,
preparatory to saying good-bye, when suddenly a thin,
whining, but remarkably clear, child's voice said loudly in
her ear, "Race you home, Mummy." She looked around her

in surprise, then decided that her mind must have wandered from the boring details of Mrs Grantham's saga, but almost immediately the voice sounded again: "Come on, Mummy, you are a slowcoach, I said, 'Race you home.'" This time Miss Arkwright was seriously disturbed, she wondered if Colonel Grantham's famous high spirits had got the better of him, but it could hardly have been so, she thought as she saw his face earnest in conversation—"The point is, Vicar, not so much whether we want to intervene as whether we've got to." She began to feel most uncomfortable and as soon as politeness allowed she made her way home.

The village street seemed particularly hot and dusty, the sunlight on the whitewashed cottages peculiarly glaring as she walked along. "One too many on a hot day that's your trouble, my dear," she said to herself and felt comforted by so material an explanation. The familiar trimness of her own little house and the cool shade of the walnut tree on the front lawn further calmed her nerves. She stopped for a moment to pick up a basket of lettuce that old Pyecroft had left at the door and then walked in. After the sunlight outside, the hall seemed so dark that she could hardly discern even the shape of the grandfather clock. Out of this shadowy blackness came the child's voice loudly and clearly but if anything more nasal than before. "Beat you to it this time," it said. Miss Arkwright's heart stopped for a moment and her lungs seemed to contract and then almost instantaneously she had seen it—a little white-faced boy, thin, with matchstick arms and legs growing out of shrunken clothes, with red-rimmed eyes and an adenoidal open-mouthed expression. Instantaneously, because the next moment he was not there, almost like a flickering image against the eye's retina.

Miss Arkwright straightened her back, took a deep breath, then she went upstairs, took off her shoes, and lay down on her bed.

It was many weeks before anything fresh occurred and she felt happily able to put the whole incident down to cocktails and the heat, indeed she began to remember that she had woken next morning with a severe headache—"You're much too old to start suffering from hangovers," she told herself. But the next experience was really more alarming. She had been up to London to buy a wedding present at Harrods and, arriving somewhat late for the returning train, found herself sitting in a stuffy and over-packed carriage. She felt therefore particularly pleased to see the familiar slate quarries that heralded the approach of Brankston Station, when suddenly a sharp dig drove the bones of her stays into her ribs. She looked with annoyance at the woman next to her—a blowsy creature with feathers in her hat—when she saw to her surprise that the woman was quietly asleep, her arms folded in front of her. Then in her ears there sounded 'Chuff, chuff, chuff, chuff," followed by a little snort and a giggle, and then quite unmistakably the whining voice saying "Rotten old train." After that it seemed to her as though for a few moments pandemonium had broken loose in the carriage—shouts and cries and a monotonous thumping against the woodwork as though someone were beating an impatient rhythm with their foot—yet no other occupant seemed in the slightest degree disturbed. They were for Miss Arkwright moments of choking and agonising fear. She dreaded that at any minute the noise would grow so loud that the others would notice, for she felt an inescapable responsibility for the incident; yet had the whole carriage risen and flung her from the window as a witch it would in some degree have been a release from the terrible sense of personal obsession, it would have given objective reality to what now seemed an uncontrollable expansion of her own consciousness into space, it would at the least have shown that others were mad beside herself. But no slightest ripple broke the drowsy torpor of the hot carriage in the August sun. She was deeply relieved when the train at last drew into Brankston and the impatience of her invisible attendant was assuaged, but no sooner had she set foot on the platform than she heard once more the almost puling whine, the too familiar "Race you home, Mummy." She knew then that whatever it was, it had come to stay, that her homecomings would no longer be to the familiar comfort of her house and servants, but that there would always be a childish voice, a childish face to greet her for one moment as she crossed the threshold.

And so it proved. Gradually at first, at more than weekly intervals, and then increasingly, so that even a short spell in the vegetable garden or with the rock plants would mean impatient whining, wanton scattering of precious flowers, overturning of baskets—and then that momentary vision, lengthened now sometimes to five minutes' duration, that sickly, cretinous face. The very squalor of the child's appearance was revolting to Miss Arkwright, for whom cheerful, good health was the first of human qualities. Sometimes the sickliness of the features would be of the thick, flaccid, pasty appearance that suggested rich feeding and late hours, and then the creature would be dressed in a velvet suit and fauntleroy collar that might have clothed an over-indulged French *bourgeois* child; at other times the appearance was more cretinous, adenoidal, and emaciated, and then it would wear the shrunken uniform and thick black boots of an institution idiot. In either case it was a child quite out of keeping with the home it sought to possess—a home of quiet beauty, unostentatious comfort, and restrained good taste. Of course, Miss Arkwright argued, it was an emanation from the sick side of herself so that it was bound to be diseased, but this realisation did not compensate for dribble marks on her best dresses or for sticky finger marks on her tweed skirts.

At first she tried to ignore the obsession with her deep reserve of stoic patience, but as it continued, she felt the need of the Church. She became a daily communicant and delighted the more "spikey" of her neighbours. She prayed ceaselessly for release or resignation. A lurking sense of sin was roused in her and she wondered if small frivolities and pleasures were the cause of her visitation; she remembered that after all it had first begun when she was drinking gin. Her religion had always been of the "brisk" and "sensible" variety, but now she began to fear that she had been over-suspicious of "enthusiasm" or "pietism." She gave up all but the most frugal of meals, distributed a lot of her clothes to the poor, slept on a board, and rose at one in the morning to say a special Anglican office from a little book she had once been given by a rather despised High Church cousin. The only result seemed to be to cause scandal to her comfortable, old-fashioned parlourmaid and cook. She mentioned her state of sin in general terms to the vicar and he lent her Neale's translations of the Coptic and Nestorian rites, but they proved of little comfort. At Christmas she rather shamefacedly and secretively placed a little bed with a

richly filled stocking in the corner of her bedroom, but the
child was not to be blackmailed. Throughout the day she
could hear faint but unsavoury sounds of uncontrolled and
slovenly guzzling, like the distant sound of pigs feeding, and
when evening came she was pursued by ever louder retching
and the disturbing smell of vomit.

On Boxing Day she visited her old and sensible friend the
bishop and told him the whole story. He looked at her very
steadily with the large, dramatic brown eyes that were so
telling in the pulpit, and for a long time he remained silent.
Miss Arkwright hoped that he would advise her quickly, for
she could feel a growing tugging at her skirt. It was obvious
that this quiet, spacious library was no place for a child, and
she could not have borne to see these wonderful, old books
disturbed even if she was the sole observer of the sacrilege.
At last the bishop spoke. "You say that the child appears ill
and depraved, has this evil appearance been more marked in
the last weeks?" Miss Arkwright was forced to admit that it
had. "My dear old friend," said the bishop and he put his
hand on hers. "It is your sick self that you are seeing, and all
this foolish abstinence, this extravagant martyrdom are making you more sick." The bishop was a Broad Churchman of
the old school. "Go out into the world and take in its beauty
and its colour. Enjoy what is yours and thank God for it."
And without more ado, he persuaded Miss Arkwright to go
to London for a few weeks.

Established at Berners', she set out to have a good time.
She was always fond of expensive meals, but her first attempt to indulge at Claridge's proved an appalling failure,
for with every course the voice grew louder and louder in
her ears. "Coo! what rotten stuff," it kept on repeating. "I

want an ice." Henceforth her meals were taken almost exclusively on Selfridge's roof or in ice-cream parlours, an unsatisfying and indigestible diet. Visits to the theatre were at first a greater success, she saw the new adaptation of *The Mill on the Floss*, and a version of *Lear* modelled on the original Kean production. The child had clearly never seen a play before and was held entranced by the mere spectacle. But soon it began to grow restless, a performance of *Hedda Gabler* was entirely ruined by rustlings, kicks, whispers, giggles, and a severe bout of hiccoughs. For a time it was kept quiet by musical comedies and farces, but in the end Miss Arkwright found herself attending only *Where the Rainbow Ends, Mother Goose*, and *Buckie's Bears*—it was not a sophisticated child. As the run of Christmas plays drew near their end she became desperate, and one afternoon she left a particularly dusty performance at the Circus and visited her old friend Madge Cleaver—once again to tell all. "Poor Bessie," said Madge Cleaver and she smiled so spiritually. "How real Error can seem," for Madge was a Christian Scientist. "But it's so *un*real, dear, if we can only have the courage to see the Truth. Truth denies Animal Magnetism, Spiritualism, and all other false manifestations." She lent Miss Arkwright *Science and Health* and promised that she would give her "absent treatment."

At first Miss Arkwright felt most comforted. Mrs Eddy's denial of the reality of most common phenomena and in particular of those that are evil seemed to offer a way out. Unfortunately, the child seemed quite unconvinced of its own non-existence. One afternoon Miss Arkwright thought with horror that by adopting a theology that denied the existence of Matter and gave reality only to Spirit she might well be gradually removing herself from the scene, whilst leaving the child in possession. After all her own considerable bulk was testimony enough to her material nature, whilst the child might well in some repulsive way be accounted spirit. Terrified by the prospect before her, she speedily renounced Christian Science.

She returned to her home and by reaction decided to treat the whole phenomenon on the most material basis possible. She submitted her body to every old-fashioned purgative, she even indulged in a little amateur blood-letting, for might not the creature be some ill humour or sickly emanation of the body itself? But this antiquarian leechcraft only produced serious physical weakness and collapse. She was forced to call in Dr Kent who at once terminated the purgatives and put her onto port wine and beefsteak.

Failure of material remedies forced Miss Arkwright at last to a conviction which she had feared from the start. The thing, she decided, must be a genuine psychic phenomenon. It cost her much to admit this for she had always been very contemptuous of spiritualism, and regarded it as socially undesirable where it was not consciously fraudulent. But she was by now very desperate and willing to waive the deepest prejudices to free herself from the vulgar and querulous apparition. For a month or more she attended séances in London, but though she received "happy" communications from enough small Indian or Red Indian children to have started a nursery school, no medium or clairvoyant could tell her anything that threw light on her little companion. At one of the séances, however, she met a thin, red-haired, pre-Raphaelite sort of lady in a long grey garment and sandals, who asked her to attend the Circle of the Seventh Pentacle in the Earllands Road. The people she found there did not attract Miss Arkwright; she decided that the servants of the Devil were either common frauds or of exceedingly doubtful morals, but the little group was enthusiastic when she told her story— How could she hope to fight such Black Powers, they asked, unless she was prepared to invoke the White Art? Although she resisted their arguments at first, she finally found herself agreeing to a celebration of the Satanic Mass in her own home. She sent cook and Annie away for a week and prepared to receive the Circle. Their arrival in the village caused a great stir, partly because of their retinue of goats and rabbits. It had been decided that Miss Arkwright should celebrate the Mass herself, an altar had been set up in the drawing room, she had bought an immense white maternity gown from Debenham's and had been busy all the week learning her words, but at the last minute something within her rebelled, she could not bring herself to say the Lord's Prayer backwards, and the Mass had to be called off. In the morning the devotees of the Pentacle left with many recriminations. The only result seemed to be that valuable ornaments were missing from the bedrooms occupied by the less reputable, whilst about those rooms in which the Devil's true servants had slept there hung an odour of goat that no fumigation could remove.

Miss Arkwright had long since given up visiting her neighbours, though they had not ceased to speculate about her. A chance remark that she had "two now to provide for" had led them to think that she believed herself pregnant. After this last visitation Lady Vernon decided that the time had come to act. She visited Miss Arkwright early one morning, and seeing the maternity gown which was still lying in the sitting room, she was confirmed in her suspicions. "Bessie dear," she said. "You've got to realise that you're seriously ill, mentally ill," and she packed Miss Arkwright off to a brain specialist in Welbeck Street. This doctor, finding nothing physically wrong, sent her to a psychoanalyst. Poor Miss Arkwright! She was so convinced of her own insanity, that she could think of no argument if they should wish to shut her up. But the analyst, a smart, grey-haired Jew, laughed when she murmured "madness." "We don't talk in those terms any more, Miss Arkwright. You're a century out of date. It's true there are certain disturbingly psychotic features in what you tell me, but nothing, I think, that won't yield to deep analysis," and deep analysis she underwent for eight months or more, busily writing down dreams at night and lying on a couch "freely associating" by day. At the end of that time the analyst began to form a few conclusions. "The child itself," he said, "is unimportant, the fact that you still see it even less so. What is important is that you now surround yourself with vulgarity and whining. You have clearly a need for these things which you have inhibited too long in an atmosphere of refinement." It was decided that Miss Arkwright should sublimate this need by learning the saxophone. Solemnly each day the poor lady sat in the drawing room—that room which had resounded with Bach and Mozart—and practised the altosax. At last one day when she had got so far as to be able to play the opening bars of "Alligator Stomp," her sense of the ridiculous rebelled and she would play no more, though her little companion showed great restlessness at the disappearance of noises which accorded all too closely with its vulgar taste.

I shall treat myself, she decided, and after long thought

she came to the conclusion that the most salient feature of
the business lay in the child's constant reiteration of the challenge "Race you home, Mummy"; with this it had started
and with this it had continued. If, thought Miss Arkwright, I
were to leave home completely, not only this house, but also
England, then perhaps it would withdraw its challenge and
depart.

In January 1938, then, she set out on her travels. All across
Europe, in museums and cafés and opera houses, it continued to throw down the gauntlet—"Race you home,
Mummy," and there it would be in her hotel bedroom. It
seemed, however, anxious to take on local colour and would
appear in a diversity of national costumes, often reviving for
the purpose peasant dresses seen only at folk-dance festivals
or when worn by beggars in order to attract tourists. For
Miss Arkwright this rather vulgar and commercial World's
Fair aspect of her life was particularly distressing. The child
also attempted to alter its own colour, pale brown it achieved
in India, in China a faint tinge of lemon, and in America
by some misunderstanding of the term of Red Indian it
emerged bright scarlet. She was especially horrified by the
purple swelling with which it attempted to emulate the
black of the African natives. But whatever its colour, it was
always there.

At last the menace of war in September found Miss Arkwright in Morocco and along with thousands of other British
travellers she hurried home, carrying, she felt, her greatest
menace with her. It was really only after Munich that she
became reconciled to its continued presence, learning gradually to incorporate its noises, its appearance, its whole personality into her daily life. She went out again among her

neighbours and soon everyone had forgotten that she had ever been ill. It was true that she was forced to address her companion occasionally with a word of conciliation, or to administer a slap in its direction when it was particularly provoking, but she managed to disguise these peculiarities beneath her normal gestures.

One Saturday evening in September 1939 she was returning home from the rectory, worried by the threat of approaching war and wondering how she could best use her dual personality to serve her country, when she was suddenly disturbed to hear a clattering of hoofs and a thunderous bellow behind her. She turned to see at some yards' distance a furious bull, charging down the village street. She began immediately to run for her home, the little voice whining in her ear, "Race you home, Mummy." But the bull seemed to gain upon her, and in her terror she redoubled her speed, running as she had not run since she was a girl. She heard, it is true, a faint sighing in her ears as of dying breath, but she was too frightened to stop until she was safe at her own door. In she walked, and, to her amazement, indeed, to her horror, look where she would, the little child was *not* there. She had taken up his challenge to a race and she had won.

She lay in bed that night depressed and lonely. She realised only too clearly that difficult as it was to get rid of him—now that the child was gone she found herself thinking of "him" rather than "it"—it would be well-nigh impossible to get him back. The sirens that declared war next morning seemed only a confirmation of her personal loss. She went into mourning and rarely emerged from the house. For a short while, it is true, her spirits were revived when

the evacuee children came from the East End, some of the
more cretinous and adenoidal seemed curiously like her lost
one. But country air and food soon gave them rosy cheeks
and sturdy legs and she rapidly lost interest. Before the year
was out she was almost entirely dissociated from the external world, and those few friends who found time amid the
cares of war to visit her in her bedroom decided that there
was little that could be done for one who showed so little
response. The vicar, who was busy translating St Gregory
Nazianzen's prayers for victory, spoke what was felt to be
the easiest and kindest verdict when he described her as
"just another war casualty."

# The Cat "I Am"

"Do you know anything about Possession?"

"Well, it's nine points of the law."

"I don't mean possessing; I mean being possessed."

"By what? You don't mean . . . ?"

"I don't know. I wish to hell I did!"

The setting was conventional; a warm wood-fire in a soundly built, open fireplace. The room finely wood-panelled, modern without flagrant departure from tradition, panels alternated with built-in bookcases filled to the floor with books, their ordered book backs making the best of wallpapers. The two men matched. They might have been supplied by the furnishers with the room; each picked to fit the big easy chair in which he lounged in tweeds cut for lounging. They even had pipes in hand and whisky on the small table that was fitted into the central wedge, which was all the two overgrown chairs permitted in the fireplace area.

Comfort, good sense, physical fitness, wide, easy interests—there wasn't an object in the large, full-furnished, well-lit, freshly warm room that did not chorus that sequence of assurances. There was nothing that looked by any possibility askance—still less uncanny. There was nothing, either, that didn't sound the same: the crackle of the fire to give the traditional sense of well-being, the murmur of a dance tune from the radio to bring the modern assurance of a world well within call—a world telling you that it was having a good time and that ease, rhythm, fun, sensible sensuality—the five senses harmonised and put to a lilt—is all there is to know and all we need to know. There was no other sound to suggest any other possibility—except that one odd, incongruous but, thank heaven, still ambiguous word, Possession.

"It all may be accident, coincidence, contingency, or whatever it is that scientists use to erase writing when it appears of itself on our walls. I hope you'll tell me it is. I know one can see cyphers everywhere, as the wilder Baconians find them in any passage of Shakespeare. And, of course, many children," he bent forward and poked the fire with rather unnecessary force, "can see faces in the fire. Eidetic imagery, don't they call it? I hope you'll tell me it's just that or something of that sort."

"How can I tell you what it really is until you tell me what you think you have experienced?" Dr Hamilton thought it no harm to show a little irritation. Innes had asked him over this evening but had never warned him he was wanted for a sideline opinion. That *is* irritating to any man who has done a long day's over-the-countryside work and not reassuring to a doctor who has watched for a number of years the way a nervous breakdown may open its attack, and who knows perhaps a little more of the patient than he likes. It was bad and vexing that Innes hadn't said he felt a bit queer and would like to consult his friend and doctor. No harm friend and doctor being the same, provided patient and friend did not confuse *his* two parts.

Innes had always been a fairly normal if not a very attractive type—a sound if not very remunerative patient and a friend with whom one would play golf and dine more than one would share confidences. He looked sane enough, but of course those stable quiet fellows, if they ever fell off the high poop of their sanity, were apt to go right down and not come up again. But he must listen, not run on. Innes was apologising. "I'm sorry to have brought you around under false pretences—at least I hope they are false. You see, I was sure they were. Every detail in itself is nothing—but together—"

Whatever it is, reflected Hamilton, that's sufficient evidence of strain. Innes is businesslike, and that's not a business-like opening. Aloud he said, "All right. An outsider"— he deliberately did not say doctor—"is certainly a better judge than oneself as to whether any odd series of events has a real, objective connection. Fire away; spin your yarn, and I'll pull you up when I think you're making hook-ups where there aren't any." He felt he had used the right tone—not merely for Innes but for himself. For he always liked to be objective even with himself, and somehow that sudden opening of Innes's, after what he'd thought was a cheerful pipe-drawing silence, had, he owned, shocked him—just the utter incongruity of the remark in this snug place from that commonplace man.

He was sure he had used the right tone as far as Innes was concerned. The man seemed relieved at once. Hamilton naturally shared his relief. His mind had already run ahead to the story's end. He knew now it was a little insomnia, domestic strain—a doctor has to diagnose the whole family of a patient—perhaps a few Freudian fear-dreams, perhaps a freak or two of amnesia. Yes, five to ten grains daily of dear old Pot. Amon. I'm young enough, he thought, to be return-

ing to the old sound sedatives—not, of course, Pot. Brom—
that was too lowering. Perhaps a little iron—often a touch of
anaemia gave one queer exhaustions and fancies.

But Innes was well under way. "They're the more intelligent and beautiful." Damn, he'd missed the beginning and
mustn't show it. "He taps against that French window over
there. And I go over and let him in. I've often sketched him
as he grooms himself." Of course, it's a cat he has! "We've
had him some six months. He isn't a success with the ladies.
Of course, she should have known, if she had thought a
moment. They can't be turned into lap-dogs or mannikins.
He's himself—at least, I was sure—well, to go on. I call him
'I Am'; he's so clear and emphatic. They're lovely, those
Siamese with their pale blue, almost transparent eyes," he
paused a moment, "and their smoky fur. But they have
strong characters. Very temperamental, in fact. He got in
some fine scratches on my wife." Innes laughed. "Tore her
lace coverlets and silk pillows, actually bit the cook, and of
course tried to eat a squawking blackbird they're trying to
tame and teach words to. Silly; let an animal be an animal, I
say. Cook said the cat deliberately bit her but she's so deaf I
expect she never saw I Am was about—though Siamese have
a step as audible as a dog's. I've often heard my wife saying
to Cook, in a voice that certainly carries into the dining-
room, 'Are you deaf?' She says Cook never even turns around
and then says she's not deaf and Mrs Innes shouldn't speak
so indistinctly."

Hamilton was not interested in hearing a patient diagnose
another patient's very different symptoms. But a description
of domestic tensions could throw a valuable sidelight on the
situation. He attended carefully as Innes went on. "It seems
that just at the point where it would have been necessary to

sacrifice the cat to save a major loss in the kitchen, I Am took himself off. I thought he'd gone for good, bagged by a passing hobo who saw there'd be a couple of meals to be got for his pelt. But in three or four days there was a tap on the bottom pane of that French window back there—I've never known another cat to do it—a smart little tap—no mewing— you could hear his claws click on the glass. That became a regular arrangement. I read in here after dinner, as a rule. Regular as clockwork, the tap would come at nine-thirty."

Hamilton glanced casually at his watch; it was nine. "I get up and let him in. He runs in and trots in front of me to the fire here. He waits till I'm settled again and then, after a look at the fire, to judge, I suppose, whether he's at the right distance from it, he settles down to groom himself. It's a regular ritual and takes considerable time: first the chest; then round the ears with the paws; next paw-drill working between the pads; that's followed with big side sweeps that get most of the coat clean; and the whole concludes with the most gymnastic pose. It must be good for the figure as well as for the fur. You hoist one back leg like a signal while, with the help of a front paw driven out behind you, you thrust your head forward and clean the fur right down on your tummy."

"Yes," said Hamilton, "yes," impatiently wondering why all this rather old-maidish cat-cataloguing. Then, with self-reproof, he realised that Innes must be spinning out his story, trying to gain time. He was edging towards some part of it that must be creepy. He was trying, with an accumulation of sane, simple, boring detail, to give a setting of re-assuring dullness to what had to come out at last. "Yes," Hamilton said encouragingly.

"Well," said Innes, "well, just four nights ago the tap came

as usual. I got up, went over there, and I could see his misty-
looking face waiting to be let in. As I opened the window, he
hopped over the threshold and trotted ahead of me to the
fireplace. I sat down. He chose his position, just about where
your feet now are, gave a lick, and then, with that queer
deliberate way cats have, as though he had suddenly remembered something he had been told but till that minute
had all but forgotten, he got up again—he had never done so
before—and went over there." Innes pointed to a bookcase
which was almost opposite the French window and the
lowest shelf of which was within an inch of the floor.

"There, almost touching the books, he began his grooming. I watched him a little and then went back to my book. I
was reading in this chair. I suppose my attention was again
disturbed by a slight tapping. The light, you see, is a good
one." He pointed up to a powerful reading lamp which was
standing behind them.

"Yes, good for the eyes," said Hamilton.

"It has, you see, a reflector, and this was throwing the
light over my shoulder. I could see that the cat had come to
the concluding phase of his drill. The hind leg was hoisted—
the whole body and head assembled, as it were, around this
raised ensign. I could see precisely what I Am was doing as
his head was pointing this way. He was grooming the inside
of his raised thigh, and I could also see what caused the
small regular noise. Every time he swept the fur with his
tongue, the upraised leg wagged and the hoisted paw, rising
over his head, tapped on the book backs behind him."

Well, Hamilton could not help reflecting, all this parlour
natural history might be reassuring, but it certainly doesn't
seem to be leading anywhere.

"Well," continued Innes, suddenly becoming hesitant, "you see, from this position I could see exactly."

"Yes."

"I've long sight, you know?"

"Yes, yes."

"So there couldn't be any doubt. The books in that row are just as they were then." Innes suddenly got up, went to the bookcase, bent down, taking a volume from the ground shelf, turned round, and handed it to Hamilton. Hamilton read aloud, *Called, I Come.*

"It may be coincidence." Innes again hesitated, as though turning over something in his mind and speaking mainly to himself.

"I don't think it is coincidence," answered the doctor. Then, with deliberate reassurance, "Really, you may take my word for it, there is nothing in *that*." He'd often known quiet emphasis to work with excited patients.

"Good, good," Innes replied almost absent-mindedly. "Then listen to this." He replaced the book and sat down again, still looking at the bookcase and no longer at Hamilton. "Of course cats are creatures of habit. What makes them change a routine, Heaven knows. Some little external accident, perhaps, psychologists would say. But once it is changed, the pattern goes on in the new place. The next night the tap came on time; the same entry was made. I was accompanied to the hearth here: then I was left, and almost but not quite, the same position as that of the night before was chosen for the grooming ritual. The cat placed himself with his back to the books and got to work, but it was against the row nearest to us, and not that farther one in which the volume named *Called, I Come* is standing. I read my book until once more the regular tapping disturbed me. I knew, of course, at once what it was. It was a distracting little sound: not sufficient to be annoying, but enough to take one's attention from the book and make one raise one's eyes, so that, over the top of the page, one could watch the toilet. The paw, hoisted over the top of the rhythmically moving head, was, under the strokes, waving to and fro; and, as on the night before, it was beating on the books immediately behind. Again I idly read the title indicated in this chance way, with this queer pointer."

Innes again got up, knelt down at the bookcase, but this time didn't take out a book; instead he pointed with his finger and read out the title: *I Cross the Frontier.*

"It's a dull book," he said. "The other book is, of course, that sentimental anthology which had such a success a couple of years ago. This is simply a poor autobiography of one of my wife's old pioneer ancestors of whom she's pointlessly proud." He stopped again.

Hamilton felt he should put another layer of reassurance on the rather quaggy ground. "No," he said judiciously, "there's certainly nothing out of the common in that either—there's not a shred of objective association between these two incidents, I'll warrant."

"You're sure?" asked Innes with an unhappy concern.

"Quite sure." The answer was professional. Hamilton now felt no doubt that this was no time for easy friendly speculation. He must be professionally authoritative. To himself he remarked: Certainly bromide: perhaps, too, castor oil—sometimes intestinal clog can  . . .

But the patient was proceeding. "I see your point: just those two points, mere incidents—yes, I know. Indeed, I'm sure they didn't disturb me. True, I remembered them, because—well, because I'm interested in cat psychology." He gave a feeble laugh. "All detail is important to a diagnostician, isn't it?" Hamilton gave only a Lord Burleigh nod. "I'm sure I'd have forgotten them, if . . . Well, the next night the same routine was followed. The usual tap, the entry, the walk to the fireplace, and the second thought that the better position was by the bookcase. But at that point a variation was introduced. It confirmed the psychologists: an outer stimulus altered the pattern. I think, indeed I'm pretty sure, I Am was just getting ready for his clean-up when his attention was distracted from himself. I can't be quite sure, for I only looked up when I heard a scrambling. He'd caught sight of one of those oddly inefficient but surprisingly nimble insects we used to call daddy longlegs. It was half-flying and half-hopping about. For some reason cats are easily aroused by them and, to chase them, even grooming or eating or sleeping by the fire will be instantly abandoned. Already the Siamese was boxing at it as it rose in the air and pouncing as it alighted on the carpet. But always the insect just managed to make a getaway. I watched the duel for a few moments, and then the daddy longlegs bobbed past a sweep of the cat's paw and skidded against the books. For a second it hung on to the top of a volume—the cat whirled round and sprang, and the fly, either driven by the impact of the blow or leaping away from it, shot into the space, of an inch or so, between the books and the shelf above them.

"That cat thrust its paw in, as far as it could reach. I watched, idly amused. It was so like an impatient human, groping for something he has dropped behind a chair or desk. You could almost hear I Am swearing under his breath.

I let him struggle, sure that he'd give up in a moment and we'd both of us go back to our quiet concerns: he with his coat, I with my thoughts. But he didn't. I could just hear the fly faintly whirring behind the books, and maybe I Am could feel it buzz against his outstretched groping toes. Anyhow he redoubled his efforts. He pushed both front paws into the crack above the books. He wedged himself in and then, with his efforts, actually began to work a couple of volumes loose.

"I let him go on: such industry seemed to deserve not to be discouraged. Perhaps he had a purpose . . ." Again Innes paused. "Well, anyhow, this partial success encouraged him. He worked away and, sure enough, the two books fell out. Now he had breached the daddy longlegs' defences. He thrust himself in, head and all, reaching behind the books, still straining to find his victim's retreat. It was a long reach, though—the books he had displaced were in the centre of that bottom left-hand row, and, naturally, the fly retreated into the back corner of the shelf. The cat had, therefore, to push himself in and, in doing so, his hind leg, thrust out to give him drive, stamped right onto a page of a book he had thrown out and which was sprawling open.

"That was too much. My love of books won against my interest in natural history. I sprang forward, pulled him out by the scruff of his neck, and rearranged the shelf. But, in replacing the books, I noticed a vexing thing. I said I thought the cat had been distracted before he could settle down to his evening wash. Well, that was painfully obvious. His hind foot, the one with which he had done the big push, had obviously been still muddily damp. For it had left a complete imprint on the margin of the page. I brought the book to the light, hoping I might be able to wipe it clean before the mud dried in."

Innes stopped. Putting his hand down beside him in the chair, he fished up a volume, opened it, and put it on the broad arm of the chair near Hamilton's. Hamilton leaned across. True enough, on the outer border of the left-hand page, about half-way down, was a blur of mud stain rather like a large, clumsy asterisk stamped with a blunt rubber pad. "And you see," went on Innes, "the page is further spoiled." That was clear, too. One of the cat's hind claws had found purchase in the paper and had made a little tear right through the page. The two men looked for a moment at the damaged leaf. Then Innes remarked in an altered tone, "Do you notice anything else about this page?"

Hamilton scanned it. "No?" he questioned. Innes sighed, but all he actually said, as he remained looking down at the open book, was: "This game fish is not only deaf but so stupid that, though it can move quickly out of range when alarmed and then keep concealed, it seems unaware of his presence: when, after four or five days of such approach, during which he has become more and more clearly visible, he can stand right over the pool and spear it easily.

"You see," he said, looking up from the page, for he had been reading from it, "what I may perhaps call the cat's asterisk or sign manual is put alongside that passage . . ." He looked up at Hamilton, but the doctor had put out his hand and taken the book. "Big Game Fish," he read out to himself. "Well, that's healthy, outdoor sport."

Paying no attention to the comment, Innes completed his own sentence . . . "and the cat's claw, like an accent stroke, is notched against the line which runs, 'After four or five days of such approach . . .'"

Hamilton cleared his throat. "Really, Innes," he said, closing the book and putting it aside, "you must take my opin-

ion. There is nothing in all this. Nothing at all." Innes turned
his head away. "Now, don't think I'm going to be stupidly
backslapping and tell you just not to have damn-fool fancies.
But, first, you must take my word for it, my professional
word, that all these little incidents which have," he paused
for a word, "have so annoyed you, are in *themselves*," he
stressed the last word, "nothing, absolutely nothing."

Innes had sunk in his chair. Hamilton hurried a little; he
must rouse the man. "And, secondly, I assure you, I give you
my word, that you were right, very right to talk it all over
with me. I want particularly to assure you that I've come
across plenty of cases like this, plenty; quite common in my
practice, quite common. Nothing to be alarmed over, if
they're understood. Due to strain, you know, subconscious of
course. Quite easy to deal with, taken in time, as you've
taken it."

All that Innes said in reply was, as he turned round slowly
and fixed his eyes on the doctor, "Then I may tell you all?"

"Why, of course, naturally, naturally, that's half the cure,
you know, especially when we've already decided that we
know the source of the little trouble—just strain, strain
that's making these queer little subjective associations appear as associations, which an onlooker can see are here," he
pointed quite gaily to his own head, "and not there." He
made a flourish which included the book, fireplace, and
bookcase.

Indeed, he might have run on with his reassuring patter
had not Innes interrupted him with, "Well, the next thing
was worse. Perhaps I'd have lacked nerve to tell you if you
hadn't told me to go ahead—at least after the way you've
treated evidence which seems to me fairly objective. For
this, I know, isn't."

That's bad, thought the doctor; it's a developing hallucination.

"The next night—the fourth," Innes remarked parenthetically, "there was the usual tap at nine-thirty. How he knows the time, I don't know; but then, I know now that I know nothing."

"Go on," said Hamilton in a quietly commanding voice.

"Well, he does know that, I know for certain," said Innes almost defiantly. "I confess I went to the window for the first time with something like real uneasiness. Damn it, I'm sure you'd have felt the same if you'd been seeing things as I couldn't help seeing them."

For a moment Hamilton felt, emotionally—not rationally —that he could sympathise in a way. He blew the thin fog of feeling out of his mind. That kind of sympathy is the end of the professional attitude; you become a patient yourself. "Well," he said almost sharply, "you went to the window."

"Yes," Innes hurried on. "I opened it; I Am ran in, trotted to the fire, waited for me to sit down. I sat down; own, I didn't take up my book; own, I hadn't been reading it before he knocked. But this time he didn't have any queer second thoughts. I began to think the act was over. He was back on the old rails. For, sure enough, he chose his spot on the hearth—there, just where your feet are—and started on his grooming. It was all so reassuring. After all, it's one of the most reassuring sights there is: that sane, methodical, pleasant body-conscious self-centredness. Women brushing their hair, they're always thinking of some man and what he'll say about it. But a cat's pleasure is sanely animal. I watched a few minutes, watched until, all clear and clean, he stretched out one paw and then the other one, found everything at ease, curled up, and went to sleep. It was such a persuasively pantomime sermon on the virtue of relaxation; he was practising so well what he preached and demonstrated that it had me convinced. I smiled at myself." Innes smiled wanly at the memory of his last relief, as the sun itself, already overwhelmed by storm clouds, throws up against them a last pallid shaft of light.

"I picked up my book and found my place. It was a good novel of detective adventure. I was soon well settled: my body snug in this chair, my mind ranging off with the story teller or now and then following its own speculations. I don't know how long I read. I suppose I must have stirred, crossed my legs or something, and that may have done it; set it off. Anyhow, I looked up over the edge of my book to the hearth. There was the cat on it. But he was no longer curled up asleep. He was awake and, as I've said, some move of mine may have done it. Anyhow, he was looking up at me."

He stopped. Hamilton cut in. "Yes, that's common in cats. I myself have often noticed it. You disturb them; they look up at you and then forget, but also forget to turn their heads. They've never been taught it's rude to stare. After all," he chuckled rather deliberately, "cats wouldn't have been told they could look at kings unless they'd first shown a taste for this bland, contemptuous interest in human self-consciousness."

Innes wasn't listening. He was getting ready to make an avowal, dreadful to himself, ridiculous to his companion. At last he collected the words, "I looked at I Am; he at me—a sort of strange staring match, I thought for a little. And then I noticed something else. You know how all cats' eyes flash when at night a car's headlights catch them, say, when they're crossing a road. You'd know also that the pale blue eyes of the Siamese are really nearly pigmentless; they are almost albinos." Hamilton grunted assent. "Well, then, perhaps you have noticed another thing. If you're sitting like this with your back to a strong light, such as this reading lamp with its reflector, and the focused light, of course, is thrown straight into the cat's eyes, then, not only are its slit-pupils nearly closed and all the eye nearly covered by the iris, but all the colour goes from the eye—it appears like a pink mirror."

"Of course," said the doctor, "you're looking right into the eye itself."

"Well, all I know is that then it gives the effect . . ." he went over the sentence again, "it gives the effect of looking into a small, lit room, lit with a warm firelight, cozy, quiet, but waiting for someone to come and occupy it." He closed his sentence with an ancient quotation: " 'empty, swept, and garnished.' I went on looking into those small binocular, stereoscopic mirrors. I suppose the cat and I were both in a kind of reciprocal trance. Anyhow, gradually I began to think that I was actually looking into a mirror and that in that mirror was reflected this room. The cat's eyes would then be showing me this room. You see," he went on more slowly, "I would be seeing this room, seeing behind me all of the other wall right along to the window."

Innes pointed over his shoulder with his left hand but kept his eyes on the hearth. "I saw it all perfectly clearly, like a view down the wrong end of a telescope. It was in minute but sharpest-cut detail. I scanned every bit of it with the lazy curiosity with which one looks into a camera obscura. Things reduced to model size are somehow always intriguing. I worked my attention along, or rather my eye shifted out to the very edge of the picture, right out to where that window," again he didn't turn around but pointed with a hooked-back finger in the direction, "terminated my view. I went to it and glanced at the curtain on the left. You see it is a heavy thick curtain and, as now, it was drawn back, since I had not replaced it when I had let in the cat. And then," Innes' voice had become a whisper and Hamilton had to lean over to catch the words, "I saw the room was— not—not quite as it had been when I had last looked at it. Something else had—been added. By the thick folds of the curtain— I had blinked my own eyes twice to see that they were not cheating me, I looked carefully twice into the mirror-eyes before I could be sure. But then I was as sure as that you're in that chair—" His voice rose to an unpleasantly shrill dismay. "There in the corner by the curtain, watching me, was something, someone, standing, ready, ready . . ."

He swung round. The panic infection of his voice was too strong for the doctor. He, too, could not keep his head from swivelling over his shoulder. He gasped with relief, and then with disgust with himself. The room was healthily empty as a meadow. He flung a glance at Innes, who with incredulous relief was also gazing at the curtain.

Hamilton sprang up, strode across the room, and shook the heavy velvet— "The commonest form of hallucination," he exclaimed. "Why, Walter Scott, that sane old tale-teller, says he was almost frightened out of his life by seeing, in the dusk, his dressing gown look like a dead friend."

"But," Innes muttered, "but it wasn't in the room itself, at least not yet, not then, that I saw it. It was in that creature's eyes."

For a moment Dr Hamilton stood by the window. He'd probably do best to go across to Innes and give him a good shaking. Hysterics are now, once again, being slapped into remembering that they are sane; he recalled reading that only a week ago, in his favourite medical journal. Maybe it's not much use to the hysteric, but what a blessed relief to the doctor. Could he really slap an old, respectable, not well-liked friend? He hesitated. What would have happened if he had acted on the notion, who knows. But in those four or five seconds in which he delayed and Innes waited, the next thing happened.

The room was empty and silent, but suddenly they were both arrested. "Bump, bump." Innes had heard it; he was half out of his chair. Yes, there could be no doubt, Hamilton glanced at his watch—nine-thirty, precisely. It was not a considered reaction, but all he could say was, "Well, that isn't a tap! it's a kind of bump."

Innes was already passing him on his way to the window. "On time" was all he said. Hamilton had only to wheel round and they were both abreast of the dark window. They looked down to the lowest pane at floor level. In the light thrown out past them by the lit room behind, they could see a faint object.

"It's I Am," said Innes. Hamilton couldn't clearly discern that it was a cat at all. If it was, it must be muffled in some way. What was obvious was that Innes was going into complete panic. There'd be an awful scene if he didn't somehow stop the whole fantasy. He gripped the bolt lever and threw open the window. Over the threshold at their feet hopped a smoke-grey cat. Of course it had been hard to see it outside, for its face was nearly hidden in black feathers. In its jaws was a fairly large bird, and the wretched creature was still alive.

With a natural reaction Hamilton struck the cat, dealing it a stinging rap on the back of the head. It sprung back, dropping its prey, and bounded out into the garden. The heap of blood-stained feathers lay on the floor a moment. Then the twisted body began to try and pull itself together. They could see that the head and neck were crushed down under the body. It was trying to get them free. Both Innes and Hamilton drew back, one shrinking to touch the mangled body, the other wondering whether he had not better step on it quickly and so break its neck. The body drew itself up; the neck and head nearly emerged. At that moment both of them heard, rising from the wreckage, a small, hoarse ghost-of-a-voice. "Are you deaf then?" it questioned.

The feathers flopped. Hamilton, with thumb and finger, lifted the limp dead body of the blackbird. Over at the fire he cleared a place in the blazing logs, dropped the carrion in, and flung after it three or four handfuls of kindling. The fire shot up with a crackle and filled the whole hearth. Then he turned to Innes. He was still looking at the small blood stain and some smeared down-feathers that clung to the carpet. "Come and sit down," he said. "Cats are cruel little beasts, but they can't help it. In the blood; merely reflex, instinct."

He owned to himself that that dirty little incident, coming where and when it did, couldn't have been more inapposite—or should he say apposite? Such questions were grotesque. Innes was having bad luck, and that was all. Here, for the first time, was a real coincidence, barging in, to fling a spot of trouble on a nervous case which had gone further than he'd first fancied and further than—in another sense of that odd word—he now quite fancied. He went towards Innes but stopped at the bookcase.

Innes swung past him and, keeping his eyes on the curtain, drew back to the chairs. But he spoke to Hamilton: "I don't blame the cat—any more than I blame the bird." Then with a sudden blaze of terror exploding into rage: "Don't you see, you hell-fool Hamilton. Don't you see? They were simply pawns, messengers. Don't you see? I've been stalked: stalked so assuredly, so cleverly that the stalker actually gives warnings that he's on my track. Dares me to shake him off. See, he's ready to start as soon as I'll call him up. Yes, he knew I'd called him. I'd wanted to kill her, my wife. Night after night, I've come in here to get away from her. Her voice, saying, 'Are you deaf'—God how I've longed to silence it. I've sat here night after night praying for a safe, sure way, a way that everyone would think natural. I know there's lots of ways. I've sat in that chair saying to myself, that if I just sit quiet and still it will steal into my mind, the perfect traceless way—just as a forgotten word comes in, while you wait, looking, as it were, in the other direction. Then the next signal, *The Frontier Is Crossed,* he's on his way. The third—then I saw he had me—I was to be the victim, not she—I'm the poor stupid fish. He gave his timetable then, from the first reply to my call till his arrival. Oh, he's a fine timekeeper. He runs on schedule. The next night he shows me he's at my shoulder, at my back, standing over me, ready to strike. Tonight, with perfect irony, in your presence—you whom I've asked to save me, you a starched shirt stuffed with stupid self-assurance—tonight he asks me,

'Am I deaf?' No, I'm not deaf; I'm not blind now. The poor fish sees and hears as the spear gets it!"

Innes's eyes were now watching something at the curtain with such intensity that Hamilton could not but believe that there was a "presence" between him and the wretched maniac. It was all the more horribly convincing as he saw Innes's eyes drawing in their focus, and, a moment after, Innes's body creeping back, as though giving way before someone approaching him. But, of course, he couldn't give way.

"Take care!" shouted Hamilton. But Innes, dreading something else far more, had stumbled back into the leaping fire.

Hamilton snatched him out. "Shock," he said, trying to pull himself together, when it was clear that there was no use trying any longer to pull the patient round. "Of course, I knew that he'd got to hate her like hell. But naturally he hadn't the nerve to pull off a murder—or even a suicide. But it's the fatal shock all right. And," he paused in his quick muttering to himself, "were all those—happenings coincidences? Better call the police. Thank heaven, they're even more spirit-proof than we doctors. Still, it's one more queer story for a posthumous case-book."

# Violence

"But what seems so odd to me, so horribly pathetic, is that such people don't resist," said Leidall, suddenly entering the conversation. The intensity of his tone startled everybody; it was so passionate, yet with a beseeching touch that made the women feel uncomfortable a little. "As a rule, I'm told, they submit willingly, almost as though—"

He hesitated, grew confused, and dropped his glance to the floor; and a smartly dressed woman, eager to be heard, seized the opening. "Oh, come now," she laughed; "one always hears of a man being *put* into a strait waistcoat. I'm sure he doesn't slip it on as if he were going to a dance!" And she looked flippantly at Leidall, whose casual manners she resented. "People are *put* under restraint. It's not in human nature to accept it—healthy human nature, that is?" But for some reason no one took her question up. "That is so, I believe, yes," a polite voice murmured, while the group at tea in the Dover Street Club turned with one accord to Leidall as to one whose interesting sentence still remained unfinished. He had hardly spoken before, and a silent man is ever credited with wisdom.

"As though—you were just saying, Mr Leidall?" a quiet little man in a dark corner helped him.

"As though, I meant, a man in that condition of mind is not insane—all through," Leidall continued stammeringly; "but that some wise portion of him watches the proceeding with gratitude, and welcomes the protection against himself. It seems awfully pathetic. Still," again hesitating and fumbling in his speech—"er—it seems to me that he should yield quietly to enforced restraint—the waistcoat, handcuffs, and the rest." He looked round hurriedly, half suspiciously, at the faces in the circle, then dropped his eyes again to the floor. He sighed, leaning back in his chair. "I cannot understand it," he added, as no one spoke, but in a very low voice, and almost to himself. "One would expect them to struggle furiously."

Someone had mentioned that remarkable book, *The Mind that Found Itself,* and the conversation had slipped into this serious vein. The women did not like it. What kept it alive was the fact that the silent Leidall, with his handsome, melancholy face, had suddenly wakened into speech, and that the little man opposite to him, half invisible in his dark corner, was assistant to one of London's great hypnotic doctors, who could, and he would, tell interesting and terrible things. No one cared to ask the direct question, but all hoped for revelations, possibly about people they actually knew. It was a very ordinary tea-party indeed. And this little man now spoke, though hardly in the desired vein. He addressed his remarks to Leidall across the disappointed lady.

"I think, probably, your explanation *is* the true one," he said gently, "for madness in its commoner forms is merely want of proportion; the mind gets out of right and proper relations with its environment. The majority of madmen are mad on one thing only, while the rest of them are as sane as myself—or you."

The words fell into the silence. Leidall bowed his agreement, saying no actual word. The ladies fidgeted. Someone made a jocular remark to the effect that most of the world was mad anyhow, and the conversation shifted with relief into a lighter vein—the scandal in the family of a politician. Everybody talked at once. Cigarettes were lit. The corner soon became excited and even uproarious. The tea-party was a great success, and the offended lady, no longer ignored, led all the skirmishes—towards herself. She was in her element. Only Leidall and the little invisible man in the corner took small part in it; and presently, seizing the opportunity when some new arrivals joined the group, Leidall rose to say his adieux, and slipped away, his departure scarcely noticed. Dr Hancock followed him a minute later. The two men met in the hall; Leidall already had his hat and coat on.

"I'm going West, Mr Leidall. If that's your way too, and you feel inclined for the walk we might go together." Leidall turned with a start. His glance took in the other with avidity—a keenly-searching, hungry glance. He hesitated for an imperceptible moment, then made a movement towards him, half inviting, while a curious shadow dropped across his face and vanished. It was both pathetic and terrible. The lips trembled. He seemed to say, "God bless you; *do* come with me!" But no words were audible.

"It's a pleasant evening for a walk," added Dr Hancock gently; "clean and dry under foot for a change. I'll get my hat and join you for a second." And there was a hint, the merest flavour of authority in his voice.

That touch of authority was his mistake. Instantly Leidall's hesitation passed. "I'm sorry," he said abruptly, "but I'm afraid I must take a taxi. I have an appointment at the Club and I'm late already." "Oh, I see," the other replied, with a kindly smile; "then I mustn't keep you. But if you ever have a free evening, won't you look me up, or come and dine? You'll find my telephone number in the book. I should like to talk with you about—those things we mentioned at tea." Leidall thanked him politely and went out. The memory of the little man's kindly sympathy and understanding eyes went with him.

"Who was that man?" someone asked, the moment Leidall had left the tea-table. "Surely he's not the Leidall who wrote that awful book some years ago?"

"Yes—*The Gulf of Darkness*. Did you read it?"

They discussed it and its author for five minutes, deciding by a large majority that it was the book of a madman. Silent, rude men like that always had a screw loose somewhere, they agreed. Silence was invariably morbid.

"And did you notice Dr Hancock? He never took his eyes off him. That's why he followed him out like that. I wonder if *he* thought anything!"

"I know Hancock well," said the lady of the wounded vanity. "I'll ask him and find out." They chattered on, somebody mentioned a *risqué* play, and talk switched into other fields, and in due course the tea-party came to an end.

And Leidall, meanwhile, made his way towards the Park on foot, for he had not taken a taxi after all. The suggestion of the other man, perhaps, had worked upon him. He was very open to suggestion. With hands deep in his overcoat pockets, and head sunk forward between his shoulders, he walked briskly, entering the Park at one of the smaller gates. He made his way across the wet turf, avoiding the paths and people. The February sky was shining in the west; beautiful clouds floated over the houses; they looked like the shoreline of some radiant strand his childhood once had known. He sighed; thought dived and searched within; self-analysis, that old, implacable demon, lifted its voice; introspection took the reins again as usual. There seemed a strain upon the mind he could not dispel. Thought circled poignantly. He knew it was unhealthy, morbid, a sign of those many years of difficulty and stress that had marked him so deeply, but for the life of him he could not escape from the hideous spell that held him. The same old thoughts bored their way into his mind like burning wires, tracing the same unanswerable questions. From this torture, waking or sleeping, there was no escape. Had a companion been with him it might have been different. If, for instance, Dr Hancock—

He was angry with himself for having refused—furious; it was that vile, false pride his long loneliness had fostered. The man was sympathetic to him, friendly, marvellously understanding; he could have talked freely with him, and found relief. His intuition had picked out the little doctor as a man in ten thousand. Why had he so curtly declined his gentle invitation? Dr Hancock *knew;* he guessed his awful secret. But how? In what had he betrayed himself?

The weary self-questioning began again, till he sighed and groaned from sheer exhaustion. He *must* find people, companionship, someone to talk to. The Club—it crossed his tortured mind for a second—was impossible; there was a conspiracy among the members against him. He had left his usual haunts everywhere for the same reason—his restaurants, where he had his lonely meals; his music hall, where he tried sometimes to forget himself; his favourite walks, where the very policemen knew and eyed him. And, coming to the bridge across the Serpentine just then, he paused and leaned over the edge, watching a bubble rise to the surface. "I suppose there *are* fish in the Serpentine?" he said to a man a few feet away.

They talked a moment—the other was evidently a clerk on his way home—and then the stranger edged off and continued his walk, looking back once or twice at the sad-faced man who had addressed him. "It's ridiculous, that with all our science we can't live under water as the fish do," reflected Leidall, and moved on round the other bank of the water, where he watched a flight of duck whirl down from the darkening air and settle with a long, mournful splash beside the bushy island. "Or that, for all our pride of mechanism in a mechanical age, we cannot really fly." But these attempts to escape from self were never very successful. Another part of him looked on and mocked. He returned ever to the endless introspection and self-analysis, and in the deepest moment of it—ran into a big, motionless figure that blocked his way. It was the Park policeman, the one who always eyed him. He sheered off suddenly towards the trees, while the man, recognising him, touched his cap respectfully. "It's a pleasant evening, sir; turned quite mild again." Leidall mumbled some reply or other, and hurried on to hide himself among the shadows of the trees. The policeman stood and watched him, till the darkness swallowed him. "He knows too!" groaned the wretched man. And every bench was occupied; every face turned to watch him; there were even figures behind the trees. He dared not go into the street, for the very taxi-drivers were against him. If he gave an address, he would not be driven to it; the man would *know*, and take him elsewhere. And something in his heart, sick with anguish, weary with the endless battle, suddenly yielded.

"There *are* fish in the Serpentine," he remembered the stranger had said. "And," he added to himself, with a wave of delicious comfort, "they lead secret, hidden lives that no one can disturb." His mind cleared surprisingly. In the water he could find peace and rest and healing. Good Lord! How easy it all was! Yet he had never thought of it before. He turned sharply to retrace his steps, but in that very second the clouds descended upon his thought again, his mind darkened, he hesitated. Could he get out again when he had had enough? Would he rise to the surface? A battle began over these questions. He ran quickly, then stood still again to think the matter out. Darkness shrouded him. He heard the wind rush laughing through the trees. The picture of the whirring duck flashed back a moment, and he decided that the best way was by air, and not by water. He would *fly* into the place of rest, not sink or merely float; and he remembered the view from his bedroom window, high over old smoky London town, with a drop of eighty feet onto the pavement. Yes, that was the best way. He waited a moment, trying to think it all out clearly, but one moment the fish had it, and the next the birds. It was really impossible to decide. Was there no one who could help him, no one in all this enormous town who was sufficiently on his side to advise him on the point? Some clear-headed, experienced, kindly man?

And the face of Dr Hancock flashed before his vision. He saw the gentle eyes and sympathetic smile, remembered the soothing voice and the offer of companionship he had refused. Of course, there was one serious drawback: Hancock *knew*. But he was far too tactful, too sweet and good a man to let that influence his judgment, or to betray in any way at all that he did know.

Leidall found it in him to decide. Facing the entire hostile world, he hailed a taxi from the nearest gate upon the street, looked up the address in a chemist's telephone-book, and reached the door in a condition of delight and relief. Yes, Dr Hancock was at home. Leidall sent his name in. A few minutes later the two men were chatting pleasantly together, almost like old friends, so keen was the little man's intuitive sympathy and tact. Only Hancock, patient listener though he proved himself to be, was uncommonly full of words. Leidall explained the matter very clearly. "Now, what is your decision, Dr Hancock? Is it to be the way of the fish or the way of the duck?" And, while Hancock began his answer with slow, well-chosen words, a new idea, better than either, leaped with a flash into his listener's mind. It was an inspiration. For where could he find a better hiding-place from all his troubles than—inside Hancock himself? The man was kindly; he surely would not object. Leidall this time did not hesitate a second. He was tall and broad; Hancock was small, yet he was sure there would be room. He sprang upon him like a wild animal. He felt the warm, thin throat yield and bend between his great hands . . . then darkness, peace, and rest, a nothingness that surely was the oblivion he had so long prayed for. He had accomplished his desire. He had secreted himself for ever from persecution—inside the kindliest little man he had ever met—inside Hancock . . .

He opened his eyes and looked about him into a room he did not know. The walls were soft and dimly coloured. It was very silent. Cushions were everywhere. Peaceful it was, and out of the world. Overhead was a skylight, and one window, opposite the door, was heavily barred. Delicious!

No one could get in. He was sitting in a deep comfortable chair. He felt rested and happy. There was a click, and he saw a tiny window in the door drop down, as though worked by a sliding panel. Then the door opened noiselessly, and in came a little man with smiling face and soft brown eyes—Dr Hancock.

Leidall's first feeling was amazement. "Then I didn't get into him properly after all! Or I've slipped out again, perhaps! The dear, good fellow!" And he rose to greet him. He put his hand out, and found that the other came with it in some inexplicable fashion. Movement was cramped. "Ah, then I've had a stroke," he thought, as Hancock pressed him, ever so gently, back into the big chair. "Do not get up," he said soothingly but with authority; "sit where you are and rest. You must take it very easy for a bit; like all clever men who have overworked—"

"I'll get in the moment he turns," thought Leidall. "I did it badly before. It must be through the back of his head, of course, where the spine runs up into the brain," and he waited till Hancock should turn. But Hancock never turned. He kept his face towards him all the time, while he chatted, moving gradually nearer to the door. On Leidall's face was the smile of an innocent child, but there lay a hideous cunning behind that smile, and the eyes were terrible.

"Are those bars firm and strong," asked Leidall, "so that no one can get in?" He pointed craftily, and the doctor, caught for a second unawares, turned his head. That instant Leidall was upon him with a roar, then sank back powerless into the chair, unable to move his arms more than a few inches in any direction. Hancock stepped up quietly and made him comfortable again with cushions.

And something in Leidall's soul turned round and looked another way. His mind became clear as daylight for a moment. The effort perhaps had caused the sudden change from darkness to great light. A memory rushed over him. "Good God!" he cried. "I am violent. I was going to do you an injury—you, who are so sweet and good to me!" He trembled dreadfully, and burst into tears. "For the sake of Heaven," he implored, looking up, ashamed and keenly penitent, "put me under restraint. Fasten my hands before I try it again." He held both hands out willingly, beseechingly, then looked down, following the direction of the other's kind brown eyes. His wrists, he saw, already wore steel handcuffs, and a strait waistcoat was across his chest and arms and shoulders.

# Entrance and Exit

These three—the old physicist, the girl, and the young Anglican parson who was engaged to her—stood by the window of the country house. The blinds were not yet drawn. They could see the dark clump of pines in the field, with crests silhouetted against the pale wintry sky of the February afternoon. Snow, freshly fallen, lay upon lawn and hill. A big moon was already lighting up.

"Yes, that's the wood," the old man said, "and it was this very day fifty years ago—February 13—the man disappeared from its shadows; swept in this extraordinary, incredible fashion into invisibility—into *some other place*. Can you wonder the grove is haunted?" A strange impressiveness of manner belied the laugh following the words.

"Oh, please tell us," the girl whispered; "we're all alone now." Curiosity triumphed; yet a vague alarm betrayed itself in the questioning glance she cast for protection at her younger companion, whose fine face, on the other hand, wore an expression that was grave and singularly rapt. He was listening keenly.

"As though Nature," the physicist went on, half to himself, "here and there concealed vacuums, gaps, holes in space" (his mind was always speculative; more than speculative

some said), "in fact, at right angles to three known ones—
'higher space,' through which a man might drop invisibly—a
new direction, as Boyle, Gauss, and Hinton might call it; and
what you, with your mystical turn"—looking toward the
young priest—"might consider a spiritual change of condition, into a region where space and time do not exist, and
where all dimensions are possible—because they are *one*."

"But, please, the story," the girl begged, not understanding these dark sayings, "although I'm not sure that Arthur
ought to hear it. He's much too interested in such queer
things as it is!" Smiling, yet uneasy, she stood closer to his
side, as though her body might protect his soul.

"Very briefly, then, you shall hear what I remember of this
haunting, for I was barely ten years old at the time. It was
evening—clear and cold like this, with snow and moonlight
—when someone reported to my father that a peculiar
sound, variously described as crying, wailing, was being
heard in the grove. He paid no attention until my sister
heard it too, and was frightened. Then he sent a groom to
investigate. Though the night was brilliant the man took a
lantern. We watched from this very window till we lost his
figure against the trees, and the lantern stopped swinging
suddenly, as if he had put it down. It remained motionless.
We waited half an hour, and then my father, curiously
excited, I remember, went out quickly, and I, utterly terrified, went after him. We followed his tracks, which came to
an end beside the lantern, the last step being a stride almost
impossible for a man to have made. All around, the snow
was unbroken by a single mark, but the man himself had
vanished. Then we heard him calling for help—above, behind, beyond us; from all directions at once, yet from none,

came the sound of his voice; but though we called back he made no answer, and gradually his cries grew fainter and fainter, as if going into tremendous distance, and at last died away altogether."

"And the man himself?" asked both listeners.

"Never returned—from that day to this has never been seen . . . At intervals for weeks and months afterwards reports came in that he was still heard crying, always crying for help. With time, even these reports ceased—for most of us," he added under his breath; "and that is all I know. A mere outline, as you see."

The girl did not quite like the story, for the old man's manner made it too convincing. She was half disappointed, half frightened.

"See! There are the others coming home," she exclaimed, with a note of relief, pointing to a group of figures moving over the snow near the pine trees. "Now we can think of tea!" She crossed the room to busy herself with the friendly tray as the servant approached to fasten the shutters. The young priest, however, deeply interested, talked on with their host, though in a voice almost too low for her to hear. Only the final sentences reached her, making her uneasy— absurdly so, she thought—till afterwards.

"—for matter, as we know, interpenetrates matter," she heard, "and two objects may conceivably occupy the same space. The odd thing really is that one should hear, but not see; that air-waves should bring the voice, yet ether-waves fail to bring the picture."

And then the older man: "—as if certain places in Nature, yes, invited the change—places where these extraordinary forces stir from the earth as from the surface of a living

Being with organs—places like islands, mountain-tops, pine-woods, especially pines isolated from their kind. You know the queer results of digging absolutely virgin soil, of course —and that theory of the earth's being *alive*—" The voice dropped again.

"States of mind also helping the forces of the place," she caught the priest's reply in part; "such as conditions induced by music, by intense listening, by certain moments in the Mass even—by ecstasy or—"

"I say, what *do* you think?" cried a girl's voice, as the others came in with welcome chatter and odours of tweeds and open fields. "As we passed your old haunted pine-wood we heard *such* a queer noise. Like someone wailing or crying. Caesar howled and ran; and Harry refused to go in and investigate. He positively funked it!" They all laughed. "More like a rabbit in a trap than a person crying," explained Harry, a blush kindly concealing his startling pallor. "I wanted my tea too much to bother about an old rabbit."

It was some time after tea when the girl became aware that the priest had disappeared, and putting two and two together, ran in alarm to her host's study. Quite easily, from the hastily opened shutters, she and the physicist saw his figure moving across the snow. The moon was very bright over the world, yet he carried a lantern that shone pale yellow against the white brilliance.

"Oh, for God's sake, quick!" she cried, pale with fear. "Quick! or we're too late! Arthur's simply wild about such things. Oh, I might have known—I might have guessed. And this is the very night. I'm terrified!"

By the time her host had found his overcoat and slipped round the house with her from the back door, the lantern, they saw, was already swinging close to the pine-wood. The night was still as ice, bitterly cold. Breathlessly they ran, following the tracks. Half-way the footsteps diverged, and were plainly visible in the virgin snow by themselves. They heard the whispering of the branches ahead of them, for pines cry even when no airs stir. "Follow me close," said the old man sternly. The lantern, he already saw, lay upon the ground unattended; no human figure was anywhere visible.

"See! The steps come to an end here," he whispered, stooping down as soon as they reached the lantern. The tracks, hitherto so regular, showed an odd wavering—the snow curiously disturbed. Quite suddenly they stopped. The final step was a very long one—a stride, almost immense, "as though he was pushed forward from behind," muttered the old man, too low to be overheard, "or sucked forward from in front—as in a fall."

The girl would have dashed forward but for his strong restraining grasp. She clutched him, uttering a sudden dreadful cry. "Hark! I hear his voice!" she almost sobbed. They stood still to listen. A mystery that was more than the mystery of night closed about their hearts—a mystery that is beyond life and death, that only great awe and terror can summon from the deeps of the soul. Out of the heart of the trees, fifty feet away, issued a crying voice, half wailing, half singing, very faint. "Help! help!" it sounded through the still night; "for the love of God, pray for me!"

The melancholy rustling of the pines followed; and then again the singular crying voice passed above their heads, now in front of them, now once more behind. It sounded everywhere. It grew fainter and fainter, fading away, it seemed, into distance that somehow was appalling . . . The grove, however, was empty of all but the sighing wind; the snow unbroken by any tread. The moon threw inky shadows; the cold bit; it was a terror of ice and death and this awful singing cry . . .

"But why *pray?*" screamed the girl, distracted, frantic with her bewildered terror. "Why *pray?* Let us *do* something to help—*do* something . . .!" She swung round in a circle, nearly falling to the ground. Suddenly she perceived that the old man had dropped to his knees in the snow and was— praying.

"Because the forces of prayer, of thought, of the will to help, alone can reach and succour him where he now is" was all the answer she got. And a moment later both were kneeling in the snow, praying, so to speak, their very heart's life out . . .

The search may be imagined—the steps taken by the police, friends, newspapers, by the whole country in fact . . . But the most curious part of this queer "Higher Space" adventure is the end of it—at least, the "end" so far as at present known. For after three weeks, when the winds of March were a-roar about the land, there crept over the fields towards the house the small dark figure of a man. He was thin, pallid as a ghost, worn and fearfully emaciated, but upon his face and in his eyes were traces of an astonishing radiance—a glory unlike anything ever seen . . . It may, of course, have been deliberate, or it may have been a genuine loss of memory only; none could say—least of all the girl whom his return snatched from the gates of death; but, at any rate, what had come to pass during the interval of his amazing disappearance he has never yet been able to reveal.

"And you must never ask me," he would say to her—and

repeat even after his complete and speedy restoration to bodily health—"for I simply cannot tell. I know no language, you see, that could express it. I was near you all the time. But I was also—elsewhere and otherwise . . ."

# Gay as Cheese

Mr Pol the barber always wore white overalls. He must have had at least six for every day. He was snowy white and freshly starched as a marguerite, his blue eyes, red face and bulbous nose appearing incongruously over the top of the bib. His shop looked like, and was, a kitchen, roughly adapted to barbering with a mirror, basin and some pictures of beautiful girls on the whitewashed walls. It was a long narrow crack of a room with the copper at one end and tottering flight of steps at the other, leading down to the street; customers waiting their turn mostly sat on the steps in the sun, risking piles and reading *Men Only*.

Mr Pol rented his upstairs room to an artist, and in the summertime when the customers had been shaved or trimmed they sometimes went on up the stairs and bought a view of the harbour, water or oil, or a nice still life. The artist had an unlimited supply of these, which he whipped out with the dexterity of a card sharper.

Both men loved their professions. When the artist was not painting fourteen-by-ten-inch squares for the trippers, he was engaged on huge, complicated panels of mermaids, sharks, all mixed up with skulls, roses and cabbages, while Mr Pol hung over the heads of his customers as if he would have liked to gild them.

"Ah, I'm as gay as cheese this morning," he used to say, bustling into his kitchen with a long, gnomish look at the first head of hair waiting to be shorn. "I'll smarten you up till you're like a new button mushroom."

"Now I'm as bright as a pearl," he would exclaim when the long rays of the early sun felt their way back to the copper with an under-water glimmer.

When Mr Pol laid hands on a customer's head he knew more about that man than his mother did at birth, or his sweetheart or confessor—not only his past misdeeds but his future ones, what he had had for breakfast and would have for supper, the name of his dog and the day of his death. This should have made Mr Pol sad or cynical, but it did not. He remained impervious to his portentous gift. Perhaps this was because the destinies of the inhabitants of a small Cornish town contained nothing very startling, and Mr Pol's divinings seldom soared higher or lower than a double twenty or a sprained ankle.

He never cut his own hair, and had no need to, for he was as bald as an egg.

"It was my own hair falling out that started me thinking on the matter," he told the artist. "All a man's nature comes out in the way his hair grows. It's like a river—watch the currents and you can tell what it's come through, what sort of fish are in it, how fast it's running, how far to the sea."

The artist grunted. He was squatting on the floor, stretching a canvas, and made no reply. He was a taciturn man, who despised the trippers for buying his pink and green views.

Mr Pol looked down at the top of his head and suddenly gave it an affectionate, rumpling pat, as one might to a large woolly dog.

"Ah, that's a nice head of hair. It's a shame you won't let me get at it."

"And have you knowing when I'm going to eat my last bite of bacon? Not likely."

"I wouldn't tell you, my handsome!" said Mr Pol, very shocked. "I'm not one to go measuring people for their coffins before they're ready to step in. I'm as close as a false tooth. There's Sam now, off his lorry, the old ruin; I could tell a thing or two about him, but do I?"

He stumped off down the stairs, letting out a snatch of hymn in his powerful baritone.

"And there's some say," he went on, as he sculpted with his shears round the driver's wicked grey head, "that you can grow turnip from carrot seed under the right moon. Who'd want to do that, I ask you?"

"Shorter round the ears," grumbled Sam, scowling down into the enamel basin.

When the night train from Paddington began to draw down the narrow valley towards the sea town, Brian and Fanny Dexter stood up stiffly from the seats where they had slept and started moving their luggage about. Brian was surly and silent, only remarking that it was damned cold and he hoped he could get a shave and a cup of coffee. Fanny glanced doubtfully at her reflection in the little greenish mirror. A white face and narrow eyes, brilliant from lack of sleep, glanced back at her.

"It'll be fine later," she said hopefully. Brian pulled on a sweater without comment. He looked rough but expensive, like a suède shoe. His thick light hair was beginning to grey, but hardly showed it.

"Lady Ward and Penelope said they'd be getting to Pengelly this week," Brian observed. "We might walk along the cliff path later on and see if they've arrived yet. We can do with some exercise to warm us and they'll be expecting us to call."

"I must do my shopping first. It's early closing, and there's all the food to lay in."

Brian shot her an angry look and she was reminded that although the ice of their marriage seemed at the moment to be bearing, nevertheless there were frightening depths beneath and it was best not to loiter in doubtful spots.

"It won't take long," she said hurriedly.

"It was just an idea," Brian muttered, bundling up a camel-hair overcoat. "Here we are, thank God."

It was still only nine in the morning. The town was grey and forbidding, tilted steeply down to a white sea. The fleet was out; the streets smelt of fish and emptiness. After they had had coffee Brian announced that he was going to get his shave.

"I'll do my shopping and meet you," suggested Fanny.

"No you bloody well won't, or you'll wander off for hours and I shall have to walk half over the town looking for you," snapped Brian. "You could do with a haircut yourself, you look like a scotch terrier."

"All right."

She threaded her way after him between the empty tables of the café and across the road into Mr Pol's shop. Mr Pol was carefully rearranging his tattered magazines.

"Good morning, my handsome," he cautiously greeted Fanny's jeans and sweater and Eton crop, assessing her as a summer visitor.

"Can you give me a shave and my wife a haircut please?" cut in Brian briskly.

Mr Pol looked from one to the other of them.

"I'll just put the kettle on for the shave, sir," he answered, moving leisurely to the inner room, "and then I'll trim the young lady, if you'd like to take a seat in the meanwhile."

Brian preferred to stroll back and lean against the doorpost with his hands in his pockets, while Mr Pol wreathed Fanny's neck in a spotless towel. Her dark head, narrow as a boy's, was bent forward, and he looked benignly at the swirl of glossy hair, flicked a comb through it and turned her head gently with the palms of his hands.

As he did so, a shudder like an electric shock ran through him and he started back, the comb between his thumb and forefinger jerking upward like a diviner's rod. Neither of the other two noticed; Brian was looking out into the street and Fanny had her eyes on her hands, which were locked together with white knuckles across a fold of the towel.

After a moment Mr Pol gingerly replaced his palms on the sides of her head with a pretence of smoothing the downy hair above the ears, and again the shock ran through him. He looked into the mirror, almost expecting to see fish swimming and seaweed floating around her. Death by drowning, and so soon; he could smell salt water and see her thin arm stretched sideways in the wave.

"Don't waste too much time on her," said Brian looking at his watch. "She doesn't mind what she looks like."

Fanny glanced up and met Mr Pol's eyes in the glass. There was such a terrified appeal in her look that his hands closed instinctively on her shoulders and his lips parted to form the words:

"There, there, my handsome. Never mind," before he saw that her appeal was directed, not to him, but to her own reflection's pathetic power to please.

"That's lovely," she said to Mr Pol with a faint smile, and stood up, shaking the glossy dark tufts off her. She sat on one of his chairs, looking at a magazine, while Brian took her place and Mr Pol fetched his steaming kettle.

"You're visiting the town?" Mr Pol asked, as he rubbed up the lather on his brush. He felt the need for talk.

"Just come off the night train; we're staying here, yes," Brian said shortly.

"It's a pretty place," Mr Pol remarked. "Plenty of grand walks if you're young and active."

"We're going along to Pengelly by the cliff path this morning," said Brian.

"Oh, but I thought you only said we *might*—" Fanny began incautiously, and then bit off her words.

Brian shot her a look of such hatred that even Mr Pol caught it, and scuttled into the next room for another razor.

"For Christ's sake *will* you stop being so damned negative," Brian muttered to her furiously.

"But the groceries—"

"Oh, to hell with the groceries. We'll eat out. Lady Ward and Penelope will think it most peculiar if we don't call— they know we're here. I suppose you want to throw away a valuable social contact for the sake of a couple of ounces of tea. I can't think why you need to do this perpetual shopping—Penelope never does."

"I only thought—"

"Never mind what you thought."

Mr Pol came back and finished the shave.

"That's a nice head of hair, sir," he said, running his hands over it professionally. "Do you want a trim at all?"

"No thanks," replied Brian abruptly. "Chap in the Burlington Arcade always does it for me. Anything wrong?"

Mr Pol was staring at the ceiling above Brian's head in a puzzled way.

"No—no, sir, nothing. Nothing at all. I thought for a moment I saw a bit of rope hanging down, but it must have been fancy." Nevertheless Mr Pol passed his hand once more above Brian's head with the gesture of someone brushing away cobwebs.

"Will that be all? Thank you, sir. Mind how you go on that path to Pengelly. 'Tis always slippery after the rain and we've had one or two falls of rock this summer; all this damp weather loosens them up."

"We'll be all right, thanks," said Brian, who had been walking out of the door without listening to what Mr Pol was saying. "Come on, Fanny." He swung up the street with Fanny almost running behind him.

"Have they gone? Damnation, I thought I could sell them a view of the cliffs," said the artist, coming in with a little canvas. "Hullo, something the matter?"

For the barber was standing outside his door and staring in indecision and distress after the two figures, now just taking the turning up to the cliff path.

"No," he said at last, turning heavily back and picking up his broom. "No, I'm as gay as cheese."

And he began sweeping up the feathery tufts of dark hair from his stone floor.

# Diamond Cut Diamond
# or The Biter Bit

## Miss Hinch
### H. S. Harrison

## The Legend of Clare
### Anonymous

## The Markhampton Miracle
### Cyril Hare

# Miss Hinch

In going from a given point on 126th Street to the subway station at 125th, it is not usual to begin by circling the block of 127th Street, especially in sleet, darkness, and deadly cold. When two people pursue such a course at the same time, moving unobtrusively on opposite sides of the street, in the nature of things the coincidence is likely to attract the attention of one or the other of them.

In the bright light of the entrance to the tube they came almost face to face, and the clergyman took a good look at her. Certainly she was a decent-looking old body, if any woman was: white-haired, wrinkled, spectacled, and stooped. A poor but thoroughly respectable domestic servant of the better class she looked, in her old black hat, wispy veil, and grey shawl; and her brief glance at the reverend gentleman was precisely what it should have been from her to him—open deference itself. Nevertheless, he, going more slowly down the draughty steps, continued to study her from behind with a singular intentness.

An express was just thundering in, which the clergyman, handicapped as he was by his clubfoot and stout cane, was barely in time to catch. He entered the same car with the woman, and chanced to take a seat directly across from her.

It must have been then after twelve o'clock, and the wildness of the weather was discouraging to travel. The car was almost deserted. Even in this underground retreat the bitter breath of the night blew and bit, and the old woman shivered under her shawl. At last, her teeth chattering, she got up in an apologetic sort of way, and moved towards the better protected rear of the car, feeling the empty seats as she went, in a palpable search for hot pipes. The clergyman's eyes followed her candidly, and watched her sink down, presently, into a seat on his own side of the car. A young couple sat between them now; he could no longer see the woman, beyond occasional glimpses of her black knees and her ancient bonnet, skewered on with a long steel hatpin.

Nothing could have seemed more natural or more trivial than this change of seats on the part of a thin-blooded and half-frozen passenger. But it happened to be a time of mutual doubt and suspicion, of alert suspicions and hair-trigger watchfulness, when men looked askance into every strange face and the smallest incidents were likely to take on an hysterical importance. Through days of fruitless searching for a fugitive outlaw of extraordinary gifts, the nerve of the city had been slowly strained to the breaking-point. All jumped, now, when anybody cried "Boo!" and the hue and cry went up falsely twenty times a day.

The clergyman pondered; mechanically he turned up his coat collar and fell to stamping his icy feet. He was an Episcopal clergyman, by his garb—rather short, very full bodied, not to say fat, bearded, and somewhat puffy-faced, with heavy cheeks cut by deep creases. Well lined against the cold though he was, however, he, too, began to suffer visibly, and presently he was forced to retreat in his turn, seeking out a new place where the heating apparatus gave a better account of itself. He found one two seats beyond the old serving-woman, limped into it, and soon relapsed into his own thoughts.

The young couple, now half the car-length away, were thoroughly absorbed in each other's society. The fifth traveller, a withered old gentleman sitting next the middle door across the aisle, napped fitfully upon his cane. The woman in the hat and shawl sat in a sad kind of silence; and the train hurled itself roaringly through the tube. After a time, she glanced timidly at the meditating clergyman, and her look fell swiftly from his face to the discarded "ten-o'clock extra" lying by his side. She removed her dim gaze and let it travel casually about the car; but before long it returned again, pointedly, to the newspaper. Then, with some obvious hesitation, she bent forward and said: "Excuse me, Father, but would you please let me look at your paper a minute, sir."

The clergyman came out of his reverie instantly, and looked up with an almost eager smile.

"Certainly. Keep it if you like: I am quite through with it. But," he said, in a pleasant deep voice, "I am an Episcopal minister, not a priest."

"Oh, sir—I beg your pardon! I thought—"

He dismissed the apology with a smile and a good-natured hand.

The woman opened the paper with decent cotton-gloved fingers. The garish head-lines told the story at a glance: "Earth Opened and Swallowed Miss Hinch—Headquarters Virtually Abandons Case—Even Jessie Dark"—so the bold capitals ran on—"Seems Stumped." Below the spread was a luridly written but flimsy narrative, "By Jessie Dark," which at once confirmed the odd implication of the caption. "Jessie Dark," it appeared, was one of those most extraordinary of the products of yellow journalism, a woman "crime expert," now in action. More than this, she was a "crime expert" to be taken seriously, it seems—no mere office-desk sleuth—but an actual performer with, unexpectedly enough, a somewhat formidable list of notches on her gun. So much, at least, was to be gathered from the paper's display of "Jessie Dark's Triumphs":

March 2, 1901. Caught Julia Victorian, alias Gregory, the brains of the "Healey Ring" kidnappers.

October 7–29, 1903. Found Mrs Trotwood and secured letter that convicted her of the murder of her lover, Ellis B. Swan.

December 17, 1903. Ran down Charles Bartsch in a Newark laundry and trapped a confession from him.

July 4, 1904. Caught Mary Calloran and recovered the Stratford jewels.

And so on—nine "triumphs" in all; and nearly every one of them, as the least observant reader could hardly fail to notice, involved the capture of a woman.

Nevertheless, it could not be pretended that the "snappy" paragraphs in this evening's extra seemed to foreshadow a new or tenth triumph for Jessie Dark at any early date; and the old serving-woman in the car presently laid down the sheet with an irrepressible sigh.

The clergyman glanced toward her kindly. The sigh was so audible that it seemed to be almost an invitation; besides, public interest in the great case was a freemasonry that made conversation between total strangers the rule wherever two or three were gathered together.

"You were reading about this strange mystery, perhaps?"

The woman, with a sharp intake of breath, answered: "Yes, sir. Oh, sir, it seems as if I couldn't think of anything else."

"Ah?" he said, without surprise. "It certainly appears to be a remarkable affair."

Remarkable indeed the affair seemed. In a tiny little room within ten steps of Broadway, at half past nine o'clock on a fine evening, Miss Hinch had killed John Catherwood with the light sword she used in her famous representation of the Father of his Country. Catherwood, it was known, had come to tell her of his approaching marriage; and ten thousand amateur detectives, athirst for rewards, had required no further "motive" of a creature so notorious for fierce jealousy. So far the tragedy was commonplace enough, and even vulgar. What had redeemed it to romance from this point on was the extraordinary faculty of the woman, which had made her celebrated while she was still in her teens. Coarse, violent, utterly unmoral she might be, but she happened also to be the most astonishing impersonator of her time. Her brilliant "act" consisted of a series of character changes, many of them done in full view of the audience with the assistance only of a small table of properties half concealed under a net. Some of these transformations were so amazing as to be beyond belief, even after one had sat and watched them. Not her appearance only, but voice, speech, manner, carriage, all shifted incredibly to fit the new part, so that on the stage the woman appeared to have no permanent form or fashion of her own, but to be only so much plastic human material out of which her cunning could mould at will man, woman, or child, great lady of the Louisan court or Tam-

many statesman with the modernest of East Side modern-
isms upon his lip.

With this strange skill, hitherto used only to enthrall huge
audiences and wring extortionate contracts from managers,
the woman known as Miss Hinch—she appeared to be without a first name—was now fighting for her life somewhere
against the police of the world. Without artifice, she was a
tall, thin-chested young woman with strongly marked features and considerable beauty of a bold sort. What she
would look like at the present moment nobody could venture
a guess. Having stabbed John Catherwood in her dressing-
room at the Amphitheatre, she had put on her hat and coat,
dropped two wigs and her make-up kit into a handbag, and
walked out into Broadway. Within ten minutes the dead
body of Catherwood was found and the chase begun. At the
stage door, as she passed out, Miss Hinch had met an acquaintance, a young comedian named Dargis, and exchanged
a word of greeting with him. That had been ten days ago.
After Dargis, no one had seen her. The earth, indeed, seemed
to have opened up and swallowed her. Yet her natural features were almost as well known as a President's, and the
newspapers of a continent were daily reprinting them in a
thousand variations.

"A very remarkable case," repeated the clergyman, rather
absently; and his neighbour, the old woman, respectfully
agreed that it was. After that she hesitated a moment, and
then added with sudden bitterness: "Oh, they'll never catch
her, sir—never! She's too smart for 'em all, Miss Hinch is."

Attracted by her tone, the stout divine inquired if she was
particularly interested in the case.

"Yes, sir—I got reason to be. Jack Catherwood's mother

and me was at school together, and great friends all our life
long. Oh, sir," she went on, as if in answer to his look of faint
surprise, "Jack was a fine gentleman, with manners and looks
and all beyond his people. But he never grew away from his
old mother—no, sir, never! And I don't believe ever a Sunday passed that he didn't go up and set the afternoon away
with her, talking and laughing just like he was a little boy
again. Maybe he done things he hadn't ought, as high-
spirited lads will, but oh, sir, he was a good boy in his
heart—a good boy. And it does seem too hard for him to die
like that—and that hussy free to go her way, ruinin' and
killin'—"

"My good woman," said the clergyman presently, "compose yourself. No matter how diabolical this woman's skill is,
her sin will assuredly find her out."

The woman dutifully lowered her handkerchief and tried
to compose herself, as bidden.

"But oh, she's that clever—diabolical, just as ye say, sir.
Through poor Jack we of course heard much gossip about
her, and they do say that her best tricks was not done on the
stage at all. They say, sir, that, sittin' around a table with her
friends, she could begin and twist her face so strange and
terrible that they would beg her to stop, and jump up and
run from the table—frightened out of their lives, sir, grown-
up people, by the terrible faces she could make. And let her
only step behind her screen for a minute—for she kept her
secrets well, Miss Hinch did—and she'd come walking out to
you, and you could go right up to her in the full light and
take her hand, and still you couldn't make yourself believe
that it was her."

"Yes," said the clergyman, "I have heard that she is remarkably clever—though, as a stranger in this part of the world, I never saw her act. I must say, it is all very interesting and strange."

He turned his head and stared through the rear door of the car at the dark flying walls. At the same moment the woman turned her head and stared full at the clergyman. When he turned back, her gaze had gone off towards the front of the car, and he picked up the paper thoughtfully.

"I'm a visitor in the city, from Denver, Colorado," he said presently, "and knew little or nothing about the case until an evening or two ago, when I attended a meeting of gentlemen here. The men's club of St Matthias' Church—perhaps you know the place? Upon my word, they talked of nothing else. I confess they got me quite interested in their gossip. So tonight I bought this paper to see what the extraordinary woman detective it employs had to say about it. We don't have such things in the West, you know. But I must say I was disappointed, after all the talk about her."

"Yes, sir, indeed, and no wonder, for she's told Mrs Catherwood herself that she's never made such a failure as this so far. It seemed like she could always catch women, up to this. It seemed like she knew in her own mind just what a woman would do, where she'd try to hide and all, and she could find them time and time when the men detectives didn't know where to look. But oh, sir, she's never had to hunt for such a woman as Miss Hinch before!"

"No? I suppose not," said the clergyman, "Her story here in the paper certainly seems to me very poor."

"*Story*, sir! Bless my soul!" suddenly exploded the old gentleman across the aisle, to the surprise of both. "You don't suppose the clever little woman is going to show her

hand in those stories, with Miss Hinch in the city and reading every line of them! In the city, sir—such is my positive
belief!"

The approach to his station, it seemed, had roused him
from his nap just in time to overhear the episcopate criti-
cism. Now he answered the looks of the old woman and the
clergyman with an elderly cackle.

"Excuse my intrusion, I am sure! But I can't sit silent and
hear anybody run down Jessie Dark—Miss Matthewson in
private life, as perhaps you don't know. No, sir! Why, there's
a man at my boarding-place—astonishing young fellow
named Hardy—Tom Hardy—who's known her for *years!* As
to those stories, sir, I can assure you that she puts in there
*exactly the opposite of what she really thinks!*"

"You don't tell me!" said the clergyman encouragingly.

"Yes, sir! Oh, she plays the game—yes, yes! She has her
private ideas, her clues, her schemes. The woman doesn't
live who is clever enough to hoodwink Jessie Dark. I look for
developments any day—any day, sir!"

A new voice joined in. The young couple down the car,
their attention caught by the old man's pervasive tones, had
been frankly listening: and it was illustrative of the public
mind at the moment that, as they now rose for their station,
the young fellow felt perfectly free to offer his contribution:
"Tremendously dramatic situation, isn't it, gentlemen?
Those two clever women pitted against each other in a life-
and-death struggle, fighting it out silently in the underground somewhere—keen professional pride on one side and
the fear of the electric chair on the other. Good heavens,
there's—"

"Oh, yes! Oh, yes!" exclaimed the old gentleman rather

testily. "But my dear sir, it's not *professional pride* that makes Jessie Dark so resolute to win. It's *sex jealousy*, if you follow me—no offence, madam! Yes, sir! Women never have the slightest respect for each other's abilities—not the slightest. No mercy for each other, either! I tell you, Jessie Dark'd be ashamed to be beaten by another woman. Read her stories between the lines, sir—as I do. Invincible determination—no weakening—no mercy! You catch my point, sir?"

"It sounds reasonable," answered the Colorado clergyman, with his courteous smile. "All women, we are told, are natural rivals at heart—"

"Oh, I'm for Jessie Dark every time!" the young fellow broke in eagerly, "especially since the police have practically laid down. But—"

"Why, she's told my young friend Hardy," the old gentleman rode him down, "that she'll find Hinch if it takes her lifetime! Knows a thing or two about actresses, she says. Says the world isn't big enough for the creature to hide from her. Well! What do you think of that?"

"Tell what we were just talking about, George," said the young wife, looking at her husband with grossly admiring eyes.

"But oh, sir," began the old woman timidly, "Jack Catherwood's been dead ten days now, and—and—"

"Woman got on my car at nine o'clock tonight," interjected the subway guard, who, having flung open the doors for the station, was listening excitedly to the symposium; "wore a brown veil and goggles. I'd 'a' bet every dollar I had—"

"Ten days, madam! And what is that, pray?" exploded the

old gentleman, rising triumphantly. "A lifetime, if necessary! Oh, never fear! Mrs Victorian was considered pretty clever, eh? Wasn't she? Remember what Jessie Dark did for her? Nan Parmalee, too—though the police did their best to steal her credit. She'll do just as much for Miss Hinch—you take it from me!"

"But how's she going to make the capture, gentlemen?" cried the young fellow, getting his chance at last. "That's the point my wife and I've been discussing. Assuming that she succeeds in spotting this woman-devil, what will she do? Now—"

"Do! Yell for the police!" burst from the old gentleman at the door.

"And have Miss Hinch shoot her—and then herself, too? Wouldn't she have to—"

"Grand Central!" cried the guard for the second time; and the young fellow broke off reluctantly to find his bride towing him strongly towards the door.

"Hope she nabs her soon, anyway," he called back to the clergyman over his shoulder. "The thing's getting on my nerves. One of these kindergarten reward-chasers followed my wife for five blocks the other day, just because she's got a pointed chin, and I don't know what might have happened if I hadn't come along and—"

Doors rolled shut behind him, and the train flung itself on its way. Within the car a lengthy silence ensued. The clergyman stared thoughtfully at the floor, and the old woman fell back upon her borrowed paper. She appeared to be re-reading the observations of Jessie Dark with considerable care. Presently she lowered the paper and began a quiet search for something under the folds of her shawl; and at length,

her hands emerging empty, she broke the silence with a
timid request:

"Oh, sir—have you a pencil you could lend me, please? I'd
like to mark something in the piece to send to Mrs Catherwood. It's what she says here about the disguises, sir."

The kindly divine felt in his pockets, and after some hunting produced a pencil—a white one with blue lead. She
thanked him gratefully.

"How is Mrs Catherwood bearing all this strain and anxiety?" he asked suddenly. "Have you seen her today?"

"Oh, yes, sir, I've been spending the evening with her
since nine o'clock, and am just back from there now. Oh,
she's very much broke up, sir."

She looked at him hesitatingly. He stared straight in front
of him, saying nothing, though conceivably he knew, in
common with the rest of the reading world, that Jack
Catherwood's mother lived, not on 126th Street, but on East
Houston Street. Possibly he might have wondered if his
silence had not been an error of judgment. Perhaps that
misstatement had not been a slip, but something cleverer?

The woman went on with a certain eagerness: "Oh, sir, I
only hope and pray those gentlemen may be right, but it
does look to Mrs Catherwood, and me too, that if Jessie Dark
was going to catch her at all, she'd have done it before now.
Look at those big, bold blue eyes she had, sir, with lashes an
inch long, they say, and that terrible long chin of hers. They
do say she can change the colour of her eyes, not for ever of
course, but put a few of her drops into them and make them
look entirely different for a time. But that chin, ye'd say—"

She broke off; for the clergyman, without preliminaries of
any sort, had picked up his heavy stick and suddenly risen.

"Here we are at Fourteenth Street," he said, nodding pleasantly. "I must change here. Good night. Success to Jessie Dark, I say!"

He was watching the woman's faded face and he saw just that look of respectful surprise break into it that he had expected.

"Fourteenth Street! I'd no notion at all we'd come so far. It's where I get out too, sir, the express is not stopping at my station."

"Ah?" said the clergyman, with the utmost dryness.

He led the way, limping and leaning on his stick. They emerged upon the chill and cheerless platform, not exactly together, yet still with some reference to their acquaintance-ship on the car. But the clergyman, after stumping along a few steps, all at once realised that he was walking alone, and turned. The woman had halted. Over the intervening space their eyes met.

"Come," said the man gently. "Come, let us walk about a little to keep warm."

"Oh, sir—it's too kind of you, sir," said the woman coming forward.

From other cars two or three blue-nosed people had got off to make the change; one or two more came straggling in from the street; but, scattered over the bleak concrete ex-panse, they detracted little from the isolation that seemed to surround the woman and the clergyman. Step for step, the odd pair made their way to the extreme northern end of the platform.

"By the way," said the clergyman, halting abruptly, "may I see that paper again for a moment?"

"Oh, yes, sir—of course," said the woman, producing it

from beneath her shawl. "I thought you had finished with it, and I—"

He said that he wanted only to glance at it for a moment; but he fell to looking through it page by page with considerable care. The woman looked at him several times. Finally she said hesitatingly: "I thought, sir, I'd ask the ticket-chopper could he say how long before the next train. I'm very late as it is, sir, and I still must stop to get something to eat before I go to bed."

"An excellent idea," said the clergyman.

He explained that he, too, was already an hour behind time, and was spending the night with cousins in Newark, to boot. Side by side, they retraced their steps down the platform, questioned the chopper with scant results, and then, as by some tacit consent, started slowly back again. However, before they had gone very far, the woman all at once stopped short and, with a white face, leaned against the wall.

"Oh, sir, I'm afraid I'll just have to stop and get a bite somewhere before I go on. You'll think me foolish, sir, but I missed my supper entirely tonight, and there is quite a faint feeling coming over me."

The clergyman looked at her with apparent concern. "Do you know, my friend, you seem to anticipate all my own wants? Your mentioning something to eat just now reminded me that I myself was all but famishing." He glanced at his watch, appearing to deliberate. "Yes—it will not take long. Come, we will find a modest eating-place together."

"Oh, sir," she stammered, "but—you wouldn't want to eat with a poor old woman like me, sir."

"And why not? Are we not all equal in the sight of God?"

They ascended the stairs together, like any prosperous parson and his poor parishioner, and, coming out into Fourteenth Street, started west. On the first block they came to a restaurant, a brilliantly lighted, tiled and polished place of the quick-lunch variety. But the woman timidly preferred not to stop here, saying that the glare of such places was very bad for her old eyes. The divine accepted the objection as valid, without argument. Two blocks farther on they found on a corner a quieter resort, an unpretentious little haven which yet boasted a "Ladies' Entrance" down the side street.

They entered by the front door, and sat down at a table, facing each other. The woman read the menu through, and finally, after some embarrassed uncertainty, ordered poached eggs on toast. The clergyman ordered the same. The simple meal was soon dispatched. Just as they were finishing it, the woman said apologetically: "If you'll excuse me, sir—could I see the bill of fare a minute? I think I'd best take a little pot of tea to warm me up, if they do not charge too high."

"I haven't the bill of fare," said the clergyman.

They looked diligently for the cardboard strip, but it was nowhere to be seen. The waiter drew near.

"Yes, sir! I left it there on the table when I took the order."

"I'm sure I can't imagine what's become of it," repeated the clergyman, rather insistently.

He looked hard at the woman, and found she was looking hard at him. Both pairs of eyes fell instantly.

The waiter brought another bill of fare; the woman ordered tea; the waiter came back with it. The clergyman

paid for both orders with a bill that looked hard-earned. The
tea proved to be very hot; it could not be drunk down at a
gulp. The clergyman, watching the woman intently as she
sipped, seemed to grow more and more restless. His fingers
drummed the tablecloth: he could hardly sit still. All at once
he said: "What is that calling in the street? It sounds like
newsboys."

The woman put her old head on one side and listened.
"Yes, sir. There seems to be an extra out."

"Upon my word," he said, after a pause. "I believe I'll go
get one. Good gracious! Crime is a very interesting thing, to
be sure!"

He rose slowly, took down his shovel hat from the hanger
near him, and, grasping his heavy stick, limped to the door.
Leaving it open behind him, much to the annoyance of the
proprietor in the cashier's cage, he stood a moment in the
little vestibule, looking up and down the street. Then he
took a few steps eastward, beckoning with his hand as he
went, and so passed out of sight of the woman at the table.

The eating-place was on the corner, and outside the
clergyman paused for half a breath. North, east, south, and
west he looked, and nowhere he found what his flying glance
sought. He turned the corner into the darker cross-street,
and began to walk, at first slowly, continually looking about
him. Presently his pace quickened, quickened so that he no
longer even stayed to use his stout cane. In another moment
he was all but running, his clubfoot pounding the icy pavement heavily as he went. A newsboy thrust an extra under
his very nose, and he did not even see it.

Far down the street, nearly two blocks away, a tall figure
in a blue coat stood and stamped in the freezing sleet; and

the hurrying divine sped straight toward him. But he did not get very near. For, as he passed the side entrance at the extreme rear of the restaurant, a departing guest dashed out so recklessly as to run full into him, stopping him dead.

Without looking at her, he knew who it was. In fact, he did not look at her at all, but turned his head hurriedly east and west, sweeping the dark street with a swift eye. But the old woman, having drawn back with a sharp exclamation as they collided, rushed breathlessly into apologies:

"Oh, sir—excuse me! A newsboy popped his head into the side door just after you went out, and I ran to him to get you the paper. But he got away too quick for me, sir, and so I—"

"Exactly," said the clergyman in his quiet deep voice. "That must have been the very boy I myself was after."

On the other side, two men had just turned into the street well muffled against the night, talking cheerfully as they trudged along. Now the clergyman looked full at the woman, and she saw that there was a smile on his face.

"As he seems to have eluded us both, suppose we return to the subway?"

"Yes, sir; it's full time I—"

"The sidewalk is so slippery," he went on gently, "perhaps you had better take my arm."

Behind the pair in the dingy restaurant, the waiter came forward to shut the door, and lingered to discuss with the proprietor the sudden departure of his two patrons. However, the score had been paid with a liberal tip for service, so there was no especial complaint to make. After listening to some unfavourable comments on the ways of clergy, the waiter returned to his table to set it in order.

On the floor in the carpeted aisle between tables lay a white piece of cardboard, which his familiar eye recognised as part of one of his own bills of fare, face downward. He stooped to pick it up. On the back of it was some scribbling, made with a blue lead-pencil.

The handwriting was very loose and irregular, as if the writer had had his eyes elsewhere while he wrote, and it was with some difficulty that the waiter deciphered this message:

Miss Hinch 14th St. Subway. Get police quick.

The waiter carried this curious document to the proprietor, who read it over a number of times. He was a dull man, and had a dull man's suspiciousness of a practical joke. However, after a good deal of irresolute discussion, he put on his overcoat and went out for a policeman. He turned west and, half-way up the block, met an elderly bluecoat sauntering east. The policeman looked at the scribbling, and dismissed it profanely as a wag's foolishness of the sort that was bothering the life out of him a dozen times a day. He walked along with the proprietor, and as they drew near to the latter's place of business, both became aware of footsteps thudding nearer up the cross-street from the south. As they looked up, two young policemen, accompanied by a man in uniform like a street-car conductor's, swept around the corner and dashed straight into the restaurant.

The first policeman and the proprietor ran in after them, and found them staring about rather vacantly. One of the arms of the law demanded if any suspicious characters had been seen about the place, and the dull proprietor said no. The officers, looking rather flat, explained their errand. It seemed that a few moments before, the third man, who was a ticket-chopper at the subway station, had found a mysterious message lying on the floor by his box. Whence it had come, how long it had lain there, he had not the slightest idea. However, there it was. The policeman exhibited a crumpled white scrap torn from a newspaper, on which was scrawled in blue pencil:

Miss Hinch Miller's Restaurant    Get police quick.

The first policeman, who was both the oldest and the fattest of the three, produced the message on the bill of fare, so utterly at odds with this. The dull proprietor, now bethinking himself, mentioned the clergyman and the old woman who had taken poached eggs and tea together, called for a second bill of fare, and departed so unexpectedly by different doors. The ticket-chopper recalled that he had seen the same pair at his station: they had come up, he remembered, and questioned him about trains. The three policemen were momentarily puzzled by this testimony. But it was soon plain to them that if either the woman or the clergyman really had any information about Miss Hinch—a highly improbable supposition in itself—they would never have stopped with peppering the neighbourhood with silly little contradictory messages.

"They're a pair of old fools tryin' to have sport with the police, and I'd like to run them in for it," growled the fattest of the officers; and this was the general verdict.

The little conference broke up. The dull proprietor returned to his cage, the waiter to his table; the subway man departed on the run for his chopping box; the three policemen passed out into the bitter night. They walked together, grumbling, and their feet, perhaps by some subconscious impulse, turned eastward toward the subway. And in the middle of the next block a man came running up to them.

"Officer, look what I found on the sidewalk a minute ago. Read that scribble!"

He held up a white slab which proved to be part of a bill of fare from Miller's Restaurant. On the back of it the three peering officers saw, almost illegibly scrawled in blue pencil:

Police! Miss Hinch 14th St. Subw

The hand trailed off on the *w* as though the writer had been suddenly interrupted. The fat policeman blasphemed and threatened arrests. But the second policeman, who was dark and wiry, raised his head from the bill of fare and said suddenly: "Tim, I believe there's something in this."

"There'd ought to be ten days on the Island in it for them," growled fat Tim.

"Suppose, now," said the other policeman, staring intently at nothing, "the old woman was Miss Hinch herself, f'r instance, and the parson was shadowing her while pretendin' he never suspicioned her, and Miss Hinch not darin' to cut and run for it till she was sure she had a clean getaway. Well, now, Tim, what better could he do—"

"That's right!" exclaimed the third policeman. " 'Specially when ye think that Hinch carries a gun, an'll use it, too! Why not have a look in at the subway station anyway, the three of us?"

The proposal carried the day. The three officers started for the subway, the citizen following. They walked at a good pace and without more talk; and both their speed and their silence had a subtle psychological reaction. As the minds of the four men turned inward upon the odd behaviour of the pair in Miller's Restaurant, the conviction that, after all, something important might be afoot grew and strengthened within each one of them. Unconsciously their pace quickened. It was the wiry policeman who first broke into an open run, but the three other men had been for twenty paces on the verge of it.

However, these consultations and vacillations had taken time. The stout clergyman and the poor old woman had five minutes' start on the officers of the law, and that, as it happened, was all that the occasion required. On Fourteenth Street, as they made their way arm in arm to the station, they were seen, and remembered, by a number of belated pedestrians. It was observed by more than one that the woman lagged as if she were tired, while the clubfooted divine, supporting her on his arm, steadily kept her up to his own brisk gait.

So walking, the pair descended the subway steps, came out upon the bare platform again, and presently stood once more at the extreme uptown end of it, just where they had waited half an hour before. Nearby a careless porter had overturned a bucket of water, and a splotch of thin ice ran out and over the edge of the concrete. Two young men who were taking lively turns up and down distinctly heard the clergyman warn the woman to look out for this ice. Far away to the north was to be heard the faint roar of an approaching train.

The woman stood nearest the track, and the clergyman stood in front of her. In the vague light their looks met, and each was struck by the pallor of the other's face. In addition, the woman was breathing hard, and her hands and feet betrayed some nervousness. It was difficult now to ignore the too patent fact that for an hour they had been clinging desperately to each other, at all costs; but the clergyman made a creditable effort to do so. He talked ramblingly, in a voice sounding only a little unnatural, for the most part of the deplorable weather and his train to Newark, for which he was now so late. And all the time both of them were incessantly turning their heads towards the station entrances, as if expecting some arrival.

As he talked, the clergyman kept his hands unobtrusively busy. From the bottom edge of his black sack-coat he drew a pin, and stuck it deep into the ball of his middle finger. He took out his handkerchief to dust the hard sleet from his hat; and under his overcoat he pressed the handkerchief against his bleeding finger. While making these small arrangements, he held the woman's eyes with his own, talking on; and, still holding them, he suddenly broke off his random talk and peered at her cheek with concern.

"My good woman, you've scratched your cheek somehow! Why, bless me, it's bleeding quite badly."

"Never mind—never mind," said the woman, and swept her eyes hurriedly towards the entrance.

"But, good gracious, I must mind! The blood will fall on your shawl. If you will permit me—ah!"

Too quick for her, he leaned forward and, through the thin veil, swept her cheek hard with the handkerchief; removing it, he held it up so that she might see the blood for herself. But she did not glance at the handkerchief, and neither did he. His gaze was riveted upon her cheek, which looked smooth and clear where he had smudged the clever wrinkles away.

Down the steps and upon the platform pounded the feet of three flying policemen. But it was evident now that the express would thunder in just ahead of them. The clergyman, standing close in front of the woman, took a firmer grip on his heavy stick and a look of stern triumph came into his face.

"You're not so terribly clever, after all!"

The woman had sprung back from him with an irrepressible exclamation, and in that instant she was aware of the police.

However, her foot slipped upon the treacherous ice—or it may have tripped on the stout cane, when the clergyman suddenly shifted its position. And in the next breath the express train roared past.

By one of those curious chances which sometimes refute all experience, the body of the woman was not mangled or mutilated in the least. There was a deep blue bruise on the left temple, and apparently that was all; even the ancient hat remained on her head, skewered fast by the long pin. It was the clergyman who found the body huddled at the side of the dark track where the train had flung it—he who covered the still face and superintended the removal to the platform. Two eye-witnesses of the tragedy pointed out the ice on which the unfortunate woman had slipped, and described their horror as they saw her companion spring forward just too late to save her.

Not wishing to bring on a delirium of excitement among the bystanders, two policemen drew the clergyman quietly aside and showed him the three mysterious messages. Much affected by the shocking end of his sleuthery as he was, he readily admitted having written them. He briefly recounted

how the woman's strange movements on 126th Street had
arrested his attention and how watching her closely on the
car, he had finally detected that she wore a wig. Unfortunately, however, her suspicions had been aroused by his
interest in her, and thereafter a long battle of wits had
ensued between them—he trying to summon the police without her knowledge; she dogging him close to prevent that,
and at the same time watching her chance to give him the
slip. He rehearsed how, in the restaurant, when he had
invented an excuse to leave her for an instant, she had made
a bolt and narrowly missed getting away; and finally how,
having brought her back to the subway and seeing the police
at last near, he had decided to risk exposing her make-up,
with this unexpectedly shocking result.

"And now," he concluded in a shaken voice, "I am naturally most anxious to know whether I am right—or have
made some terrible mistake. Will you look at her, officer, and
tell me if it is indeed—she?"

But the fat policeman shook his head over the well-known
ability of Miss Hinch to look like everybody else in the
world but herself.

"It'll take God Almighty to tell ye that, sir—saving your
presence. I'll leave it f'r headquarters," he continued, as if
that were the same thing. "But, if it is her, she's gone to her
reward, sir."

"God pity her!" said the clergyman.

"Amen! Give me your name, sir. They'll likely want you in
the morning."

The clergyman gave it: Rev. Theodore Shaler, of Denver;
city address, a number on East 126th Street. Having thus
discharged his duty in the affair, he started sadly to go away,
but passing by the silent figure stretched on a bench under

the ticket-seller's overcoat, he bared his head and stopped
for one last look at it.

The parson's gentleness and efficiency had already won
favourable comments from the bystanders, and of the first
quality he now gave a final proof. The dead woman's balled-
up handkerchief, which somebody had recovered from the
track and laid upon her breast, had slipped to the floor; and
the clergyman, observing it, stooped silently to restore it
again. This last small service chanced to bring his head close
to the head of the dead woman; and as he straightened up
again, her projecting hatpin struck his cheek and ripped a
straight line down it. This in itself would have been a trifle,
since scratches soon heal. But it happened that the point of
the hatpin caught under the lining of the clergyman's perfect beard and ripped it clean from him; so that, as he rose
with a suddenly shrill cry, he turned upon the astonished
onlookers the bare, smooth chin of a woman, curiously long
and pointed.

There were not many such chins in the world, and the
urchins in the street would have recognised this one. Amid a
sudden uproar which ill became the presence of the dead,
the police closed in on Miss Hinch and handcuffed her with
violence, fearing suicide, if not some new witchery; and at
the station-house an unemotional matron divested the
famous impersonator of the last and best of all her many
disguises.

This much the police did. But it was everywhere understood that it was Jessie Dark who had really made the
capture, and the papers next morning printed pictures of the
unconquerable little woman and of the hatpin with which
she had reached back from another world to bring her
greatest adversary to justice.

ANONYMOUS

# The Legend of Clare

This is a traditional story told by an old Suffolk story-
teller about a well known country house in that county,
Clare Priory. It was written down by the then owner
of the Priory, Lady Barker, in 1902.

According to tradition, the Friars Hermits of the
Order of Saint Augustine became established at Clare,
in Suffolk, in 1248. For more than a hundred and fifty
years the Priory grew in size and wealth, and its fame
spread far beyond its own boundaries. But in later
years the fortunes of the community declined, and before the dissolution, in 1538, it was in a poor state, not
only in material wealth, but also in reputation, due to
the lax behaviour of the friars.

It was early in the fifteenth century that the friars of Clare
finished the building of their beautiful house. Not only was
the masonry and wood-work complete, but the church walls
were covered with frescoes, and the windows were glazed
with coloured glass. Nothing was lacking for the stately and
imposing service of the church, or the seemly ordering of the
friars' establishment. A long line of generous donors had
provided for them all that was necessary for the life of a
religious community and it only remained for the brothers to

carry out the intentions of their founders and live the religious life unhampered by worldly cares and distractions.

But unfortunately for the community Galfridus was appointed Prior. He was not what the world would call an evil man, but he was careless and easy-going, and he made no effort to keep himself, or to force on others, the strict observance of the Ancient Rule. Neither did he set much store by the words of Brother Giles, who held that it is impossible for a man to grow in virtue without carefulness and much labour.

Now when a community of men who have always been accustomed to absolute and unquestioning obedience to their superior are suddenly left to do very much as they please, it is hardly to be wondered at if some go woefully astray. And such was the case at Clare.

At this time Hugh of Bury was the Sacrist. In his charge were all the sacred vessels, the vestments, and the jewels and the treasures of the church. He held the keys of the old iron chest with its maze of locks, where those not in daily use were stored, and where the offerings made by the pious for the service of the High Altar were kept for safety. He was a quick and active man, and managed, in addition to the fulfilment of his duties, to take part in both the piety of the pious and the sports of the pleasure seekers. Whereby among his brethren he passed as a good friar and a good sportsman too. Yet he was not liked by his companions, though few could have given any reason for their dislike. He never failed to join in the daily chanting of the Psalms, though it is true he sometimes sang them out of tune. And none guessed that when the brothers met in the Chapter House and confessed their sins to each other, he mentioned only his virtues or sometimes a small failing, and of his sins he said no word at all. And even the brothers who most loved a little gossip knew of no tale to tell against the Sacrist, except that he was surly and ill-natured, and much occupied with business in the town.

One afternoon he sat by the river Stour with a rod in his hand, catching fish. There were other friars nearby, some walking up and down the river bank keenly interested in their sport, others sitting half idly musing, now throwing their lines, now gazing into the placid stream, or watching the light of the setting sun play round the ring of ripples when a fish jumped or a brother threw a line. A little occasional talk broke the stillness of the evening, as one would ask another his luck or foretell the morrow's weather. As the daylight faded, one by one they pulled in their lines and drifted back to the Friary, till Hugh alone was left. He had been sitting for some time too much absorbed in his own thoughts to heed his fishing rod. His face looked lined and care-worn and from his expression it was not hard to guess that his thoughts brought him more sorrow than joy.

Unfortunately his steps had strayed from the straight and narrow way, and he now found himself surrounded by a multitude of difficulties, and anxieties, from which he was vainly seeking to find escape. Looking back over the past few years, he was able to trace with startling clearness the steps that had led him down the path of evil to his present terrible position. Today for the first time he fully realised how matters stood, and as he tried to think, his difficulties seemed to grow and his evil deeds to increase, till they blotted out all other thoughts from his mind. For, though he scarcely dared acknowledge the fact even to himself, the truth was that the sacred treasure for which he—the Sacrist —was responsible, no longer lay safely stored in the great iron chest. He tried to turn his thoughts from the present to the future, but the more he thought, the more difficult his path seemed to grow. He cursed himself for his folly in ever having allowed matters to drift into such a pass, and even more for his inability to find a way out. He tried to comfort himself with the thought that for the present he was safe, for he knew that Prior Galfridus asked few questions, and seldom interfered in the business of the Friary. But Galfridus might die, and a new Prior be appointed; would he not examine the treasure and see that all was in order? Or there might even be danger in the immediate future: there was the Pope's Legate who had lately visited the Abbey of Saint Edmund, he might visit the friars and inspect their house. The more he thought, the more difficult his path became. Moreover there was not only the possibility of discovery but in the immediate future he needed more money for his own purposes. How could he obtain it?

As he sat and thought the light faded and faded in the west till the shadows in the river became deep purple and at last disappeared altogether for lack of light to show them. Then with a sigh and shudder he gathered himself together and prepared to depart. But as he turned he saw a figure approaching him. The new-comer was tall and wrapped in a habit whose colour he could not distinguish and whose form he did not recognise. He could only see that this seeming monk kept his cowl closely drawn round his head; and the folds of his habit were so long that they lay on the grass and covered his feet. Hugh wondered for a moment how his feet were shod, were they sandalled or bare?

"Good evening, brother," said the stranger in a kindly voice, "methinks you find your cares a burden towards the evening time."

"All should bethink them of the day's passing while the sun is setting," replied Hugh with pious unction. "And the cares of a friar are not always easy to explain in the Chapter House."

"Neither can comfort always be gathered in confession," replied the tall stranger.

"It is true," said Hugh, "and to each heart its own bitterness." He wondered as he spoke who the tall monk could be, and to what order he belonged. Instinctively he felt himself drawn to the stranger and he longed to ask his help. Yet he knew in his heart that the help he sought was not such as could be given by the wearer of the habit of religion.

"But wherefore suffer the bitterness when there is no need?" said the stranger. "Are you not Sacrist to the Friary yonder?"

"Truly," said Brother Hugh, "I am the Sacrist."

"And therein lies both your trouble and your help, is it not so, brother?"

"Therein lies my trouble," replied Hugh, "but I can see no help."

"Ah! I grieve for you, good friar, I have been Sacrist myself, and I know the difficulties. One wishes for a little money for one's private—one's private charities, is it not so? The Prior is hard, he will allow no money for his Sacrist's use—the offerings at the High Altar must suffice. But perhaps these are already spent—there is the jewelled cope left by some great nobleman to the Friary (in the hope of saving his soul thereby). It is only worn in procession at the crowning of the King, why should it not earn a little money for its care-taker? Say, am I not right, brother? It might be given in charge of that Jewish moneylender, he will lend a large sum on the security of such a treasure—and the money can always be repaid before the next coronation. Let me see your face, brother, do I not speak the truth, the very truth of what might be?"

"The truth of what might be," murmured Hugh cautiously.

"Nay—the truth of what is, good brother."

"Are you man or devil?" cried Hugh, "that you know so much and taunt me with my woes."

"I am your friend and brother," said the stranger softly. "I would not taunt you, nay, I am come to help you in your trouble, for is there not a way out of all troubles? Let me show you a way and I will help you."

The stranger leaned forward and spoke in silky purring voice, but his eyes glittered like the eyes of a tiger in the darkness.

"Have you never thought of the candles, O Brother Hugh? Mice eat candles. You have a goodly store in your sacristy tonight. You sell them to the pious that they may light them before the sacred shrine, do you not?—and you provide them for the use of the brothers when they come in their habits and their night-boots to chaunt the midnight office. Why not hide these candles and ask for a fresh supply because the mice have eaten yours. These, too, you might sell to the pious that they may light them before the shrine. Do you follow me, brother? But when their prayer is said, and they go out into the fields to work, why should their candle burn to waste? O careless Sacrist, why so thoughtless for the care of your goods! One candle might bring to you the price of three or four, if you but blow it out and return it to your store at once, and you would have sufficient money to spend in the town whenever you wish to go, and yet be able to set by a sum each week to satisfy the rapacious Jew, when the time comes that the cope must be returned. Think for one moment of my scheme, O brother! All those candles you now have, and all that fresh supply the Priory will give you, can be sold again and again, and you need but account for one burning. You might even find a friend to sell some in the town for you, for who has not need of candles? See how much money you can make by your wisdom and your industry."

"Indeed, good stranger, I thank you most heartily for your advice," cried Hugh. Then on second thought he added, "Yet, were it not a grievous sin to do as you suggest?"

"If you dislike my advice do not take it," said the stranger hotly. "Consult your brothers in the Chapter House tomorrow if that be more to your liking."

"Nay, nay, kind friend," said the Sacrist, "indeed I see the wisdom of your counsel. You have helped me out of woeful difficulties, and I know not how to thank you sufficiently or how to reward your kindness."

"I do but help you from the love I bear your soul," replied the stranger with a queer little chuckling laugh. "Yet one bargain I will make. The first candle that you take from the shrine, half burned, shall be mine. You shall keep it in your charge, but you shall remember it is mine. So long as it stands secure and unburned in your cell, you shall succeed with your plan, but should you light that candle and burn it out for any cause whatever, in the moment that the flame flickers to death you shall become mine for ever and for ever and for ever!"

"You need not fear, kind brother," said Hugh. "I will keep your candle for you and more than one if you wish. It is surely but small payment for the knowledge of such a wise plan."

But before he finished speaking the stranger had turned and vanished into the darkness. Hugh now hurried along the river bank, his mind full of the stranger's words. The scheme did not present many difficulties, and he soon realised that with care and ingenuity he could set by a small sum each day for his own use. He passed through the passage of the dormitory, walking softly that he might not disturb the brothers who had already gone to rest, then turning into the cloisters he walked past the Chapter House, and half opened the church door. The moon was rising, and the church was neither dark nor light, but filled with a dim gloom. Hugh paused a moment, for the silent stillness seemed to shut him out. Then, laughing at his folly, he entered the church, and walked boldly up the familiar chancel. Yet as he went it seemed to him that someone followed. He turned once and looked round, but saw nothing; then he listened. There was a queer click, click just behind him. He felt sure the stranger monk was in the church with him, though invisible in the darkness, and he thought to himself, At least the stranger goes not barefoot, his footfall has almost the ring of metal. But as he approached the High Altar the sound ceased, and Hugh was again conscious of being alone in the church. He hastened through his task, prepared the books and the candles for the midnight service, lighted the four great cressets that should have been lighted an hour before, and passed into the sacristy. Here he gathered together all the store of candles he had in charge; he tied them into a bundle with a wrapper of matting and hid them under his habit. Then he locked the sacristy door and again passed through the church and the cloister and went to his own rooms.

The days passed into weeks and the weeks into months, and the stranger's scheme succeeded better than the Sacrist had dared to hope. Everything was in his favour: at the yearly market a friend in the town had undertaken the sale of his superfluous candles. There had been moreover much sickness and disease in Clare, and the faithful had lighted many candles before the shrine in their anxiety and distress. Every day the Sacrist was able to enter his accounts with satisfaction to himself, and others, and yet to reserve a sum of money for his own use. But the first candle that he took half burned from the shrine, he set apart for the stranger, according to his promise. He stood it on the window ledge in his chamber, and sometimes as he looked at it he wondered how, and when, its owner would come and fetch it. But as time passed by he almost forgot the stranger, and the candle slipped into a corner and was forgotten—both out of sight and out of mind.

All this time Prior Galfridus had continued to govern the Friary in his careless and easy-going way. Gradually by mismanagement the funds of the community grew less and less, till the Prior became alarmed and determined to examine the affairs of the household and try to discover why there was so much less money in the treasury than in former times. He himself looked into all the accounts and examined carefully all the stores and provisions and he soon discovered that there was waste and extravagance on every side. The cellarer's accounts did not tally; the larderer failed to keep any proper control over the provisions in his charge; and the Sacrist used many more candles than in former days. Prior Galfridus was very angry, and determined to put a stop to this waste and extravagance.

The next morning, in the solemn gathering at the Chapter House, he spoke to the brothers of the careless mismanagement of their officers and servants which was bringing the Friary to ruin. He spared no blame from the Sacrist to the cook's-boy, and when he had freely spoken his mind, he apportioned fit punishment for each offender and left the Chapter House in wrath.

Now the punishment that fell to the share of Sacrist Hugh was one that was particularly distasteful to him. He should live on bread and water for a fortnight, and not leave the precincts of the Friary for a month—such had been the Prior's judgment.

Prior Galfridus had left the Chapter House in wrath, but he was not one to trouble himself unnecessarily over things that were past, and so soon as the Chapter was over his wrath began to cool. He sent for his falconer and his hawks, and determined to forget his worries in a day of sport. In a few minutes the courtyard was filled with noise and clatter; servants ran to and fro, horses were saddled, dogs barked, and every friar who could obtain permission prepared to follow the Prior over the meadows.

Sacrist Hugh stood watching with a surly inward wrath as the cheery train of huntsmen passed through the gateway, then turning he sauntered to the cloisters, and sat down in a shady corner to consider what should be done next.

The more he thought, the less he liked the position of

affairs. The Prior had but discovered a very small portion of his misdeeds, in the extravagant use of candle-wax. What would happen if the Prior should inspect the Sacristy and discover the absence of the jewelled cope? There were other sins, too, that the Prior might discover, which were so black that Sacrist Hugh hardly dared acknowledge them even to himself. After a while he changed his shady seat for one in the sunshine, for there was a bite of autumn in the air. He sat with his hands folded, his head bent, and his eyes on the ground in the prescribed attitude of contemplation, and so he remained till it was time for dinner. But dinner for the misguided Sacrist meant only bread and water, and neither his hunger nor his misery were much appeased when he had finished his meal. During the afternoon he attended to some of his duties, but they were considerably reduced and time hung heavily on his hands. In the Chapter House that morning he had handed over the keys of his store cupboard where the candles were kept to the sub-Sacrist, and it was now no longer his duty to arrange for the lighting of the Church, the cloisters, or the other buildings.

Just as it was growing dusk he heard the sound of a horn in the distance, for the huntsmen were returning homeward over the water meadows. The sound reminded him of an unfulfilled request the cellarer had made to him in the morning, that he would put out a fresh supply of salt for use at the refectory supper. He slipped the cellar key from his girdle, and was hastening through the great kitchen when he remembered that the cellar would be quite dark by now, and he had no light with him. He did not wish to ask his subordinate for a candle, and remembering the long forgotten candle of the stranger, he hastened to his chamber in search of it. There, after some looking, he found it, lying in a corner half covered with dust. Retracing his steps hurriedly, he lit his candle and entered the cellar. He soon found a great jar of salt, and took a sufficient supply for the supper, but while he was covering the jar again his eye fell on a fat larded capon, lying on a dish with a dressing of garlic around it. Now Sacrist Hugh was hungry, and he did not stop to think, but standing his candle on the shelf, he fell to and devoured that larded capon before his conscience had time to awaken. But just as he was making an end of his meal the first huntsman clattered into the yard; he picked up his salt, left the cellar in a hurry, slammed the door behind him, and quite forgot his candle.

The Prior, who had had but poor sport, was not in a happy frame of mind, though he was somewhat comforted by remembering that he had ordered a larded capon for his supper. He flung his reins to a lad in the yard, and going straight to his own chamber he called for meat and wine.

Now according to the legend it was just eight o'clock when the Prior returned from his hawking, and suddenly three things happened simultaneously at different parts of the Friary.

In the Prior's parlour, a server set the bare bone of what had been a larded capon before the Prior.

In the cellar a candle flickered, guttered, and went out.

On the refectory steps the Sacrist was met by a stranger with a long habit which covered his feet.

The next moment the brothers in the refectory heard a piercing scream, followed by another and another. The sound was so wild and so piercing that for a moment they looked at each other in terror, none moving from where he stood. Then someone opened the door and they rushed out to find what the sound could be. They were met by a cloud of smoke and a smell of sulphur. The staircase was in total darkness, but they saw an even darker shadow pass down the stairs, and they heard a sound like the clank of a cloven hoof. When they had fetched lights they found the Sacrist lying at the foot of the stairs. His head was dashed to pieces on the stone step, and a look of horror was in his eyes such as no brother had ever seen before. They raised him gently from the ground and carried him to the Infirmary where they laid him on a bed. But he was quite dead and his flesh was seared as if he had been through a flame of fire. (Afterwards it was whispered that Prior Galfridus had called upon the Devil to fetch the friar who had eaten his capon; but that is as may be.)

The good brothers sang many masses for the peace of his soul, though some maintained that it was a mere waste of time, for the Devil himself had come to fetch him. And there was a stain of blood left on the bottom step of the stone staircase which no brother could remove. They scrubbed the step, they scraped the step, they sprinkled it with Holy Water, but still the stain remained. And there it is, I doubt not, to this day. Though lately, when the house was repaired, the steps were so worn that the workmen had to cut some part of the centre of each step away and put in new stone treads to make them safe to walk upon. And the new stone tread on the bottom step has covered the stain, but I doubt not it is there all the same.

# The Markhampton Miracle

William White, formerly Detective-Inspector of the Mark-shire Constabulary, and now the senior partner in White's Private Inquiry Agency, called by appointment at the offices of Mark's Footballs Pools two days after Boxing Day. He was taken at once to the room of the managing director of that famous and profitable concern where he found a very worried and very puzzled man.

"I have called you in, Mr White," the managing director explained, "to investigate, in strict confidence, what appears to be the largest fraud that has ever been perpetrated in the history of this firm—I may say, in the history of football pools."

"Yes, sir," said White. If the managing director had not been so preoccupied with his own concerns he might have noticed that White seemed rather downcast at his opening words.

"The fraud relates to our Ten Results Pool on matches played on Boxing Day," he went on.

"Quite, sir." White looked even gloomier than before.

"We have reason to think that some of the winning entries were faked."

"There was more than one all-correct line, then, sir?"

"Yes, more than one. To be accurate, there were"—he consulted some papers on his desk—"one correct line sent in from Middlesbrough, one from Redruth and 53,619 from Markhampton and its suburbs."

"*How* many, did you say, sir?"

"Fifty-three thousand six hundred and nineteen."

"But that's impossible, sir."

"Exactly. In the whole country outside this city there were just two correct entries out of approximately three-quarters of a million. The Markhampton figures speak for themselves. It is a fraud on a colossal scale. How was it done! That's what I've called you in to find out."

White was silent for a moment.

"Well, sir," he said finally, "you know as well as I do that there are just two ways in which a fraud on the Pools is attempted, as a rule. Either you fake the date stamp on the envelope containing the entry, so as to make it appear that it was posted before the matches were played, when in fact it was posted afterwards—"

"That's quite out of the question in this case. A single dishonest clerk in the post office might try it just once to win for himself or to oblige a pal, but it couldn't possibly be done on this scale. Besides, the winning entries came from all over the district. Every post office in the neighbourhood would have to be involved."

"The other type of fraud," White went on, "is, of course, an inside job. One of your employees adds the winning line to an entry and slips it in among the others."

The managing director shook his head.

"You can see for yourself that that won't do," he said. "Even if my staff weren't honest—which they are—and I

have a pretty strict internal security service, I may tell
you—have you considered how long it would take to mark
fifty thousand entries? Short of a conspiracy among half the
girls in my office, it's simply out of the question. You'll have
to think of something else."

"Well, at the moment, sir, there's nothing else I can think
of. Except that by some extraordinary freak all these entries
are genuine."

"Tcheh!" said the managing director.

Mrs White greeted her husband eagerly when he got home
that evening.

"Well?" she said. Then her face fell as she saw his discon-
solate expression. "Is there anything wrong?" she asked.

"Something funny's happened to the Ten Results entries,"
he said. "Mark's want me to look into it."

"Oh, Willie, isn't that just your luck? When you told me
they'd sent for you I thought it meant something good for
you. Emily will be so disappointed, too. She'd set her heart
on something wonderful for you this Christmas."

White was staring absently at an old copy of the *Mark-
shire Herald* which lay open on the kitchen table. He read
the headlines automatically. Then he said:

"Where is Emily? I want a word with her."

"She's playing next door with Susan Berry. Can't it wait
till she comes in?"

"No time like the present. Besides, I might have a talk to
Susan too, while I'm about it."

White went next door. He had his talk to Emily and Susan
and to Mr Berry also. He extended his inquiry to his next-
door neighbour on the other side, and then to various houses

further down the street. Next day he pursued his investigations among his friends and acquaintances, and outwards in
an ever-widening circle. All the people he questioned were
married men with young families, and everything he heard
served to confirm the wild surmise that had come into his
mind when he had glanced at the newspaper headlines.

Finally he paid two additional visits—one to the offices of
the *Markshire Herald,* the other to a dignified old house in
Markhampton cathedral close.

Within three days he was back in the offices of Mark's
Pools.

"I have investigated the matter you complained of, sir," he
told the managing director.

"Yes?"

"One person is responsible for the winning lines in the Ten
Results Pool for Boxing Day. I interviewed him last night,
and he admits everything."

"Who is it? I shall prosecute, whoever it is."

"As to prosecuting, sir, I'm not so sure. The man in question is the Reverend Canon Furbelow."

"Canon Furbelow! Mr White, are you trying to make a
fool of me?"

"Not at all, sir. He is the culprit, though he admits that he
would not have been as successful as he was if he had not
had the assistance of a journalist who writes for the *Herald*
under the name of John Straight."

"But this is preposterous! Canon Furbelow is against pools
or betting of any sort. Why, I'm told he's been known to
preach sermons against them."

"Quite so, sir. A very powerful preacher is the Canon. It
seems that it's his preaching that's at the bottom of the
trouble in this case."

The managing director mopped his brow with his handkerchief.

"One of us is certainly mad," he said. "Possibly both. Will you kindly explain?"

"Canon Furbelow," said White, "conducted a series of children's services during Advent. They were very popular, and the cathedral was crowded for each of them. He has a wonderful way with children, has the Canon. My little girl Emily went to them. She was very much impressed by him."

"Confound your little girl Emily!" said the managing director rudely. "Will you kindly get to the point—if you have one?"

"I'm just coming to it, sir," said White calmly. "His last sermon on the Sunday before Christmas was particularly eloquent. It attracted a good deal of attention. The journalist I mentioned just now happened to be in the cathedral on that occasion, and he made it the subject of a very striking article, which was read and commented on all over the city. Luckily the national newspapers didn't take it up, or the damage would have been even greater than it was. I have a copy of the article here, sir, if you would care to see it."

The managing director waved it angrily away.

"Unless it forecasts the results of the Boxing Day League matches, I don't," he said.

"It doesn't mention the football, sir. What the sermon and the article dealt with was the beauty of unselfishness. Canon Furbelow reminded the children that at Christmas time they would all, quite rightly, be looking forward to the good things they were going to get—their presents and parties and so on. But, he told them, these were not the things they ought to ask for when they said their prayers. They should ask for things for others, and especially for those nearest and dearest to them. What a wonderful thing it would be, he said, if on Christmas Eve every child in Markhampton were to kneel down and pray that their parents should have their dearest wish granted to them. He drew a beautiful picture of all those innocent, unselfish supplications floating up to heaven together at that holy time of the year. The Canon has a great faith in the power of prayer, sir, and a great gift for imparting his faith to others.

"And the children did what he told them, sir. And thanks to John Straight his words went all over Markhampton and reached thousands of homes where the people didn't go to church. The children's prayers were heard and their parents got their heart's desire. And 53,619 of us had set our hearts on the Ten Results Pool," he concluded a little bitterly.

The managing director was silent for a time. Then he said, "You don't believe all this stuff, do you?"

White shrugged his shoulders.

"I don't know what else there is to believe," he said. "Canon Furbelow believes it, anyway. By the way, sir, he was asking me—how much will the dividend on the Ten Results work out at?"

"Two shillings and fourpence."

"I told him it would be round about that figure. He said there was a moral in that. I believe he means to make it the theme of his sermon next Sunday. Good day, sir."

# In Time and Space

The Second Death
GRAHAM GREENE

Many-Coloured Glass
LUCY M. BOSTON

The Riddle
WALTER DE LA MARE

Balaam
ANTHONY BOUCHER

Vindicae Flammae
GERALD HEARD

# The Second Death

She found me in the evening under the trees that grew
outside the village. I had never cared for her and would
have hidden myself if I'd seen her coming. She was to blame,
I'm certain, for her son's vices. If they were vices, but I'm
very far from admitting that they were. At any rate he was
generous, never mean, like others in the village I could
mention if I chose.

I was staring hard at a leaf or she would never have found
me. It was dangling from the twig, its stalk torn across by
the wind or else by a stone one of the village children had
flung. Only the green tough skin of the stalk held it there
suspended. I was watching closely, because a caterpillar was
crawling across the surface making the leaf sway to and fro.
The caterpillar was aiming at the twig, and I wondered
whether it would reach it in safety or whether the leaf
would fall with it into the water. There was a pool under-
neath the trees, and the water always appeared red, because
of the heavy clay in the soil.

I never knew whether the caterpillar reached the twig,
for, as I've said, the wretched woman found me. The first I
knew of her coming was her voice just behind my ear.

"I've been looking in all the pubs for you," she said in her old shrill voice. It was typical of her to say "all the pubs" when there were ony two in the place. She always wanted credit for trouble she hadn't really taken.

I was annoyed and I couldn't help speaking a little harshly. "You might have saved yourself the trouble," I said, "you should have known I wouldn't be in a pub on a fine night like this."

The old vixen became quite humble. She was always smooth enough when she wanted anything. "It's for my poor son," she said. That meant that he was ill. When he was well I never heard her say anything better than "that dratted boy." She'd make him be in the house by midnight every day of the week, as if there were any serious mischief a man could get up to in a little village like ours. Of course we soon found a way to cheat her, but it was the principle of the thing I objected to—a grown man of over thirty ordered about by his mother, just because she hadn't a husband to control. But when he was ill, though it might be with only a small chill, it was "my poor son."

"He's dying," she said, "and God knows what I shall do without him."

"Well, I don't see how I can help you," I said. I was angry, because he'd been dying once before and she'd done everything but actually bury him. I imagined it was the same sort of dying this time, the sort a man gets over. I'd seen him about the week before on his way up the hill to see the big-breasted girl at the farm. I'd watched him till he was like a little black dot, which stayed suddenly by a square box in a field. That was the barn where they used to meet. I have very good eyes and it amuses me to try how far and how clearly they can see. I met him again some time after mid-

night and helped him get into the house without his mother
knowing, and he was well enough then—only a little sleepy
and tired.

The old vixen was at it again. "He's been asking for you,"
she shrilled at me.

"If he's as ill as you make out," I said, "it would be better
for him to ask for a doctor."

"Doctor's there, but he can't do anything." That startled
me for a moment, I'll admit it, until I thought, "The old
devil's malingering. He's got some plan or other." He was
quite clever enough to cheat a doctor. I had seen him throw
a fit that would have deceived Moses.

"For God's sake come," she said, "he seems frightened."
Her voice broke quite genuinely, for I suppose in her way
she was fond of him. I couldn't help pitying her a little, for I
knew that he had never cared a mite for her and had never
troubled to disguise the fact.

I left the trees and the red pool and the struggling caterpillar, for I knew that she would never leave me alone, now
that her "poor boy" was asking for me. Yet a week ago there
was nothing she wouldn't have done to keep us apart. She
thought me responsible for his ways, as though any mortal
man could have kept him off a likely woman when his appe-
tite was up.

I think it must have been the first time I had entered their
cottage by the front door, since I came to the village ten
years ago. I threw an amused glance at his window. I
thought I could see the marks on the wall of the ladder we'd
used the week before. We'd had a little difficulty in putting
it straight, but his mother slept sound. He had brought the
ladder down from the barn, and when he'd got safely in, I

carried it up there again. But you could never trust his word. He'd lie to his best friend, and when I reached the barn I found the girl had gone. If he couldn't bribe you with his mother's money, he'd bribe you with other people's promises.

I began to feel uneasy directly I got inside the door. It was natural that the house should be quiet, for the pair of them never had any friends to stay, although the old woman had a sister-in-law living only a few miles away. But I didn't like the sound of the doctor's feet, as he came downstairs to meet us. He'd twisted his face into a pious solemnity for our benefit, as though there was something holy about death, even about the death of my friend.

"He's conscious," he said, "but he's going. There's nothing I can do. If you want him to die in peace, better let his friend go along up. He's frightened about something."

The doctor was right. I could tell that as soon as I bent under the lintel and entered my friend's room. He was propped up on a pillow, and his eyes were on the door, waiting for me to come. They were very bright and frightened, and his hair lay across his forehead in sticky stripes. I'd never realised before what an ugly fellow he was. He had got sly eyes that looked at you too much out of the corners, but when he was in ordinary health, they held a twinkle that made you forget the slyness. There was something pleasant and brazen in the twinkle, as much as to say, "I know I'm sly and ugly. But what does that matter? I've got guts." It was that twinkle, I think, some women found attractive and stimulating. Now when the twinkle was gone, he looked a rogue and nothing else.

I thought it my duty to cheer him up, so I made a small

joke out of the fact that he was alone in bed. He didn't seem to relish it, and I was beginning to fear that he, too, was taking a religious view of his death, when he told me to sit down, speaking quite sharply.

"I'm dying," he said, talking very fast, "and I want to ask you something. That doctor's no good—he'd think me delirious. I'm frightened, old man. I want to be reassured," and then after a long pause, "someone with common sense." He slipped a little farther down in his bed.

"I've only once been badly ill before," he said. "That was before you settled here. I wasn't much more than a boy. People tell me that I was even supposed to be dead. They were carrying me out to burial, when a doctor stopped them just in time."

I'd heard plenty of cases like that, and I saw no reason why he should want to tell me about it. And then I thought I saw his point. His mother had not been too anxious once before to see if he were properly dead, though I had little doubt that she made a great show of grief—"My poor boy. I don't know what I shall do without him." And I'm certain that she believed herself then, as she believed herself now. She wasn't a murderess. She was only inclined to be premature.

"Look here, old man," I said, and I propped him a little higher on his pillow, "you needn't be frightened. You aren't going to die, and anyway I'd see that the doctor cut a vein or something before they moved you. But that's all morbid stuff. Why, I'd stake my shirt that you've got plenty more years in front of you. And plenty more girls too," I added to make him smile.

"Can't you cut out all that?" he said, and I knew then that

he had turned religious. "Why," he said, "if I lived, I wouldn't touch another girl. I wouldn't, not one."

I tried not to smile at that, but it wasn't easy to keep a straight face. There's always something a bit funny about a sick man's morals. "Anyway," I said, "you needn't be frightened."

"It's not that," he said. "Old man, when I came round that other time, I thought that I'd been dead. It wasn't like sleep at all. Or rest in peace. There was someone there, all round me, who knew everything. Every girl I'd ever had. Even that young one who hadn't understood. It was before your time. She lived a mile down the road, where Rachel lives now, but she and her family went away afterwards. Even the money I'd taken from mother. I don't call that stealing. It's in the family. I never had a chance to explain. Even the thoughts I'd had. A man can't help his thoughts."

"A nightmare," I said.

"Yes, it must have been a dream, mustn't it? The sort of dream people do get when they are ill. And I saw what was coming to me too. I can't bear being hurt. It wasn't fair. And I wanted to faint and I couldn't, because I was dead."

"In the dream," I said. His fear made me nervous. "In the dream," I said again.

"Yes, it must have been a dream—mustn't it?—because I woke up. The curious thing was I felt quite well and strong. I got up and stood in the road, and a little farther down, kicking up the dust, was a small crowd, going off with a man—the doctor who had stopped them burying me."

"Well?" I said.

"Old man," he said, "suppose it was true. Suppose I had been dead. I believed it then, you know, and so did my mother. But you can't trust her. I went straight for a couple of years. I thought it might be a sort of second chance. Then things got fogged and somehow . . . it didn't seem really possible. It's not possible. Of course it's not possible. You know it isn't, don't you?"

"Why, no," I said. "Miracles of that sort don't happen nowadays. And anyway, they aren't likely to happen to you, are they? And here of all places under the sun."

"It would be so dreadful," he said, "if it had been true, and I'd got to go through all that again. You don't know what things were going to happen to me in that dream. And they'd be worse now." He stopped and then, after a moment, he added as though he were stating a fact: "When one's dead there's no unconsciousness any more for ever."

"Of course it was a dream," I said, and squeezed his hand. He was frightening me with his fancies. I wished that he'd die quickly, so that I could get away from his sly, bloodshot and terrified eyes and see something cheerful and amusing, like the Rachel he had mentioned, who lived a mile down the road.

"Why," I said, "if there had been a man about working miracles like that, we should have heard of others, you may be sure. Even poked away in this God-forsaken spot," I said.

"There were some others," he said. "But the stories only went round among the poor, and they'll believe anything, won't they? There were lots of diseased and crippled they said he'd cured. And there was a man, who'd been born blind, and he came and just touched his eyelids and sight came to him. Those were all old wives' tales, weren't they?" he asked me, stammering with fear, and then lying suddenly still and bunched up at the side of the bed.

I began to say, "Of course, they were all lies," but I

stopped, because there was no need. All I could do was to go downstairs and tell his mother to come up and close his eyes. I wouldn't have touched them for all the money in the world. It was a long time since I'd thought of that day, ages and ages ago, when I felt a cold touch like spittle on my lids and opening my eyes had seen a man like a tree surrounded by other trees walking away.

LUCY M. BOSTON

# Many-Coloured Glass

The Mayor's ball was to be held in the Costume wing of the Museum. This was occasionally used for concerts of chamber music, and as the Mayor was also a director, it had been found possible to allow its use for a private dance to celebrate an unusual occasion. The Mayor's only son was not merely coming of age, but had recently returned with an Olympic medal. A crowd of local enthusiasts had surrounded the station for his arrival, and newspaper photographs of his smiling response to the town's welcome were pinned up in every girl's office or bedroom.

Only a minority could hope for an invitation to the ball. The Mayor, Sir Joshua Waters, was fanatical about having public functions well done. He dreamed of being remembered as a mayor who had style. His invitations therefore were sent chiefly to those who could afford a real costume, or if their name made an invitation essential he would tactfully suggest the use of costumes "not included in the showcases," which in fact he had himself bought for the occasion. He let it leak out that he hoped guests would pay proper attention to the period of their dress. Everyone was to come as a character out of Jane Austen's books. He had bad dreams about important people in scruffy rag-bag get-up. Important people should look important.

Jane Austen's period had been chosen because the largest of the Costume Museum's many rooms was given to the period 1750–1830, also because in the attics of family mansions round about some relics—wedding dresses, uniforms or riding coats—might still be found. Sir Joshua was to appear stern but benign as Sir Thomas Bertram of Mansfield Park, his son Philip as Mr Darcy, both specially tailored. As he looked at his son with pride, he congratulated himself that a desirable engagement would almost certainly be settled on the night. He had given his son a hint that the opportunity should be used.

As the hour approached Sir Joshua took a tour round the Museum to see that everything was in order. The main room faced the terrace and, beyond that, the road. The tall Georgian windows were uncurtained, so that the people outside could watch the show. All round the walls were glass-fronted cases, each containing a period scene—a morning call, a christening, a family dinner, a stolen rendezvous, the sailor's farewell. Each scene had the furniture proper to it, with looking-glasses on the wall to show the other side of the costumes. There all the dummies sat or stood, in their best clothes and with their best manners, fixed forever as if waiting for the last trump. Normally they were lit by concealed electricity, but for this occasion candlesticks and candelabra had been put in the cases, adding more animation than one would expect, and chandeliers hung at intervals down the main room. The custodian was going round lighting everything up. The buffet was in the next room and the previous century, and there the inappropriate dummies had been hidden by screens. Sir Joshua tasted the food and wine and gave his last instructions, which included a strict warning to the doorman to admit no one without an invitation card. He took a last look of surprised pleasure at his own face graced by a discreet period wig, and prepared to receive his guests.

Crowds of the uninvited began to gather outside before the first guests arrived. Usually the majority of such on-lookers are staid housewives come to have a free look and good matter for gossip, but this time, because of the fame of Philip Waters, there were packed ranks of youths and girls. The police had difficulty in keeping a way open for the arriving cars.

Sir Joshua could be satisfied with his guests. Their arrival was a real pageant. The less-young ladies in the excitement of their vast bonnets with ostrich plumes, their pelisses, empire busts and trailing skirts, by behaving according to their natures while forced to a different stance and move-ment by the altered balance of their rig, and chattering the more from this slight physical frustration, showed how truly Jane Austen had observed the species. The local repertory theatre had contributed a contingent of curled and dandified soldiers, sailors and clerics with young ladies on their arms. The local beauty was cheered when, as Emma, she was handed out by Mr Knightley.

Meanwhile Ann, the as-yet-not-quite-official girl-friend of the hero of the evening, was sitting in her taxi as it inched along towards the entrance. She had not seen Philip since his victorious return, and was surprised by the disturbance in her feeling—a pounding excitement which was not wholly delight. A sudden volley from part of the crowd of WE WANT PHILIP was taken up and grew to an enveloping roar, which filled her with near terror. She hated publicity, and caught herself thinking that however wonderful it was that Philip was such a star, she almost wished he had been unsuccessful and that they were going somewhere together quietly as before. The stamping chant of the young men was broken by the thin screams of girls, and Ann realised that Philip must have come to the top of the steps to wait for her. At this her panic redoubled, and also her excitement, suddenly indivisible from the hypnosis of the mob.

From somewhere near came counter shouts: "Down with heroes! Down with snobs!" The Commissionaire opened her door, letting her out at close quarters in front of a crush of typical students, dishevelled, unwashed, buttonless, bold-eyed or shifty, defying every human tradition. After all, savages, she thought, are as clean as cats. She half rose to begin the tricky business of stepping out of a taxi with shawl, fan and reticle, the invitation card and the fare ready in her hand. With one foot projecting, her glance lit on a slight, very young man who seemed the animating centre of the student group. His face was surrounded by long frizzy chestnut hair such as Leonardo's angels have—though less celestially ordered; this was a wild halo, and his expression was to match, being of such seraphic freedom and gaiety that at sight of it everything else went out of her mind. There was a second's pause—long enough for the gaiety to evaporate and for eyes suddenly grave with joy to look into hers, which must have met them with the same expression.

The surprise was so great that she tripped on her long skirt, and was saved from falling by a delicate but grubby hand. Then the gaiety came back, but Philip was there, proprietary.

No wonder the girls had shrieked as for a matador. Philip was really a figure to stun. Starting from the top, his hair had been drilled by the barber to fall in casual manly sweeps. It was fair and it shone. His face was held rigidly high by his built-up coat-collar and his stock, so that it was presented like something by Phidias on a stand. His shoulders were not too wide for grace, his chest and ribs so well adapted for holding and controlling breath that it was fascinating to watch the easy inflation and deflation under a coat that fitted like a second skin.

The coat was cut away in front, as was then the fashion, well above the waistline and so exposed his hips and the whole line of his faultless Olympic legs in close-fitting cream jersey cloth.

If Mr Darcy was thought arrogant because of his long tradition of eminence and responsibility, Philip Waters was arrogant unconsciously by virtue of his superlative physique and the qualities needed for successful competition. These, after all, he knew to be admirable things.

As he stood now at the top of the steps waving his acknowledgement to the crowd, he felt it was good to be able to offer a girl a part in his glory, even if only a walking-on part. He ran down the steps to meet Ann and, falling into the staginess of the occasion, bowed to kiss her hand.

"Go on, give her a proper one!" they yelled.

"All in good time," he called back good-humouredly, and led her up on his arm, very well pleased with their entry. He would have been less pleased if he had known that she had hardly been aware of their progress from the taxi to the big swinging doors. She could find no place, in the course and expectation of her life till now, for the experience of that timeless mutual look, too accidental to be given a meaning, yet it vibrated among her thoughts like a spring wind in an

unawakened wood. How was she to orientate her actions
now?

Inside, it was a brilliant scene. The idea of acting up to the
period was taking hold of the guests. They bowed and curt-
sied to the Mayor and also to each other as they gathered in
groups along the side of the room, where the impression of
numbers was doubled by the dummies entertaining each
other behind the glass of their cases, and indeed seeming to
entertain the Mayor's guests too, since these were reflected
in the looking-glasses in their sets and must therefore be
supposed to be present with them. The sailor's farewell, for
instance, gained poignancy from a group of his mates waiting for him outside the display case.

Philip took Ann round with him on his arm as he went to
do his duty to his father's guests and to receive from them
the congratulations due to him.

"Aren't you lucky!" said the girls to Ann, rolling up their
eyes. "Isn't he absolute heaven! You needn't blush, Ann,
you're not the only person who thinks so."

The ball was to be opened by the old dance, Sir Roger de
Coverley, followed by a waltz, which, though never stated to
have been danced by Jane Austen's characters, was, nevertheless, growing in popularity during her lifetime.

For Sir Roger, two long lines were formed up the centre of
the room. Philip led Ann to her position at the end and the
innocent stylised flirtation began—the long solo journey
down the centre to circle round one's opposite number without touching, with nothing but breathless smiles and the
play of eyes, approaching and retreating several times, to
achieve in the end a hand-in-hand gallop down the whole
length and a parting bow. Such childish fun! Any booby

could learn the steps, but Philip's hand was cool and hard, his look correctly genial, almost royal, and he moved with economy where other men romped or charged. Ann was glad of the formality of the dance, for she still had no idea what she might, in the course of the evening, let herself in for.

When later she and Philip were waltzing, her indecisions were far more acute, for he waltzed of course, as he well knew, divinely, travelling faster than any of the weaving, circling couples. Ann was swirled through the no-space of the crowd, guided by those inimitable shoulders and hips, feeling the pressure of his long light legs. She began to be intoxicated by the masterly movement and her own perfect submission to it. The dancers that passed across the mirrors in the cased sets imparted now a sense of movement to the lay figures, since they also had reflections which shifted to the dancers' eyes as they turned. If the figures themselves did not move, at least they seemed deep in thought, dreaming or remembering. In the overmantel behind the bent head of a girl reading a letter Ann saw for a moment Philip's face bent over her own with an expression of deep satisfaction. With her, or with himself? And what was that girl remembering? But questions were left behind as they moved and swung together, while in the plate-glass front of the imitation world a swirl of much thinner, broken, half-recognised dreams flickered as they passed.

Every perfect waltz should end with a kiss. It is written into the last note. Philip drew her into the recess of one of the big windows. Because of the dark beyond it, the window seemed to those inside more like a huge pier-glass in which they saw only their bright selves like transfers on the surface, behind which a few wandering and irrelevant lights

were passing through space. Philip's back was against the
glass as he drew Ann's waist close to his, but she became
aware that there was an outside world and tried to penetrate
beyond the festive bubble in which she was enclosed, to the
shadowy colourless movements out there, where the dark
bulk of the trees only made the reflected chandeliers hang
more brilliantly as if on the boughs. As Philip's hold tight-
ened, suddenly she found and interpreted that crowded
limbo, and what might have been the misty blur round a
dim light was the Leonardo hair round a white face at a few
yards' distance, watching what to him was ultra clear.

"What are you looking at?" said Philip. "Attend to me!"

"It's too public here. All your admirers are still out there."

"Good luck to them."

"No, Philip, not now. Not here. *Oh dear,* that was a lovely
waltz."

"Why *Oh dear,* in that tone? Why not 'you dear!' or 'my
dear,' my dear?"

"I don't know what I am saying or doing," she answered.

"Then you want a few more drinks and you'll be saying
what you really mean and won't know you've done it. I shall
like that. There'll be more waltzes and I shall want them all.
But I shall have to leave you once or twice to dance with
Father's old ladies. My father's position depends largely on
the proper observances. My manager's a bit of a bully about
public relations too. But I can't leave you now—let's dance
this."

This time it was a popular tune of the moment, and very
strange and improper indeed did the dancing look in these
most mannered costumes, as if Dionysus had got into the
Assembly Rooms at Bath. The high bonnets with ostrich

plumes and flying ribbons tossed and jigged, the bundles of curls flew up and down, the bosoms in front and sashes behind, the coat-tails and fobs and seals all jigged and swung, fichus slipped awry, trailing skirts were trodden on and ultimately had to be held knee high in mittened hands. Sir Thomas Bertram would not have approved at all, and indeed Sir Joshua shook his head, though this was not a giddy teenage dance and the stateliness of the Museum had a sobering effect.

"I must go now," said Philip. "Forgive me. There's my manager—I'll bring him to look after you till I come back. You needn't be jealous. I'm going to be horribly bored. Wait here by the door so that we can find you."

Ann leant thankfully in the comparative coolness of the doorway, which gave on to the entrance lobby. In spite of the drumming from the ballroom her ear caught the aggressive distaste in the doorman's voice saying, "Can I see your invitation card?" No "Sir," she noticed.

The reply came with airy irreverent authority.

"Afraid I haven't one with me."

"I can't admit anyone without it. And fancy dress was specified."

"What do you suppose this is? Every banquet presupposes a beggar."

The accent undermined the doorman's confidence. You never could tell.

"Well, Sir, shall I bring Sir Joshua to speak to you?"

"Don't bother."

Ann had come into the lobby, sure of whom she would see. She now came forward trading—with a pang of shame—on her being known as Philip's partner.

The boy bounded in and took her hand.

"Aren't we in luck," he said as he led her in.

In a moment they were dancing to the latest, wildest, most rhythmic hit, and from the start it was an inspired partnership. Their eyes never left each other, but their responding movements were as free as thought, as unexpected and as playful. They were two separate and equal people sharing an immense exhilarating Now-ness. This was laughter, this was delight, this was—most surprisingly—a flowering tenderness, and the rhythm was simply their lively young blood racing on its circuit.

If the other dancers noticed the infiltration of something not on the programme, it was only as an increase in their own acceptance of pleasure, but Sir Joshua had seen instantly that the style of his dance was ruined. He had devastated the doorman, who pleaded that Mr Philip's young lady had overruled him.

"Torn jeans, no shirt under his sweater, beach shoes—no socks—it's an outrage! Spoils the whole show."

"His rags are clean," the Mayor's partner replied soothingly. "Admittedly only from being washed by him in his own hand-basin. And he has an eerie charm."

"Where's Philip's manager? He ought to be able to deal with this. The press photographer is here, and you can be sure they'll make more out of Ann dancing with that layabout than of Philip. Ah, there he is—excuse me."

Meanwhile the dance had ended. In the recess where Ann had evaded Philip's kiss she received the lips of the stranger, and knew that he was now the magnet of her life, no other consideration whatsoever had either weight or pull.

"I shan't be able to stay here," he said. "Meet me in the

garden behind the Museum as soon as you can. Here comes the irate Sir Joshua with a bodyguard—I must make my obeisance to him, and leave with dignity."

Ann laughed with delight at this picture, but Philip was disentangling himself from the beautiful Emma on the other side of the room. A waltz was beginning, and from Philip's face it was going to be a furious one. Oh, *no*, thought Ann, as for the first time her predicament fully dawned on her. She began to slip away through the crowd, looking in her white and silver dress like a darting fish, and the other guests with unexpected sympathy moved to let her pass.

She fled through the empty rooms of the Museum opening one out of the other. She did not know where the door into the garden was, but if locked that would be on the inside. How long, she wondered, would it take her Romeo to go round and climb the garden wall, or however he meant to get in after he had been turned out?

The sound of the waltz grew fainter behind her. In a corridor that she judged must lead to the back she stopped to collect her thoughts. Her heart was choking her. She sat down on a bench and hid her hot face in her hands, in confusion but not in doubt.

When she opened her eyes they were confronted by a musical box against the opposite wall—one of those early Bavarian toys where mechanical figures perform to the tune.

"How odd," she thought. The little stage showed a group of fiddlers, two couples in costumes like those of the ball she had just quitted, and in a doorway at the side, a gypsy or beggarman.

Very faintly the distant waltz came to her ears, but no footsteps ringing in the abandoned halls.

With her hand pressed to her unsteady heart, acting under a sudden compulsion, she pushed down the lever. Delicate plucked music started up; the fiddlers sawed with their clumsy arms in time to an ethereal waltz. The couples moved jerkily out and each raised an arm to clasp its partner. To various clicks and rumbles from under the floor they began to revolve with each other and to orbit round the room. Their movements were sinister because of being both reluctant and predestined. Here they were and this was what they must do. Almost at once, however, there was a whirring sound, a hesitation while the tiny figures stood quivering, then with a click and a jerk their motion was resumed. A moment later it was clear that something was going wrong. The fiddlers fiddled and the tinny music continued but there were sounds of misengagement, of metals in opposition, so that Ann was afraid she ought never to have set it in motion; the machine was out of order and might churn itself up. One of the couples divided—the lady flung off on an orbit of her own while her partner revolved on the spot, holding out his arms. To continued protest from the machinery the driven doll circled near the door. The beggarman had till now stood motionless except for an arm that jerked up and down, hat in hand, but now he was propelled forward, and after they had each twirled with arms outstretched, they met face to face and proceeded as partners. The whirring quickened as they sped round, while the abandoned partner revolved helplessly in the centre, wrenching against his imprisoning connection. He swayed this way and that as they passed him in apparently smooth working order. They passed the second couple, now ominously stationary. The beggarman seemed to have charmed his weird little stage, until they came again to the faulty point where she had first broken away. Inevitably she did so again, leaving him in the grip of the cogs near his enemy. These two then revolved round each other till they were face to face when the box gave a screech and the legitimate partner fell upon the beggarman. The music stopped, and the last sounds were repeated metallic thuds as the beggarman's head was knocked against the floor.

And now Ann saw her own spectral face filling up the glass front of the box like a transparent stage-curtain. It wavered. She leant against the wall, appalled.

When she again began to consider where she was and what she was doing, she heard a confused murmur from the ballroom. It was like the sound in a sea-shell, not a party noise at all, and no music. From far away, but growing nearer and nearer and nearer, as in a nightmare, came the horrible tocsin of an ambulance. At the peak of sound it stopped, and there followed an interval of a silence more suggestive and heart-stopping than even the terror of its approach, before it set off again with its burden.

Ann leapt to her feet and began to run as if she could run after it. Then the band in the ballroom struck up with compelling desperation, as obviously taking action to avoid calamity as the ambulance itself.

# The Riddle

So these seven children, Ann and Matilda, James, William and Henry, Harriet and Dorothea, came to live with their grandmother. The house in which their grandmother had lived since her childhood was built in the time of the Georges. It was not a pretty house, but roomy, substantial, and square; and a great cedar tree outstretched its branches almost to the windows.

When the children were come out of the cab (five sitting inside and two beside the driver), they were shown into their grandmother's presence. They stood in a little black group before the old lady, seated in her bow-window. And she asked them each their names, and repeated each name in her kind, quavering voice. Then to one she gave a work-box, to William a jack-knife, to Dorothea a painted ball; to each a present according to age. And she kissed all her grandchildren to the youngest.

"My dears," she said, "I wish to see all of you bright and gay in my house. I am an old woman, so that I cannot romp with you; but Ann must look to you, and Mrs Fenn too. And every morning and every evening you must all come in to see your granny; and bring me smiling faces, that call back to my mind my own son, Harry. But all the rest of the day, when school is done, you shall do just as you please, my dears. And there is only one thing, just one, I would have you remember. In the large spare bedroom that looks out on the slate roof there stands in the corner an old oak chest; aye, older than I, my dears, a great deal older; older than my grandmother. Play anywhere else in the house, but not there." She spoke kindly to them all, smiling at them; but she was very old, and her eyes seemed to see nothing of this world.

And the seven children, though at first they were gloomy and strange, soon began to be happy and at home in the great house. There was much to interest and to amuse them there; all was new to them. Twice every day, morning and evening, they came in to see their grandmother, who every day seemed more feeble; and she spoke pleasantly to them of her mother, and her childhood, but never forgetting to visit her store of sugar-plums. And so the weeks passed by . . .

It was evening twilight when Henry went upstairs from the nursery by himself to look at the oak chest. He pressed his fingers into the carved fruit and flowers, and spoke to the dark-smiling heads at the corners; and then, with a glance over his shoulder, he opened the lid and looked in. But the chest concealed no treasure, neither gold nor baubles, nor was there anything to alarm the eye. The chest was empty, except that it was lined with silk of old-rose, seeming darker in the dusk, and smelling sweet of pot-pourri. And while Henry was looking in, he heard the softened laughter and the clinking of the cups downstairs in the nursery; and out at the window he saw the day darkening. These things brought strangely to his memory his mother who in her glimmering white dress used to read to him in the dusk; and he climbed into the chest; and the lid closed gently down over him.

When the other six children were tired with their playing,

they filed into their grandmother's room for her good-night
and her sugar-plums. She looked out between the candles at
them as if she were uncertain of something in her thoughts.
The next day Ann told her grandmother that Henry was not
anywhere to be found.

"Dearie me, child. Then he must be gone away for a time,"
said the old lady. She paused. "But remember, all of you, do
not meddle with the oak chest."

But Matilda could not forget her brother Henry, finding
no pleasure in playing without him. So she would loiter in
the house thinking where he might be. And she carried her
wooden doll in her bare arms, singing under her breath all
she could make up about it. And when one bright morning
she peeped in on the chest, so sweet-scented and secret it
seemed that she took her doll with her into it—just as Henry
himself had done.

So Ann, and James, and William, Harriet and Dorothea
were left at home to play together. "Some day maybe they
will come back to you, my dears," said their grandmother,
"or maybe you will go to them. Heed my warning as best
you may."

Now Harriet and William were friends together, pretending to be sweethearts; while James and Dorothea liked wild
games of hunting, and fishing, and battles.

On a silent afternoon in October, Harriet and William
were talking softly together, looking out over the slate roof
at the green fields, and they heard the squeak and frisking of
a mouse behind them in the room. They went together and
searched for the small, dark hole from whence it had come
out. But finding no hole, they began to finger the carving of
the chest, and to give names to the dark-smiling heads, just
as Henry had done. "*I* know! let's pretend you are Sleeping

Beauty, Harriet," said William, "and I'll be the Prince that squeezes through the thorns and comes in." Harriet looked gently and strangely at her brother but she got into the box and lay down pretending to be fast asleep, and on tiptoe William leaned over, and seeing how big was the chest, he stepped in to kiss the Sleeping Beauty and to wake her from her quiet sleep. Slowly the carved lid turned on its noiseless hinges. And only the clatter of James and Dorothea came in sometimes to recall Ann from her book.

But their old grandmother was very feeble, and her sight dim, and her hearing extremely difficult.

Snow was falling through the still air upon the roof; and Dorothea was a fish in the oak chest, and James stood over the hole in the ice, brandishing a walking-stick for a harpoon, pretending to be an Esquimau. Dorothea's face was red, and her wild eyes sparkled through her tousled hair. And James had a crooked scratch upon his cheek. "You must struggle, Dorothea, and then I shall swim back and drag you out. Be quick now!" He shouted with laughter as he was drawn into the open chest. And the lid closed softly and gently down as before.

Ann, left to herself, was too old to care overmuch for sugar-plums, but she would go solitary to bid her grandmother goodnight; and the old lady looked wistfully at her over her spectacles. "Well, my dear," she said with trembling head; and she squeezed Ann's fingers between her own knuckled finger and thumb. "What lonely old people, we two are, to be sure!" Ann kissed her grandmother's soft, loose cheek. She left the old lady sitting in her easy chair, her hands upon her knees, and her head turned sidelong towards her.

When Ann was gone to bed she used to sit reading her

book by candlelight. She drew up her knees under the
sheets, resting her book upon them. Her story was about
fairies and gnomes, and the gently-flowing moonlight of the
narrative seemed to illumine the white pages, and she could
hear in fancy fairy voices, so silent was the great many-
roomed house, and so mellifluent were the words of the
story. Presently she put out her candle, and, with a confused
babel of voices close to her ear, and faint swift pictures
before her eyes, she fell asleep.

And in the dead of night she rose out of her bed in dream
and, with eyes wide open yet seeing nothing of reality,
moved silently through the vacant house. Past the room
where her grandmother was snoring in brief, heavy slumber,
she stepped lightly and surely, and down the wide staircase.
And Vega the far-shining stood over against the window
above the slate roof. Ann walked into the strange room
beneath as if she were being guided by the hand towards the
oak chest. There, just as if she were dreaming it was her bed,
she laid herself down in the old-rose silk, in the fragrant
place. But it was so dark in the room that the movement of
the lid was indistinguishable.

Through the long day, the grandmother sat in her bow-
window. Her lips were pursed, and she looked with dim,
inquisitive scrutiny upon the street where people passed to
and fro, and vehicles rolled by. At evening she climbed the
stair and stood in the doorway of the large spare bedroom.
The ascent had shortened her breath. Her magnifying spectacles rested upon her nose. Leaning her hand on the doorpost she peered in towards the glimmering square of
window in the quiet gloom. But she could not see far,
because her sight was dim and the light of day feeble. Nor

could she detect the faint fragrance as of autumnal leaves. But in her mind was a tangled skein of memories—laughter and tears, and children long ago become old-fashioned, and the advent of friends, and last farewells. And gossiping fitfully, inarticulately, with herself, the old lady went down again to her window-seat.

ANTHONY BOUCHER

# Balaam

"What is a *man?*" Rabbi Chaim Acosta demanded, turning his back on the window and its view of pink sand and infinite pink boredom. "You and I, Mule, in our respective ways, work for the salvation of *men*—as you put it, for the brotherhood of *man* under the fatherhood of God. Very well, let us define our terms: Whom, or, more precisely, *what,* are we interested in saving?"

Father Aloysius Malloy shifted uncomfortably and reluctantly closed the *American Football Yearbook* which had been smuggled in on the last rocket, against all weight regulations, by one of his communicants. I honestly like Chaim, he thought, not merely (or is that the right word?) with brotherly love, nor even out of the deep gratitude I owe him, but with special individual liking; and I respect him. He's a brilliant man—too brilliant to take a dull post like this in his stride. But he *will* get off into discussions which are much too much like what one of my Jesuit professors called "disputations."

"What did you say, Chaim?" he asked.

The rabbi's black Sephardic eyes sparkled. "You know very well what I said, Mule; and you're stalling for time. Please indulge me. Our religious duties here are not so arduous as we might wish; and since you won't play chess . . ."

". . . and you," said Father Malloy unexpectedly, "refuse to take any interest in diagramming football plays . . ."

*"Touché.* Or am I? Is it my fault that as an Israeli I fail to share the peculiar American delusion that football means something other than rugby and soccer? Whereas chess—" He looked at the priest reproachfully. "Mule," he said, "you have led me into a digression."

"It was a try. Like the time the whole Southern California line thought I had the ball for once and Leliwa walked over for the winning TD."

"What," Acosta repeated, "is *man?* Is it by definition a member of the genus *H. sapiens* inhabiting the planet Sol III and its colonies?"

"The next time we tried the play," said Malloy resignedly, "Leliwa was smeared for a ten-yard loss."

The two *men* met on the sands of Mars. It was an unexpected meeting, a meeting in itself uneventful, and yet one of the turning points in the history of *men* and their universe.

The *man* from the colony base was on a routine patrol—a patrol imposed by the captain for reasons of discipline and activity-for-activity's-sake rather than from any need for protection in this uninhabited waste. He had seen, over beyond the next rise, what he would have sworn was the braking blaze of a landing rocket—if he hadn't known that the next rocket wasn't due for another week. Six and a half days, to be exact, or even more exactly, six days, eleven hours, and twenty-three minutes, Greenwich Interplanetary. He knew the time so exactly because he, along with half the garrison, Father Malloy, and those screwball Israelis, was due for rotation then. So no matter how much it looked like a rocket, it couldn't be one; but it was something happening on his patrol, for the first time since he'd come to this god-forsaken hole, and he might as well look into it and get his name on a report.

The *man* from the spaceship also knew the boredom of the empty planet. Alone of his crew, he had been there before, on the first voyage, when they took the samples and set up the observation outposts. But did that make the captain even listen to him? Hell, no; the captain knew all about the planet from the sample analyses and had no time to listen to a guy who'd really been there. So all he got out of it was the privilege of making the first reconnaissance. Big deal! One fast look around reconnoitring a few googols of sand grains and then back to the ship. But there was some kind of glow over that rise there. It couldn't be lights; theirs was the scout ship, none of the others had landed yet. Some kind of phosphorescent life they'd missed the first time round . . . ? Maybe now the captain would believe that the sample analyses didn't tell him everything.

The two *men* met at the top of the rise.

One *man* saw the horror of seemingly numberless limbs, of a headless torso, of a creature so alien that it walked in its glittering bare flesh in this freezing cold and needed no apparatus to supplement the all but non-existent air.

One *man* saw the horror of an unbelievably meagre four limbs, of a torso topped with an ugly lump like some unnatural growth, of a creature so alien that it smothered itself with heavy clothing in this warm climate and cut itself off from this invigorating air.

And both *men* screamed and ran.

"There is an interesting doctrine," said Rabbi Acosta, "advanced by one of your writers, C. S. Lewis . . ."

"He was an Episcopalian," said Father Malloy sharply.

"I apologise." Acosta refrained from pointing out that Anglo-Catholic would have been a more accurate term. "But I believe that many in your church have found his writings, from your point of view, doctrinally sound? He advances the doctrine of what he calls *hnaus*—intelligent beings with souls who are the children of God, whatever their physical shape or planet of origin."

"Look, Chaim," said Malloy with an effort towards patience. "Doctrine or no doctrine, there just plain aren't any such beings. Not in this solar system anyway. And if you're going to go interstellar on me, I'd just as soon read the men's microcomics."

"Interplanetary travel existed only in such literature once. But of course if you'd rather play chess . . ."

"My speciality," said the man once known to sports writers as Mule Malloy, "was running interference. Against you I need somebody to run interference."

"Let us take the sixteenth psalm of David, which you call the fifteenth, having decided, for reasons known only to your God and mine, that psalms nine and ten are one. There is a phrase in there which, if you'll forgive me, I'll quote in Latin; your Saint Jerome is often more satisfactory than any English translator. *Benedicam Dominum, qui tribuit mihi intellectum.*"

"*Blessed be the Lord, who schools me,*" murmured Malloy, in the standard Knox translation.

"But according to Saint Jerome: *I shall bless the Lord, who bestows on me*—just how should one render *intellectum?*—not merely *intellect*, but *perception, comprehension*

. . . what Hamlet means when he says of *man: In appre-hension how like a god!*"

Words change their meanings.

Apprehensively, one *man* reported to his captain. The captain first swore, then scoffed, then listened to the story again. Finally he said, "I'm sending a full squad back with you to the place where—maybe—you saw this thing. If it's for real, these mother-dighting, bug-eyed monsters are going to curse the day they ever set a God-damned tentacle on Mars." The *man* decided it was no use trying to explain that the worst of it was it *wasn't* bug-eyed; any kind of eyes in any kind of head would have been something. And they weren't even quite tentacles either . . .

Apprehensively, too, the other *man* made his report. The captain scoffed first and then swore, including some select remarks on under-hatched characters who knew all about a planet because they'd been there once. Finally he said, "We'll see if a squad of real observers can find any trace of your egg-eating, limbless monsters; and if we find them, they're going to be God-damned sorry they ever were hatched." It was no use, the *man* decided, trying to explain that it wouldn't have been so bad if it *had* been limbless, like in the picture tapes; but just *four* limbs . . .

"What is a *man?*" Rabbi Acosta repeated, and Mule Mal-loy wondered why his subconscious synapses had not earlier produced the obvious appropriate answer.

"*Man,*" he recited, "*is a creature composed of body and soul, and made to the image and likeness of God.*"

"From that echo of childish singsong, Mule, I judge that is a correct catechism response. Surely the catechism must follow it up with some question about that likeness? Can it be a likeness in"—his hand swept up and down over his own body with a graceful gesture of contempt—"*this* body?"

"*This likeness to God,*" Malloy went on reciting, "*is chiefly in the soul.*"

"Aha!" The Sephardic sparkle was brighter than ever.

The words went on, the centres of speech following the synaptic patterns engraved in parochial school as the needle follows the grooves of an antique record, "*All creatures bear some resemblance to God inasmuch as they exist. Plants and animals resemble Him in so far as they have life . . .*"

"I can hardly deny so profound a statement."

"*. . . but none of these creatures is made to the image and likeness of God. Plants and animals do not have a rational soul, such as man has, by which they might know and love God.*"

"As do all good *hnaus*. Go on; I am not sure that our own scholars have stated it so well. Mule, you are invaluable!"

Malloy found himself catching a little of Acosta's excitement. He had known these words all his life; he had recited them the Lord knows how many times. But he was not sure that he had ever listened to them before. And he wondered for a moment how often even his Jesuit professors, in their profound consideration of the $x^n$'s of theology, had ever paused to reconsider these childhood ABC's.

"*How is the soul like God?*" he asked himself the next catechistic question, and answered, "*The soul is like God because it is a spirit having understanding and free will and is destined . . .*"

"Reverend gentlemen!" The reverence was in the words only. The interrupting voice of Captain Dietrich Fassbänder

differed little in tone from his normal address to a buck
private of the Martian Legion.

Mule Malloy said, "Hi, Captain." He felt half relieved,
half disappointed, as if he had been interrupted while un-
wrapping a present whose outline he was just beginning to
glimpse. Rabbi Acosta smiled wryly and said nothing.

"So this is how you spend your time? No Martian natives,
so you have to keep in practice trying to convert each other,
is that it?"

Acosta made a light gesture which might have been polite
acknowledgment of what the captain evidently considered a
joke. "The Martian day is so tedious we have been driven to
talking shop. Your interruption is welcome. Since you so
rarely seek out our company, I take it you bring some news.
Is it, God grant, that the rotation rocket is arriving a week
early?"

"No, damn it," Fassbänder grunted. (He seemed to take a
certain pride, Malloy observed, in carefully not tempering
his language for the ears of clergymen.) "Then I'd have a
German detachment instead of your Israelis, and I'd know
where I stood. I suppose it's all very advisable politically for
every state in the UW to contribute a detachment in rotation; but I'd sooner either have my regular legion garrison
doubled, or two German detachments regularly rotating.
That time I had the pride of Pakistan here . . . Damn it,
you new states haven't had time to develop a military
tradition!"

"Father Malloy," the rabbi asked gently, "are you acquainted with the sixth book of what you term the Old
Testament?"

"Thought you fellows were tired of talking shop," Fassbänder objected.

"Rabbi Acosta refers to the Book of Joshua, Captain. And I'm afraid, God help us, that there isn't a state or tribe that hasn't a tradition of war. Even your Prussian ancestors might have learned a trick or two from the campaigns of Joshua—or for that matter, from the Cattle Raid on Cooley, when the Hound of Cullen beat off the armies of Queen Maeve. And I've often thought, too, that it'd do your strategists no harm to spend a season or two at quarterback, if they had the wind. Did you know that Eisenhower played football, and against Jim Thorpe once, at that? And . . ."

"But I don't imagine," Acosta interposed, "that you came here to talk shop either, Captain."

"Yes," said Captain Fassbänder, sharply and unexpectedly. "My shop and, damn it, yours. Never thought I'd see the day when I . . ." He broke off and tried another approach. "I mean of course, a chaplain is part of an army. You're both army officers, technically speaking, one in the Martian Legion, one in the Israeli forces; but it's highly unusual to ask a man of the cloth to . . ."

"To praise the Lord and pass the ammunition, as the folk legend has it? There are precedents among my people, and among Father Malloy's as well, though rather different ideas are attributed to the founder of his church. What is it, Captain? Or wait, I know: We are besieged by alien invaders and Mars needs every able-bodied man to defend her sacred sands. Is that it?"

"Well . . . God damn it . . ." Captain Fassbänder's cheeks grew purple. ". . . YES!" he exploded.

The situation was so hackneyed in 3V and microcomics

that it was less a matter of explaining it than of making it seem real. Dietrich Fassbänder's powers of exposition were not great, but his sincerity was evident and in itself convincing.

"Didn't believe it myself at first," he admitted. "But he was right. Our patrol ran into a patrol of . . . of *them*. There was a skirmish; we lost two men but killed one of the things. Their small arms use explosive propulsion of metal much like ours; God knows what they might have in that ship to counter our A-warheads. But we've got to put up a fight for Mars; and that's where you come in."

The two priests looked at him wordlessly, Acosta with a faint air of puzzled withdrawal, Malloy almost as if he expected the captain to start diagramming the play on a blackboard.

"You especially, Rabbi. I'm not worried about your boys, Father. We've got a Catholic chaplain on this rotation because this bunch of legionnaires is largely Poles and Irish-Americans. They'll fight all right, and we'll expect you to say a field Mass beforehand, and that's about all. Oh, and that fool gunner Olszewski has some idea he'd like his A-cannon sprinkled with holy water; I guess you can handle that without any trouble.

"But your Israelis are a different problem, Acosta. They don't know the meaning of discipline—not what we call discipline in the legion; and Mars doesn't mean to them what it does to a legionnaire. And, besides, a lot of them have got a . . . hell, guess I shouldn't call it superstition, but a kind of . . . well, reverence—awe, you might say— about you, Rabbi. They say you're a miracle-worker."

"He is," said Mule Malloy simply. "He saved my life."

He could still feel that extraordinary invisible power (a "forcefield" one of the technicians later called it, as he cursed the shots that had destroyed the machine past all analysis) which had bound him helpless there in that narrow pass, too far from the dome for rescue by any patrol. It was his first week on Mars, and he had hiked too long, enjoying the long, easy strides of low gravity and alternately meditating on the versatility of the Creator of planets and on that Year Day long ago when he had blocked out the most famous of All-American line-backers to bring about the most impressive of Rose Bowl upsets. Sibiryakov's touchdown made the headlines; but he and Sibiryakov knew why that touchdown happened, and he felt his own inner warmth . . . and was that sinful pride or just self-recognition? And when he was held as no line had ever held him and the hours passed and no one on Mars could know where he was, and when the patrol arrived they said, "The Israeli chaplain sent us." And later Chaim Acosta, laconic for the first and only time, said simply, "I knew where you were. It happens to me sometimes."

Now Acosta shrugged and his graceful hands waved deprecation. "Scientifically speaking, Captain, I believe that I have, on occasion, a certain amount of extrasensory perception and conceivably a touch of some of the other *psi* faculties. The Rhinists at Tel Aviv are quite interested in me; but my faculties too often refuse to perform on laboratory command. But "miracle-working" is a strong word. Remind me to tell you some time the story of the guaranteed genuine miracle-working rabbi from Lwow."

"Call it miracles, call it ESP, you've got something, Acosta . . ."

"I shouldn't have mentioned Joshua," the rabbi smiled. "Surely you aren't suggesting that I try a miracle to win your battle for you?"

"Hell with that," snorted Fassbänder. "It's your men. They've got it fixed in their minds that you're a . . . a saint. No, you Jews don't have saints, do you?"

"A nice question in semantics," Chaim Acosta observed quietly.

"Well, a prophet. Whatever you people call it. And we've got to make men out of your boys. Stiffen their backbones, send 'em in there knowing they're going to win."

"Are they?" Acosta asked flatly.

"God knows. But they sure as hell won't if they don't think so. So it's up to you."

"What is?"

"They may pull a sneak attack on us, but I don't think so. Way I see it, they're as surprised and puzzled as we are; and they need time to think the situation over. We'll attack before dawn tomorrow; and to make sure your Israelis go in there with fighting spirit, you're going to curse them."

"Curse my men?"

"*Potztausend Sapperment noch einmal!*" Captain Fassbänder's English was flawless, but not adequate to such a situation as this. "Curse *them!* The . . . the *things,* aliens, the invaders, whatever the *urverdammt* bloody hell you want to call them!"

He could have used far stronger language without offending either chaplain. Both had suddenly realised that he was perfectly serious.

"A formal curse, Captain?" Chaim Acosta asked. "Anathema maranatha? Perhaps Father Malloy would lend me bell, book, and candle?"

Mule Malloy looked uncomfortable. "You read about such things, Captain," he admitted. "They were done, a long time ago . . ."

"There's nothing in your religion against it, is there, Acosta?"

"There is . . . precedent," the rabbi confessed softly.

"Then it's an order, from your superior officer. I'll leave the mechanics up to you. You know how it's done. If you need anything . . . what kind of bell?"

"I'm afraid that was meant as a joke, Captain."

"Well, these *things* are no joke. And you'll curse them tomorrow morning before all your men."

"I shall pray," said Rabbi Chaim Acosta, "for guidance . . ." But the captain was already gone. He turned to his fellow priest. "Mule, you'll pray for me too?" The normally agile hands hung limp at his side.

Mule Malloy nodded. He groped for his rosary as Acosta silently left the room.

Now entertain conjecture of a time when two infinitesimal forces of *men*—one half-forgotten outpost garrison, one small scouting fleet—spend the night in readying themselves against the unknown, in preparing to meet on the morrow to determine, perhaps, the course of centuries for a galaxy.

Two *men* are feeding sample range-finding problems into the computer.

"That God-damned Fassbänder," says one. "I heard him talking to our commander. 'You and your men who have never understood the meaning of discipline . . . !' "

"Prussians," the other grunts. He has an Irish face and an American accent. "Think they own the earth. When we get

through here, let's dump all the Prussians into Texas and let
'em fight it out. Then we can call the state Kilkenny."

"What did you get on that last? . . . Check. Fassbänder's
discipline is for peace—spit-and-polish to look pretty here in
our sandy pink nowhere. What's the pay-off? Fassbänder's
great-grandfathers were losing two world wars while mine
were creating a new nation out of nothing. Ask the Arabs if
we have no discipline. Ask the British . . ."

"Ah, the British. Now *my* great-grandfather was in the
IRA . . ."

Two *men* are integrating the electrodes of the wave-hurler.

"It isn't bad enough we get drafted for this expedition to
nowhere; we have to have an egg-eating Nangurian in
command."

"And a Tryldian scout to bring the first report. What's
your reading there? . . . Check."

" 'A Tryldian to tell a lie and a Nangurian to force it into
truth.' " the first quotes.

"Now, brothers," says the *man* adjusting the microvernier
on the telelens, "the Goodman assures us these monsters are
true. We must unite in love for each other, even Tryldians
and Nangurians, and wipe them out. The Goodman has
promised us his blessing before battle . . ."

"The Goodman," says the first, "can eat the egg he was
hatched from."

"The rabbi," says a *man* checking the oxyhelms, "can take
his blessing and shove it up Fassbänder. I'm no Jew in his
sense. I'm a sensible, rational atheist who happens to be an
Israeli."

"And I," says his companion, "am a Rumanian who believes in the God of my fathers and therefore gives allegiance to His state of Israel. What is a Jew who denies the God of Moses? To call him still a Jew is to think like Fassbänder."

"They've got an edge on us," says the first. "*They* can breathe here. These oxyhelms run out in three hours. What do we do then? Rely on the rabbi's blessing?"

"I said the God of my fathers, and yet my great-grandfather thought as you do and still fought to make Israel live anew. It was his son who, like so many others, learned that he must return to Jerusalem in spirit as well as body."

"Sure, we had the Great Revival of orthodox religion. So what did it get us? Troops that need a rabbi's blessing before a commander's orders."

"Many men have died from orders. How many from blessings?"

"*I fear that few die well who die in battle . . .*" the *man* reads in Valkram's great epic of the siege of Tolnishri.

"*. . . for how* [the *man* is reading on the eve of Agincourt in his micro-Shakespeare] *can they charitably dispose of anything when blood is their argument?*"

"*. . . and if these do not die well* [so Valkram wrote] *how grievously must their bad deaths be charged against the Goodman who blesses them into battle . . . ?*"

"And why not?" Chaim Acosta flicked the question away with a wave of his long fingers.

The bleep (even Acosta was not so linguistically formal as to call it a bubble jeep) bounced along over the sand towards the rise which overlooked the invader's ship. Mule

Malloy handled the wheel with solid efficiency and said nothing.

"I *did* pray for guidance last night," the rabbi asserted, almost as if in self-defence. "I . . . I had some strange thoughts for a while; but they make very little sense this morning. After all, I am an officer in the army. I do have certain obligations to my superior officer and to my men. And when I became a rabbi, a teacher, I was specifically ordained to decide questions of law and ritual. Surely this case falls within that authority of mine."

Abruptly the bleep stopped.

"What's the matter, Mule?"

"Nothing . . . Wanted to rest my eyes a minute . . . Why did you become ordained, Chaim?"

"Why did you? Which of us understands all the infinite factors of heredity and environment which lead us to such a choice? Or even, if you will, to such a being chosen? Twenty years ago it seemed the only road I could possibly take; now . . . We'd better get going, Mule."

The bleep started up again.

"A curse sounds so melodramatic and medieval; but is it in essence any different from a prayer for victory, which chaplains offer up regularly? As I imagine you did in your field Mass. Certainly all of your communicants are praying for victory to the Lord of Hosts—and as Captain Fassbänder would point out, it makes them better fighting men. I will confess that even as a teacher of the law, I have no marked doctrinal confidence in the efficacy of a curse. I do not expect the spaceship of the invaders to be blasted by the forked lightning of Yahveh. But my men have an exaggerated sort of faith in me, and I owe it to them to do anything possible to strengthen their morale. Which is all the legion or any other army expects of chaplains anyway; we are no longer priests of the Lord, but boosters of morale—a type of sublimated Y.M.C.A. secretary. Well, in my case, say Y.M.H.A."

The bleep stopped again.

"I never knew your eyes to be so sensitive before," Acosta observed tartly.

"I thought you might want a little time to think it over," Malloy ventured.

"I've thought it over. What else have I been telling you? Now please, Mule. Everything's all set. Fassbänder will explode completely if I don't speak my curse into this mike in two minutes."

Silently Mule Malloy started up the bleep.

"Why did I become ordained?" Acosta backtracked. "That's no question really. The question is why I remained in a profession to which I am so little suited. I will confess to you, Mule, and to you only, that I have not the spiritual humility and patience that I might desire. I itch for something beyond the humdrum problems of a congregation or an army detachment. Sometimes I have felt that I should drop everything else and concentrate on my *psi* faculties, that they might lead me to this goal I seek without understanding. But they are too erratic. I know the law, I love the ritual, but I am not good as a rabbi, a teacher, because . . ."

For the third time the bleep stopped, and Mule Malloy said, "Because you are a saint."

And before Chaim Acosta could protest, he went on, "Or a prophet, if you want Fassbänder's distinction. There are all kinds of saints and prophets. There are the gentle, humble, patient ones like Francis of Assisi and Job and Ruth—or do you count women? And there are God's firebrands, the ones of fierce intellect and dreadful determination, who shake the history of God's elect, the saints who have reached through sin to salvation with a confident power that is the reverse of the pride of Lucifer, cast from the same ringing metal."

"Mule . . . !" Acosta protested. "This isn't you. These aren't your words. And you didn't learn these in parochial school . . ."

Malloy seemed not to hear him. "Paul, Thomas More, Catherine of Siena, Augustine," he recited in rich cadence. "Elijah, Ezekiel, Judas Maccabeus, Moses, David . . . You are a prophet, Chaim. Forget the rationalising double talk of the Rhinists and recognise whence your powers come, how you were guided to save me, what the 'strange thoughts' were that you had during last night's vigil of prayer. You are a prophet—and you are not going to curse *men,* the children of God."

Abruptly Malloy slumped forward over the wheel. There was silence in the bleep. Chaim Acosta stared at his hands as if he knew no gesture for this situation.

"Gentlemen!" Captain Fassbänder's voice was even more rasping than usual over the telecom. "Will you please get the blessed lead out and get up that rise? It's two minutes, twenty seconds, past zero!"

Automatically Acosta depressed the switch and said, "Right away, Captain."

Mule Malloy stirred and opened his eyes. "Was that Fassbänder?"

"Yes . . . But there's no hurry, Mule. I can't understand it. What made you . . . ?"

"I don't understand it, either. Never passed out like that before. Doctor used to say that head injury in the Wisconsin game might—but after thirty years . . ."

Chaim Acosta sighed. "You sound like my Mule again. But before . . ."

"Why? Did I say something? Seems to me like there was something important I wanted to say to you."

"I wonder what they'd say at Tel Aviv. Telepathic communication of subconscious minds? Externalisation of thoughts that I was afraid to acknowledge consciously? Yes, you said something, Mule; and I was as astonished as Balaam when his ass spoke to him on his journey to . . . Mule!"

Acosta's eyes were blackly alight as never before, and his hands flickered eagerly. "Mule, do you remember the story of Balaam? It's in the fourth book of Moses . . ."

"Numbers? All I remember is that he had a talking ass. I suppose there's a pun on *Mule?*"

"Balaam, son of Beor," said the rabbi with quiet intensity, "was a prophet in Moab. The Israelites were invading Moab, and King Balak ordered Balaam to curse them. His ass not only spoke to him; more important, it halted and refused to budge on the journey until Balaam had listened to a message from the Lord . . .

"You were right, Mule. Whether you remember what you said or not, whether your description of me was God's truth or the telepathic projection of my own ego, you were right in one thing: These invaders are *men*, by all the standards that we debated yesterday. Moreover they are *men* suited to Mars; our patrol reported them as naked and unprotected in this cold and this atmosphere. I wonder if they have scouted this planet before and selected it as suitable; that could have been some observation device left by them that trapped you in the pass, since we've never found traces of an earlier Martian civilisation.

"Mars is not for us. We cannot live here normally; our scientific researches have proved fruitless; and we maintained an inert, bored garrison only because our planetary ego cannot face facts and surrender the symbol of our 'conquest of space.' These other *men* can live there, perhaps fruitfully, to the glory of God and eventually to the good of our own world as well, as two suitably populated planets come to know each other. You were right; I cannot curse *men*."

"GENTLEMEN!"

Deftly Acosta reached down and switched off the telecom. "You agree, Mule?"

"I . . . I . . . I guess I drive back now, Chaim?"

"Of course not. Do you think I want to face Fassbänder now? You drive on. At once. Up to the top of the rise. Or haven't you yet remembered the rest of the story of Balaam? He didn't stop at refusing to curse his fellow children of God. Not Balaam.

"He blessed them."

Mule Malloy had remembered that. He had remembered more, too. The phonograph needle had coursed through the grooves of Bible study on up to the thirty-first chapter of Numbers with its brief epilogue to the story of Balaam:

*And Moses sent them to the war . . . and they warred against the Midianites, as the Lord commanded Moses; and they slew all the males . . . Balaam also the son of Beor they slew with the sword.*

He looked at the tense face of Chaim Acosta, where exultation and resignation blended as they must in a man who knows at last the pattern of his life, and realised that Chaim's memory, too, went as far as the thirty-first chapter.

And there isn't a word in the Bible as to what became of the ass, thought Mule Malloy, and started the bleep up the rise.

# Vindicae Flammae

"You are a Catharist," said the Inquisitor. "I aim at perfection," the prisoner answered. He answered as though desirous of helping an inquirer. His two guards had pushed him forward roughly; they feared him as men fear a plague-carrier. They had, however, held on to him fiercely until that moment, hanging on to him as dogs to a boar that is being pulled down. So they had gripped him from the moment they had hauled him out of the bottle-like dungeon into which he had been dropped when brought into the small town. Now they shoved him away. But not only did he come forward as though of his own will, his wrists were unreddened and his long gown fell undisturbed to his feet.

"He is an Anti-Christ," cried the Dominican, looking across to the old Bishop.

The Bishop's stool had been set in the new paved space outside the Church. The Church front itself was new. The whole town square had, indeed, just been rebuilt. "Clean as cauterised flesh," had said the monk, as he looked round; "a fittingly purged area for pure faith to grow. The very seeds of heresy are sterilised, calcined."

"He said they should both grow till His judgment," the Bishop whispered to himself. He thought of his flock torn in half, one half set to devour the other. He had loved human souls, for in them, surely, was the love of God. But he had seen lovers of God and His dear Son hunt down women and young boys who surely couldn't know the rights and wrongs of what they held, but surely could suffer and, in God's merciful name, had been made to suffer. Then came the war, the frightful climax of the struggle.

He had returned, an old man broken-hearted, to oversee a new town built on calcined human bones, a shepherd of sheep, half of whom he must never even know whether they were dead or living, must never even murmur their names before the Throne of Grace at the Giving of Thanks for the blessed sacrifice which had forgiven mankind. He tried to forget, and when people came to him saying, "One of *them* is in the district," he would reply, "Pray that evil may depart from all of us, from all men, pray." And he would fall on his knees until the informer left him, until the bell rang telling him to begin again *coram populo* his task of open intercession, counsel and sacrifice.

But the "Hound of God," the *Domini canis,* had come into the district scenting blood. Could the Lamb have a pack of hounds? He must obey; what was he but a simple bishop, absolutely servile by Holy Obedience before the Servant of the Servants of God, the Bishop of Bishops. Had not the Pope ordered this crusade, this investigation, this inquisition? And this lean devoted man, who was now calling to him across the little square, he had not been in the small town a week before his red worried eye had picked a trail. Here now was his quarry. The hound was baying the *morte* of the poor creature it had cornered . . .

He had had to see them die. Some died mute, just fell

down in the flames, seeming to melt in their fury like pathetic wax; others, in a kind of terrible defiance, summoned all their strength and under the whipping torture of the fire seemed to tear their souls out of their writhing flesh: and others, O poor children, just wept and howled and screamed, flinging the awful faggots from their bodies until they could no more, and their cries shrivelled to moans lost in the crackle of the bonfire.

He had ordered that he would never have a fire again in his room. The people thought it was mortification, and it stood him in good stead. But it was that always in the cheerful noise he heard suffocating moans, through the warming blaze he saw look out at him those terrible eyes— of his flock, his children. The pictures of past trials had flashed across his memory. He roused himself. He must confront the prisoner now placed well forward. As long as he was part of the crowd which surrounded him, the Bishop need not face the victim's eyes. Now he must look into those eyes, so soon—

The Bishop looked up. But already he was being regarded. The face which looked at him was not merely without fear—it was without sorrow or concern. He was aware that someone was regarding him with complete sympathy and interest. With a relief too profound for him to be troubled with seeking for its reason, he turned to the Inquisitor. The monk had already called back the prisoner's attention.

"Your people have striven to destroy the Catholic Church and its Faith."

"I cannot answer for a people. I am here to answer for myself. Together with the Catholic Church, I have striven for the life of union with God."

"Heresy! You will not follow the Church but be an equal."

"I believe that many doctors of the Church have taught what I would practise."

"It is heresy to interpret the Church to herself. The witnesses are ready against you."

"I do not deny that I have had many friends among those who strove after perfection, who were of true sanctity, and who have been—released."

"Bishop, what need have we of further witnesses? He has condemned himself. He has called heretics holy."

The Bishop looked at the two men, he who was deserted and doomed, and he who had life in him and was using it as a power to inflict death. "Son, our Holy Father has given you authority to—cut off from the Church those whom you convict." He looked round at the crowd. He saw the faces blank with a dull expectancy. They were waiting the close of an act to which they were now well accustomed. "Father, forgive us, we know not what we do," he said to himself.

The Dominican went through the form of words needed to make cruelty credal. The Bishop watched him: here was a man, given up to doing his duty, performing a function. He recalled when, as a young man, he had gone hawking, coming on his kestrel when it had brought down a pigeon. The raptor looked up at him from its kill with its keen golden eye, then, with a fierce but un-angry efficiency, began to tear the still trembling flesh off its victim's body. In the level sunlight the Inquisitor's eye seemed as keen and as unperceiving as the hawk's. The Bishop turned his own to the condemned man, for he was already condemned, so little time does fearful suspicion take to create irrevocable certainty. But the speed of his doom had neither stunned nor surprised him. He was regarding the crowd with the quiet interest the Bishop had once seen on the face of a great physician from Montpelier who was observing a flock of infected villagers whom the local leeches forbade him to treat. There was in his look a compassion that was completely without heartbreak or any emotional distress. He knew they were diseased; he would do anything he was permitted, to remedy their condition. Meanwhile he had faced the causes of human suffering, so that he could wait.

At that word suffering, the Bishop realised what was now to come with such an intensity that the condemned man turned as though drawn by a cry. The Bishop rose. His chaplain fell in behind him. The deacon followed. The guards laid hold again of the creature they shunned and loathed. The Inquisitor walked beside the Bishop.

"The execution?" he asked. "Until the severed limb is consumed there is danger of the contagion spreading."

"He is confined: tomorrow is the Feast of the Epiphany. Until this thanksgiving to our Father and His Son for the compassion of the Godhead to us poor darkened sinners be over, until the evening at least, that other act of faith may wait."

"Zeal is a blessed offering to God," the monk declared. The Bishop replied nothing. They entered the small, gaunt palace together. "I have an office to say," the monk excused himself.

In his own apartment the Bishop signed to his chaplain to stay. He sat looking at the empty hearth. His lips were moving. He was saying the office for the dying. Then, "My faithful son, I have been your confessor. I know your heart as mine, and I know it is, as mine, crucified with our dear Lord for this poor rent people of ours. See, say it is my order, that the executioner build up ample fuel. The authorities may order burning; they can exact no more. Now go and leave me."

The door closed and the old man walked to his oratory. He knelt on the stone. The crucifix stood above him. Hour by hour in the gloom his eyes remained fixed on it. As the moon rose its light fell on the face of the Crucified. Without wonder he saw it was the condemned man's; without wonder he saw outline themselves in the gloom on either side of the cross two other crosses. On one hung himself, on the other the Dominican. All night he pleaded, "Lay it not to our charge: remember us when Thou comest into Thy King-dom."

He was aroused by his chaplain who had been kneeling by him, intoning Amen and rising to help his master to rise. The day passed.

"My father," spoke the chaplain to him three times through the long hours, "believe that the Divine Mercy has answered your prayer."

The hour was come, "the hour of the evening sacrifice." The lean crowd was gathered again. His stool was set. The Dominican had mounted his pulpit at the other side and began his sermon. The crowd was opening at the square's other end. The guards entered with the victim. At the upper end stood the stake. Yes, his order had been well served. Like an oblation from the woods, the branches and boughs nearly hid the black post and its chains. The Inquisitor paused to give his audience a moment to see the point of his remarks.

And at that moment the prisoner's voice filled the whole place. With a compelling shock of praise it broke out over the stillness. *"Sursum Corda."* The great *Gloria* rose with exultation. The monk looked across at the Bishop; the Bishop raised his hands, joining in the holy words. The chaplain, reading his thought, crossed quickly in front of the procession. "The Bishop rejoices in the condemned one's contrition. He cannot order a penitent who is reciting the office to be silent."

The figures moved on. The guards handed the prisoner to the executioners. He mounted the pyre. They secured him among the branches. He thanked them and touched the sprays caressingly. They left him mounted above them alone. The voice of praise rang out like a summons to the celebration of triumph. The torches dipped to the fringes of pine-needles and resinous shrubs. A fragrant scent of wild incense swept the court, the smoke swirled like an autumn mist, the flames ran bright as sunbeams, up the sprays and branches. Like a rising tempest of applause the conflagration roared up and around the raised figure in the midst, but always the great voice in a paean of adoration rose above the tempest.

Then from the Bishop's side two figures moved out and forward. The chaplain and the deacon ran towards the pillar of flame which now rose with a single drive. Their voices joined that of the chanter within the fierce glory. Reaching the hill of fire they ran up it, lightly, the flames plaiting under their feet. He who was in the midst had had his hands raised in triumphant worship, but as they rose to his side he drew each of them to him. Together the three stood in the heart of the splendour.

The Inquisitor and the Bishop had followed. They now stood striving to pierce through the veil of fire which swept

up before them. The flame rose too fast and clear to be
smoke-capped, a flood of light which shook itself free, a
tongue of glory which spoke to the blue overarching quiet-
ness of the sky, and was gone. The steadfast blue seemed to
tremble as though an invisible curtain had opened and
closed before its mystery could be guessed.

"My father, my father," cried the Bishop, "the chariots of
Israel and the horsemen thereof." Their eyes, drawn up, now
with the sunk flame sank down. Nothing but a quiet bed of
incandescent charcoal remained, lighting with its glow the
dusk of the square. On his knees, bent to the hot earth,
the monk was repeating, "O ye Fire and Flame, Bless ye the
Lord, Praise Him and Magnify Him for Ever." The Bishop,
his arms held high, cried with the gratitude of answered
prayer, "Oh, Ananias, Azarias and Misael, Bless ye the Lord,
Praise Him and Magnify Him for Ever."